X THE UNKNOWN

Shaun Hutson is one of the UK's best known horror writers. He is the author of more than sixty books. He lives in Buckinghamshire.

SHAUN HUTSON

X 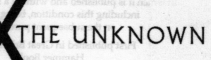 THE UNKNOWN

HAMMER

AN EXCLUSIVE MEDIA COMPANY

Published by Hammer Books 2012

2 4 6 8 10 9 7 5 3 1

Copyright © Shaun Hutson, 2012

First published in Great Britain in 2012 by
Hammer Books
Random House, 20 Vauxhall Bridge Road
London SW1V 2SA

www.randomhouse.co.uk

Addresses for companies within The Random House Group Limited can
be found at: www.randomhouse.co.uk/offices.htm

The Random House Group Limited Reg. No. 954009

A CIP catalogue record for this book
is available from the British Library

ISBN 978-0-099-55622-0

Peterborough
City Council

60000 0000 69950	
Askews & Holts	Jul-2012
HOR	£6.99

MIX
Paper from
responsible sources
FSC® C016897

Typeset in Palatino (11/14 pt) by SX Composing DTP, Rayleigh, Essex
Printed and bound by CPI Group (UK) Ltd, Croydon, CR0 4YY

Author's Introduction

Xthe Unknown was originally released in 1956 and was probably one of Hammer's first real horror films (even though it appears perhaps more science fiction-orientated at first glance). It has a Gothic feel to it that would become a trademark of the studio's output in the years to follow. It was given its title to exploit the audience appeal of the X-certificate category that the British Board of Film Censors had brought in five years earlier, in the same way as the movie version of *The Quatermass Xperiment* had been opportunistically titled shortly before. But, whatever its title's roots, *X the Unknown* is first and foremost a monster movie, in my opinion; it just happens to feature a very uncon-ventional monster.

I'd always liked the film and wondered if I could somehow 'freshen up' the story and make it more accessible to a modern readership while retaining its appeal for a more traditional audience. I was also delighted to be given the chance to work on the novelisation of a film that is even older than I am!

The biggest dilemma, in my humble opinion, when doing a novelisation is the problem of how faithful to be to the script you're working from. Obviously some things have to be changed but I think that the basic structure of the screenplay should be retained. You shouldn't start inventing loads of new characters and scenes that weren't there originally just because you feel like indulging in a bit of artistic licence. However, in certain circumstances some fine-tuning is almost unavoidable. *X the Unknown* is a case in point. When it was made (in the 1950s) the subjects of nuclear war, radioactivity and that kind of thing were of far more immediate concern than they are now. After all, the Second World War had only been over for slightly more than ten years and people had seen the modern super-powers rushing to develop and accumulate nuclear weapons. Films in America and the rest of the world would reflect this trend in their depiction of creatures sent out of control by exposure to radiation (films like *Tarantula*, *Them*, *The Black Scorpion* and *Godzilla*, to name but four) but Hammer did it particularly well with *X the Unknown* because the movie's scale was smaller and hence – especially for a British audience – more accessible and more credible.

My first consideration was whether or not to leave the story set in the 1950s. I decided to update it to a modern-day setting and try to make it more relevant to today. Hence the references to the war in Afghanistan and to events like the earthquake and tsunami in Japan in 2011. Many people will read the book without ever having seen the film so it had to retain both a contemporary feel and the Gothic qualities of the original. This meant having to change quite a bit of the dialogue so that it read more convincingly. Also, all the military equip -

ment that is featured had to be updated. In the film the army wander around on foot most of the time and seem to have one helicopter to cover the whole of Scotland! Policemen have to find public phones to use to alert others to various dangers. Obviously nowadays there is a mobile phone in everyone's pocket and lots of the action had to be adapted to take account of such technological advances. But for the most part I wanted to keep the same structure and remain true to what the original scriptwriter (Jimmy Sangster) had created, especially as that structure worked so well. Otherwise the most noticeable change I made was to the age of the main character, Doctor Royston, who was played in the film by Dean Jagger who was then fifty-three. I thought it might work better if this character was younger in the novelisation so that was why I made that particular alteration. I hope readers agree with my choice.

Other than such changes I've stayed true to the original (with the addition of some new characters here and there and a new subplot that I hope renders the action more contemporary) because it has all the trade - marks of a Hammer film and you don't mess with those if you've got any sense. It's a classic case of 'If it ain't broke, don't fix it' and this most definitely wasn't broke!

When I did the novelisation for *Twins of Evil* I inserted a number of Hammer 'in-jokes' (characters named after Hammer creations from other films that the studio had made and that kind of thing) for connoisseurs of the genre and lovers of Hammer and I couldn't resist doing the same again here. Diehard fans will doubtless notice them – or, at least, I hope they do. They are my personal homage and nod of respect to the studio and what it produced.

So I hope you enjoy reading *X the Unknown* as much as I did writing it. The film is a wonderful reminder of the beginning of Hammer as an unstoppable and unparalleled force in the world of horror films. One of the first steps in what was to become a golden age for the genre and for that company in particular. Their masterful interpretations of *Dracula*, *Frankenstein* and *The Mummy* would follow in the next two or three years and achieve worldwide success and acclaim but before these classics they gave us *X the Unknown*. And it's one hell of a monster movie!

SHAUN HUTSON

This book is dedicated with love to the
memory of my dad.

'Imagination is more important than knowledge'

Albert Einstein

One

It was like walking through an open sewer.

The stench was appalling. It clogged Private Vic Dawson's nostrils and no matter how hard he tried to mask the rancid odour by breathing through his mouth the effect was useless. He hawked and spat, then stood motionless for a moment as he tried once again to get his bearings in the darkness. He squinted through the night but could barely see more than two or three feet in any direction when he took his night-vision goggles off. With them on everything glowed neon green but prolonged wear gave him headaches. Whether others suffered like this Dawson had never thought to ask but he hated wearing the bloody things and now chose to push them up onto the top of his helmet. He'd had them on for more than an hour already and his head was pounding.

Dawson took a step to his right and promptly sank up to his knee in the marshy ground.

'Bollocks,' he hissed under his breath.

The ground had been glutinous enough even before the sudden downpour that had fallen twenty minutes earlier. Now it was like a swamp. There were stretches of firmer ground here and there but for the most part the terrain was unstable and boggy and Dawson was sure that he was crossing the worst of it. Just his luck to get stuck with the shittiest part of the area. If he didn't have bad luck he wouldn't have any luck at all, he told himself. Still muttering, he dragged his leg clear of the sucking ooze and planted his foot before him, hoping he would find some of the more solid earth.

Away to his right something moved and he spun round, sliding his night-vision goggles back into place to help him locate the source of the sound. A large frog had emerged from one of the deeper pools of rancid water and it sat among some reeds for a moment before sliding back into the enveloping blackness. Dawson shook his head and walked on, glancing down at the Geiger counter he carried.

It was clicking quietly but sporadically. Sometimes the sounds would cease altogether, only to begin again after a few more seconds. Dawson aimed the probe at to the ground straight head of him, frowning when the needle on the meter moved as the clicking intensified. He stood still again, holding the device a couple of feet above the soil, sweeping it around him in a circle. The clicking was louder immediately in front of him. He trudged on again, slipping calf deep into the sucking mud.

That same appalling stench still filled his nostrils and he remembered that it was methane. Marsh gas. Small clouds of it were released every time he moved, expelled by the earth like reeking breath from rotten lungs. It was, he also remembered, highly combustible. Best not light a cigarette, then, he mused as he struggled on. And a cigarette was the one thing he really wanted right now. His decision to give up had not been taken lightly. It was costing him far too much and he knew it was no good for his health but he'd been smoking since he was thirteen, for Christ's sake. Ten years later and he was smoking thirty a day, sometimes more. His dad had died of pancreatic cancer a year earlier but that wasn't what had prompted his decision to pack it in. After all, he'd told himself, pancreatic cancer wasn't caused by smoking anyway. It was the financial consideration that had decided him. His pay didn't stretch to the luxury of so many cigarettes. He'd thought about just cutting down but had then decided he might as well go the whole hog and just give up tobacco completely. So far it wasn't proving too successful and the more stressed he got the more he needed a cigarette. Right now he would happily have smoked an entire packet without a second thought.

There were more sounds around him. Something was moving through water away to his left now and Dawson was beginning to wonder exactly how deep the bog was that he was clumping about in. Deep enough to drown a man? He swallowed hard as he visualised himself sinking lower into the mud, the foul sludge filling his lungs as it drew him into its depths. He shook his head as if to dispel the vision, almost managing a smile at his own overactive imagination.

The Geiger counter crackled loudly.

He looked at the needle on the Series 900 mini-monitor. It shot halfway across the perspex-covered screen and stayed there as the sounds from the machine grew louder. Dawson pushed the probe further ahead of him and the crackling grew louder.

He nodded to himself and pressed on, trying to ignore the filthy water that was seeping into his boots as it had been for the last hour or more. The quicker he found what he was looking for the quicker he would be able to get out of this fucking place. He could dry his boots and his uniform, put his feet up and have a cup of tea in pleasant warm surroundings rather than trekking about like an idiot through this stinking marsh.

There were more crackling sounds from the Geiger counter and as Dawson inspected the screen he saw that the needle had hit the maximum level and was staying there.

'Got you,' he murmured to himself, setting the device down on the ground beside him. He pulled the small shovel from his pack and drove it repeatedly into the ground, the constant noise from the counter an accompaniment to his digging. It took less than a minute before the shovel struck something that sounded metallic.

Dawson dropped to his knees, using his bare hands to scrape away the last of the soggy earth. Then he stood upright and raised both arms in the air triumphantly. He reached for the two-way radio clipped to his belt and pressed the transmit button. There was a hiss of static.

'Object located,' he said into the mouthpiece, his voice echoing through the night.

More static, then another voice.

'Well, aren't you a clever boy?'

The second voice cut through the blackness. It was

one that Dawson recognised immediately. He slipped off his night-vision goggles as he saw the unmistakable figure of Sergeant Michael Coulson striding towards him, his own two-way clutched in his hand.

'It's only taken you an hour to find the fucking thing,' Coulson said, peering down at the small metal cylinder that Dawson's digging had uncovered. 'I'd better ring the *Guinness Book of Records*.'

'How did you find me so quickly?' Dawson wanted to know.

'I've been about fifty yards behind you ever since you left,' Coulson told him.

'I can't see a thing out here, sarge,' Dawson protested.

'That's why you've got night-vision goggles, you dozy bastard. Try using them.'

'They give me a headache.'

'Oh, diddums,' Coulson said mockingly.

'Why are we doing this, anyway? Yomping through shit on a moor in the middle of nowhere trying to find . . .' Dawson paused. 'What exactly are we trying to find again, sarge?'

'Radioactive material,' Coulson reminded him. 'There've been reports that the Taliban might have got hold of some weapons-grade uranium and they intend to use it in dirty bombs out in Afghanistan. Where the fuck they got it no one knows but the last thing our boys need out there is to find out that they've placed some in an IED. This kind of exercise will help you when you get out there.'

'Thanks for reminding me,' Dawson said wearily.

'When do you ship out?'

'Four days.'

'First tour?'

Dawson nodded.

'You'll be all right,' Coulson insisted. 'Just do as you're told and keep your eyes open when the time comes.' The two men looked at each other silently for a moment, then the NCO. spoke again. 'Now, that thing needs to be buried again so one of your mates can find it,' Coulson went on. 'So move it. Get it buried and we'll get you back to base.'

'That's very nice of you, sarge,' Dawson said, grinning.

'Don't push it,' Coulson told him, raising one eyebrow.

'Is the whole platoon out here tonight?' Dawson wanted to know.

'No, just B Company. A and C company are out here tomorrow night. You should be grateful you pulled this shift – there's thunderstorms forecast for tomorrow night.'

'If this exercise is supposed to help us in Afghanistan then shouldn't we be doing it in the same kind of conditions? Not fucking around in a swamp.'

'Well, there aren't too many deserts around here – in case you hadn't noticed – so this kind of terrain will have to do for now.' The NCO nodded towards the metal cylinder. 'Now get that fucking thing buried again so the next silly sod can try and find it.'

'Who's next, then?'

'Lansing,' Coulson said. The sergeant looked around, then pointed to a slight incline about thirty yards ahead.

'Stick it in there somewhere, that'll do. When you've finished there's a truck about five hundred yards over that way.' He gestured to his right. 'I'll be waiting there. And don't be too long – we haven't got all night.'

Dawson nodded, listening to the sounds of the sergeant's footfalls as he headed off across the sodden marshland. The private waited a moment. Then he set off towards the area of ground Coulson had indicated, carrying the small metal cylinder. The Geiger counter was clicking constantly now due to the proximity of the cylinder and Dawson was beginning to wonder exactly how much radioactive shit was inside it to trigger the detector. He decided that the quicker he buried the bloody thing the better. There was a broken stone wall running across the firmer ground and Dawson nodded to himself. Weeds and grass grew thickly around the base of the construction and, when the private pulled some of the vegetation away, a large centipede wriggled into view and scrambled away over one of his boots.

He set the cylinder down and began digging.

The Geiger counter crackled a little more loudly.

Two

The woman sat up sharply in bed, her breath coming in gasps.

She blinked hard to clear her vision, then ran both hands over her belly, careful not to exert too much pressure on the area that was giving her such sudden and intense pain. She pushed the sheet back, kicking it off her completely as she exposed her stomach further by pulling up the T-shirt she wore.

'What's wrong?'

The male voice came from beside her and the man slowly rolled over to face her, wincing when he saw the light from the bedside lamp that the woman had switched on.

'Nikki, what's the matter?' he persisted, rubbing his eyes and propping himself up on one elbow. He could see that she was gently rubbing her belly but when he looked at her face he saw an expression of distress on it.

'The pain woke me up,' she told him a little breathlessly.

'Pain where?'

She indicated the area she was gently rubbing.

'What if there's something wrong with the baby, Paul?' she insisted. 'It's not the first time I've had this pain.'

'You never said anything before.'

'It hasn't been this bad before. I thought it was natural. I expected aches and pains during pregnancy but nothing as bad as this.'

'Do you want me to call the doctor?'

She shook her head.

'Not yet,' she told him. 'I want to see if it goes away. If it goes away that means there's nothing wrong.' She smiled. 'That's what my mum always says, anyway.'

Paul Coleman sat up against the headboard and slid his arm around her shoulder.

'And what if it doesn't go away?' he demanded.

Nikki Cross didn't answer him. She merely sat there, gazing down at her belly as if hoping that the pain would stop simply because she wished it to. She swallowed hard and tentatively pressed the area around her navel with the fingertips of one hand. The skin there was taut, almost shiny in the dull glow cast by the bedside lamp.

'Why didn't you tell me before that you'd been having pains?' he asked.

'Because I knew you'd worry and, like I said, I expected a few aches and pains during pregnancy.'

'You're barely three months gone, Nikki. If it's bad now imagine what it's going to be like later. I don't want to see you like this. When you have the scan tomorrow morning tell them about this.'

She nodded but then winced again and sucked in a sharp breath.

Paul Coleman reached towards the bedside table, his hand closing over his mobile phone.

'Fuck this,' he snapped. 'I'm calling the doctor.'

Nikki looked at him, a smile flickering on her lips.

'It's stopped,' she said, the smile broadening. 'The pain's stopped.'

Paul looked at her warily.

'Just like that?' he asked.

She nodded.

'It's gone,' Nikki told him. She ran her fingertips over her belly, relieved that the pain had disappeared. She took a deep breath and nodded once more. 'Gone.'

'Honestly?'

'Cross my heart.'

She waited a moment, then lay down again, her head propped against the pillow.

'You wouldn't lie to me, would you?' he persisted.

She reached out and touched his cheek with her fingertips.

'I'm fine,' she said, sliding her hand around the back of his head and pulling him towards her. They kissed lightly at first, their lips barely touching then she pressed her face more urgently to his and they kissed deeply. When they parted both of them were breathing heavily. She smiled up at him. 'I love you,' she whispered.

'I love you too,' he murmured and they embraced. 'That's why I worry about you.'

'There's no need to worry,' she assured him.

And, for the rest of that night at least, there wasn't.

Three

Sergeant Mike Coulson glanced down at the map spread across the bonnet of the Land Rover 90GS and ran one index finger over it. The map itself was sheathed in a thin plastic cover to prevent the paper beneath getting too wet or being otherwise damaged and on this clear transparent skin small red and black adhesive dots had been stuck. They showed the positions of the men of Coulson's company who were out on the marshy moorlands that night. He glanced at each one in turn, aware of which man each marker signified. Of those shown, the red dots indicated men equipped with Geiger counters and it was these to which Coulson paid particular attention.

He was in contact with all the men by two-way radio and his own was clipped to his belt. It crackled every now and then as the men contacted him or he spoke to them, guiding, cajoling or insulting where he felt neces - sary. In the passenger seat of the vehicle itself, his gaze fixed to his own map, sat Lieutenant James Bannerman. Despite the fact that, at thirty-four, Bannerman was barely three years older than Coulson, he had wisps of grey in his otherwise jet-black hair that made it look as if he'd brushed against a freshly painted wall.

Bannerman was somewhat dismayed by these streaks of grey because his entire family, his mother had informed him, had gone grey early. Some as early as their thirties. It was a prospect that the lieutenant didn't relish but then, he reasoned, there was nothing he could do about this genetic aberration so there wasn't too much point in worrying about it. What will be will be, as his mother was so fond of telling him. What she hadn't mentioned was that he might acquire the nickname 'Badger'. Something which had happened in the last year when the greying process seemed to have speeded up. Bannerman smiled to himself as he thought about it. It was, he comforted himself, at least inoffensive – unlike some of the nicknames the men had for other officers.

When he heard the crackle of static from Coulson's two-way radio he swung himself out of the Land Rover and wandered around to join the NCO who looked at him and shrugged, shaking his head wearily.

'So what kind of reading are you getting off the counter?' Coulson said into the mouthpiece.

'It's pretty quiet,' the voice at the other end said. 'No change since I started looking. Over.'

'Then look somewhere else,' Coulson said. 'Over and out.'

He made a small mark on his map with a felt-tip pen, drawing a line across one of the red dots before him.

'How's the search going?' Bannerman asked. 'Anyone else found the cylinder yet?'

'Not yet, sir, but it shouldn't be too long.'

'If they had better equipment they might find it

quicker,' the officer muttered. 'Bloody politicians' cutbacks. It's a wonder they haven't asked the men to find it with a magnifying glass and a magnet.'

Coulson grinned.

'As long as they don't cut back on our equipment once we get to Afghanistan, sir,' the sergeant observed.

'If they could get away with it they would. They're only interested in saving money. They couldn't care less if we're fighting a war with one hand tied behind our back.'

'That's politicians for you, sir.'

'My father said it was the same in his day. He was a soldier, too.'

'Officer, sir?'

'Captain in the Household Cavalry.'

'My old man was in the army but he never made it past corporal. My whole family were army men, all the way back to the First World War. My great-grandad was wounded at Passchendaele. My dad used to say that was a proper war.'

'I don't suppose it matters what kind of war it is. You can get killed anywhere, can't you?'

'Very true, sir.'

'I lost a friend the last time I was in Afghanistan. Bloody IED went off right next to him. Killed him instantly. He left behind a wife and two kids.'

'I'm sorry, sir. He wasn't the first and he won't be the last, either.'

'Unfortunately.'

Bannerman glanced down at the map. As he did several spots of rain fell onto the plastic that covered it.

He looked up at the night sky, his eyes focusing on the banks of thick cloud there.

There was a crackle and then a somewhat muted voice was audible from Coulson's two-way.

'Come in . . . calling . . . found something.'

The sergeant pulled the two-way from his belt.

'Who is this?' he asked. 'You're breaking up. Say again.'

'It's Lansing, sarge,' the voice went on. *'I thought . . . found something . . . keep looking.'*

'Give me your coordinates,' Coulson insisted.

The radio crackled.

'Lansing, give me your coordinates,' Coulson repeated.

'They probably got the radios from the same place they got the Geiger counters,' Lieutenant Bannerman offered.

'Where was that, sir? Argos?'

Both men laughed.

The two-way crackled into life again.

'Lansing again . . . my coordinates . . . as follows . . .' the voice began.

As the soldier at the other end of the two-way relayed his position, both Coulson and Bannerman peered at the map, the sergeant finally jabbing his finger at the point indicated.

'What the fuck are you doing there?' Coulson snapped. 'You're way off course.'

'Readings from . . . counter. . . Seems to be pretty strong . . . see much here. I'll check it again. Over.'

'Yeah, you do that and let me know,' Coulson

instructed. 'You're nowhere near the bloody thing. Over and out.' He sucked in a deep breath. 'Lansing reckons he's getting strong readings but that's impossible. He's at least a mile from the cylinder.'

'Perhaps he's reading it wrong – either that or he's given you the wrong coordinates,' Bannerman offered. 'Let me speak to him.' The officer held out his hand for the two-way and Coulson passed it over. 'Lansing, come in – this is Lieutenant Bannerman. Can you give me your coordinates again, over?'

There was only silence at the other end.

'Lansing, can you hear me?' Bannerman went on.

There was a stab of static so loud that it forced the officer to hold the two-way away from his ear for a moment. For a second he looked at the radio as if it was about to explode, then carefully put it back against his head.

'Lansing,' he said. 'Come in, over.'

'. . . Sir . . . can hear you . . . those coordinates . . . gave you are correct . . . and I'm still . . . very strong readings from the counter . . .' the other man said, his voice occasionally swallowed by a harsh crackle. 'Wait a minute . . . something . . . don't know what it is . . . moving . . . the ground is moving . . .'

Bannerman looked at Coulson and frowned. The sergeant merely shook his head.

'. . . the Geiger counter . . . reading is at maximum . . .' Lansing went on.

'Lansing, that's impossible – you're nowhere near the source of radiation,' Bannerman assured him.

'. . . getting louder . . . can't see what it is . . . there's *something moving just ahead . . . to get out . . . oh . . . God.'*

'Lansing, what can you see?' Bannerman urged.

Silence.

'Lansing,' the officer said again.

'Help me . . . I can't . . . Jesus . . . Jesus . . .'

Even through the two-way Bannerman and Coulson could hear the rumbling. It was drowned out seconds later by a deafening scream.

Four

The rotor blades of the Merlin HC3 cut effortlessly through the night. The helicopter's spotlights were aimed at the ground below. Inside the body of the aircraft Sergeant Coulson periodically glanced out of a window, staring down towards the marshland beneath him in the hope of seeing something caught in the beams of white light as they criss-crossed the dark earth. But they illuminated nothing except the sodden ground and the clumps of trees that punctuated it. In the rear of the Merlin a single medical orderly sat, his chin resting on his knees as he gazed blankly into space. He'd been aboard the chopper when it had touched down to pick up Coulson and Bannerman a short time earlier. Fortunately the journey from the base had taken less than ten minutes: time was of the essence in their race to reach Lansing and find out just what had caused the sounds that had been relayed over his radio.

The helicopter banked to the right and Coulson looked across at Lieutenant Bannerman whose attention was also focused down towards the ground, an expression of concern etched on his face. Those sounds that the men had heard over the two-way a short time earlier still echoed in their ears like the last vestiges of some vile nightmare. The rumbling that had grown louder and louder in the background. The rattles and hisses of static and finally the screams of fear from Private Lansing before the radio had finally died.

The two men had said little to each other from the time they'd boarded the helicopter. It was as if neither of them had the words to express the thoughts tumbling through their heads or, more to the point, as if neither man wanted to give voice to those thoughts. What had been the source of the low and steadily building sound? Bannerman knew it wasn't an earthquake. Not here in the heart of Buckinghamshire. Coulson felt the same way but was therefore even more tormented and puzzled by the sounds he'd heard, not least by the scream of fear that had ended the contact. He knew Lansing well as a good soldier and a reliable man. A man that his companions could depend on. Not one who folded under pressure or who couldn't cope with whatever was thrown at him. Not the kind of man who scared easily. And especially not on an exercise in the middle of some fucking marshland in Buckingham - shire. What the hell had Lansing seen or encountered that had made him scream like he had?

Coulson looked in the direction of the medic and saw that the man was still seemingly preoccupied with his own thoughts. He sat quietly at the back of the aircraft, occasionally rubbing his hands together as if to restore lost circulation.

In the cockpit of the helicopter the co-pilot checked their position on one of the many illuminated screens before him.

'Coming up in five hundred yards,' he said, flicking a switch to his left.

The pilot eased back on the throttle and the Merlin slowed, then began to descend.

Coulson and Lieutenant Bannerman felt the change in speed and altitude and again exchanged glances, realising that they were close to the place where they had last made contact with Private Lansing. Both men knew that this particular mystery was about to be solved one way or another.

The Merlin suddenly lurched violently to one side.

'What the fuck?' Coulson snapped, grabbing at one of the straps that lined the walls of the helicopter's interior.

Bannerman also steadied himself, almost tumbling sideways as the chopper careened through the air as if it had been grabbed by some giant invisible hand. The medic wasn't so lucky. He let out a startled yelp and slammed into one wall. He groaned and put a hand to his head, aware that the other two men were looking at him with concern.

'Are you all right?' Coulson asked.

The medic nodded briefly.

The pilot wrestled with the controls and managed to bring the Merlin level again but it took all his strength to do it.

'What the hell was that?' he rasped, his tone a mixture of anger and surprise.

'Something electrical?' the co-pilot offered none too convincingly. He too was taken aback by the sudden movement. They were far too low for it to be turbulence and nothing had registered on any of the gauges or dials. 'Maybe a thermodraught.'

'In terrain like this?' the pilot asked, a note of disbelief in his voice. 'It was more as if we hit something,' he went on, guiding the Merlin lower, relieved when he felt it touch down on the marshy ground below. He flicked a switch on the dashboard and two of the chopper's forward-mounted spotlights sent their powerful beams cutting through the blackness of the night. In their brilliant cold white glare the pilot could see a thick veil of what looked like smoke hanging about a hundred yards to the left. It was like a dirty curtain suspended across the marshland.

'Marsh gas?' the co-pilot offered.

'It could be,' the pilot conceded. 'But as dense as that?'

As Coulson, Bannerman and the medic scrambled from the Merlin they saw it too. There was a pungent odour in the air as well that none of them could immediately identify. However, the soldiers were more concerned with finding Private Lansing and they set off immediately in the direction of the smoke, knowing that the last set of coordinates he'd given lay beyond that curtain of grey.

The three men hurried across the marshy ground as best they could, struggling through the deeper areas where they sometimes sank up to their knees in stagnant reeking water and mud. Coulson pulled the two-way from his belt and pressed it to his face.

'Lansing, come in,' he said urgently.

No answer.

'We're coming to get you,' he went on. 'We'll be with you in less than two minutes.'

There wasn't even a hiss of static by way of reply. Nothing. Just silence.

Coulson snapped the two-way back onto his belt.

'Have you got any idea what might have caused his injuries?' the medic asked, trudging alongside the sergeant.

'We're not even sure that he *is* injured,' Bannerman replied. 'We heard something and then a scream. He sounded as if he'd been hurt but we won't know until we find him.'

The medic nodded, not entirely satisfied with the explanation. But he wasn't going to argue with an officer and tell him he was being too vague. The trio moved on.

The rumbling came from beneath them.

All three men heard it and, seconds later, felt it. The ground beneath their feet shuddered gently and again that deep menacing sound reached their ears.

'That's what we heard over the radio,' Coulson remarked.

Bannerman merely nodded, standing motionless for a moment.

'What's going on out here?' the medic asked, his voice cracking a little.

'Trust me, we're as curious as you,' Bannerman told him, ears alert for the slightest noise.

The smell that all three men had been aware of upon leaving the Merlin was now even stronger and so too was the density of the mist that was hanging over the terrain. It moved like smoke, twisting and writhing in the air as they passed through it. The odour was unpleasant but bearable and it reminded Coulson of the caustic, pungent smell of bleach. It wasn't the sewer-like stink of marsh gas that he'd been expecting. Whatever this veil of grey was that they were now enveloped by it wasn't methane. He didn't know whether he was grateful for that or not.

'Lansing.'

It was Bannerman who had called the man's name. The shout seemed to hang in the air for a moment before it died away in the night.

They moved on when they heard no reply. There was a slight rise ahead of them and they moved towards that, hoping the ground there would be firmer and more stable. It was covered by thick clusters of bushes and reeds, some of them growing to waist height.

It was from within one of these clumps of vegetation that they heard the moans.

'There!' Coulson snapped, jabbing a finger in the direction of the pitiful sounds. All three men hurried towards the source of the groans, ignoring the low rumbling that came from beneath them once more.

Private Lansing was lying on his back, his eyes open wide and staring at the sky, his lips trembling. When he saw the other men standing over him he shot out a hand to them and tried to sit up, his eyes bulging even more in their sockets.

'Help me,' he panted. 'Please.'

The hand that he raised towards them was burned in several places, the flesh seared black. The damage was so severe on the palm and fingers that nerves and even bone had been exposed. Similarly on Lansing's face there were large areas of charred flesh, some of which had already begun to blister and suppurate. Thick yellowish pus oozed from three particularly large and swollen protuberances on the left cheek and just above the eye. More boils were forming both on and beneath the flesh of the chin and the neck. Portions of his uniform were also scorched and blackened and even the soles of his boots were smoking. He looked as if he'd just crawled out of a furnace.

The medic stood transfixed for a second until he shook himself free of his shock and dropped to his knees beside the immobile man.

'These look like chemical burns,' he said as he pulled gauze and cotton wool from a small pouch on his belt. 'But that's impossible out here. What kind of chemicals could he have come into contact with?'

'The ground opened up,' Lansing gasped suddenly, sitting bolt upright. He stared ahead as if he was watching what had happened being rerun on a giant invisible screen in front of him.

The medic steadied him and held him as the injured soldier looked around in terrified bewilderment.

'Can you tell us what happened?' Bannerman wanted to know.

'I heard something,' Lansing panted. 'I tried to tell you on the radio, then . . .' He shook his head, his body shaking. 'It came out of the ground.' The words dis - solved into frantic sobs. 'It came out of the ground.'

'What did?' Coulson insisted.

'I tried to run,' Lansing sobbed. 'But I couldn't get away.' He looked at the other men. 'Please help me.'

'Tell us what you saw,' Coulson said quietly, touching the injured man's arm gently. 'Take your time.'

'He can't tell you anything – he's in deep shock,' the medic insisted. 'His pulse is through the roof. So is his blood pressure. We'll be lucky if he doesn't die of a heart attack.'

'Can't you give him something to calm him down?' Coulson demanded. 'He's one of my men – for Christ's sake help him.'

'I'm trying,' the medic snapped. 'He needs sedating.'

'Then do it,' Coulson rasped. 'Do whatever you have to do but fucking help him.'

Lansing screamed uncontrollably, the sound cutting through the night and raising the hairs on the backs of the other men's necks. The medic held him close for a moment the way a mother might hold a terrified child and the screams stopped momentarily. They were replaced by a low and unnerving whimpering sound. Lansing was staring fixedly at the gently sloping ground ahead, his eyes wide with pain and terror.

'What you saw – is it over that ridge?' Coulson asked.

Lansing nodded.

'Kill it,' he gasped, sinking backwards as he was enveloped by the merciful oblivion of unconsciousness.

Coulson shot Lieutenant Bannerman a questioning glance but neither man spoke.

'We've got to get him back to base as quickly as possible,' the medic urged, wrapping bandages around one of Lansing's hands. 'If we don't he's got no chance.'

Bannerman nodded, pulling the two-way from his belt.

'This whole area is going to have to be sealed off,' he murmured.

'I want to know what he saw. I want to know what did that to him,' Coulson said angrily, heading off up the incline in the direction of Lansing's wide-eyed stare. The officer hesitated a moment, glancing down at the injured soldier. Then, satisfied that everything possible was being done by the medic, he joined the sergeant, both of them squinting through the darkness. Neither of them had any idea exactly what they were looking for. However, as they reached the top of the incline they both froze in their tracks, their stares riveted on what lay beyond.

'Jesus Christ,' Coulson breathed.

Bannerman said nothing. He merely stood shaking his head in total and utter disbelief.

'What the fuck is *that*?' Coulson murmured.

Bannerman wished he could tell him.

Five

She had counted eleven helicopters in the last five minutes.

Each one was probably carrying troops or equipment from the nearby base – but where were they going at half past three in the morning?

Claire Reece stood at the bedroom window, drawing on her cigarette. She ran a hand through her hair and wrapped the sheet more tightly around herself. There was a chill in the night air and she shivered a little as she peered through the open window and up at the dark sky, watching as three more helicopters sped past overhead. They looked like Chinooks. Big, bulky craft used for carrying troops. Claire smiled and took another drag on her cigarette, complimenting herself on her ability to recognise military vehicles and thinking how it seemed to have become second nature because there was a large army base only ten miles away. Helicopters, trucks, weapons. She could have identified most of them on sight as could many of the residents of the town. The sight of soldiers among them was commonplace and, she felt, somewhat reassuring too. And reassurance was something she needed in her life right now.

She took another drag on her cigarette and continued gazing out of the window, noticing that her hand was shaking slightly. Fear? She swallowed hard. If she was honest with herself that was exactly what she was feeling. The appointment was scheduled for ten the next morning and she already felt as if she was preparing for some kind of final judgement. If the doctor felt the need then they would recommend some kind of procedure or investigation. Why did they always use words like 'procedure' or 'investigation'? Did they feel that it somehow lessened the impact of what they were going to do? Did they believe that it diluted the feelings of trepidation? Because if they did then she would like to inform them that it didn't. Not in her case.

The doctor at the surgery had told her that the lump he'd found in her right breast was tiny. It was more than likely a cyst. He'd been adamant about that. She could still hear him telling her now, his voice echoing inside her subconscious. A cyst. Nothing more. But at her age (she'd be thirty-nine next birthday) – in fact, at any age – they had to know. They might have to perform a biopsy, and even if it did turn out to be something more than a cyst then they could start treatment early and everything should be fine. 'Should' being the operative word.

Easy for the doctor to say, Claire thought. He wasn't the one facing a minor procedure (that word again) and possibly a week or so of worry waiting for the results. She took a final drag on her cigarette and threw the butt out of the window, pausing there for a moment before she turned back towards the bed.

As she walked, the sheet she'd wrapped around herself trailed in her wake like some kind of mock wedding dress. She draped it back over the bed and climbed in, moving close to the figure that slept there. He stirred as she pressed her naked body against him, snaking her arms around him, trailing one hand across his broad chest.

'Shit, your hands are cold,' he grunted. 'Where have you been?'

'I was having a fag,' she told him.

'Oh, Claire,' Stephen Reece sighed. 'I thought you were going to give up.'

'What do you mean, "Oh, Claire"?' she said indignantly. 'It's a bit late to give up now, isn't it? I'm having a bloody examination tomorrow to see if the lump in my breast is cancerous. Don't you think that's a little bit like shutting the stable door after the horse has bolted? Anyway, I always smoke more when I'm nervous.'

He moved to face her, brushing some strands of hair from her cheek.

'Everything will be fine,' Reece told her.

'I wish I was as confident as you.'

'Even if it's something else, they'll catch it early and—'

'I know all about that,' she said, sharply, cutting him off. 'I know that there's nothing to worry about and all the other bullshit that they give you but I'm the one it's happening to, Steve. No one else.'

'I know – and whatever happens I'll be here, you know that.'

A single tear welled up in her eye and rolled down

her face. Reece brushed it away with an index finger.

'What if it is that?' she said, softly. 'What if it is cancer? What if it's malignant? They might have to take my breast off.'

'Then you'll have one great boob instead of two, won't you? What do you think's going to happen? If the worst comes to the worst do you think I'm going to leave you? Do you think I'm going to walk out just because of that? It was your arse and legs that attracted me in the first place, anyway – so what's the problem?' He smiled, hoping that his clumsy attempts at humour might lighten her mood too.

Claire moved closer to him.

'Whatever happens we'll see it through together,' he told her.

'I don't want to say anything to the kids until I know one way or the other. No point in worrying them. Not yet.'

Reece nodded.

Outside, the sound of more helicopters made him glance towards the window.

'Where the hell are they going at this time of the morning?' he muttered.

'It must be important. Loads have already gone over. I counted them while I was having a fag.'

'Probably just an exercise. Nothing to worry about.'

Six

Even though no exact measurements had yet been taken, even an untrained eye could see that the giant split that now scarred the ground was at least fifty yards long and half that in width. It's depth could only be guessed at. How far down this chasm reached was so far unknown.

Standing on the ridge that overlooked the abyss, Lieutenant James Bannerman still found it hard to believe what lay before him. This rip in the ground wasn't in some earthquake-ravaged part of a desolate and uninhabited region of the globe – it was in the middle of marshland in Buckinghamshire. Not an area exactly renowned for its seismic instability and tendency to split wide open. And yet that was what had happened. From what the officer saw he could only assume that there had been some kind of earth tremor which had caused this breach in the ground.

Thin wisps of vapour were still rising from the hole and in fact much of the marshland round about was covered by a layer of mist that Bannerman could only guess was steam. Perhaps, he told himself, the movement of the earth that had caused the rift had generated sufficient heat to evaporate some of the water in the marshes. But, then again, he wasn't an expert. Who knew what had really caused the damage and what it had left behind? Better-educated men than he would have to supply the answers.

Could the heat generated by the movement of the earth also explain the burns sustained by Private Lansing? It was possible but unlikely. And even if it was so, what had caused the soldier's hysteria? He'd said he'd seen something moving. Did he mean the earth itself? Or had the shock of being caught in an earth-quake terrified him so much that he'd imagined seeing something rising from the ground?

Bannerman shook his head slightly. A negative answer to his own internal questions. The Merlin that had ferried the injured man back to the base had long since left. Only when Lansing's injuries had been treated properly would they have any chance of finding out what had actually happened.

Now the lieutenant watched as dozens of troops moved around before him, each with a specific task to perform and each, he guessed, as puzzled by what they saw as he was himself. The air was filled with the sound of whirring rotor blades as helicopters came and went and, off to his right, the rumble of heavy lorries added to the cacophony as more soldiers and equipment arrived. A number of spotlights had been set up and the entire area was bathed in cold white light. Some of the lights were aimed at the chasm itself, their piercing rays illuminating the edges of the chasm.

Through the din the lieutenant heard an even louder sound and glanced around to see a huge vehicle making its way across the terrain towards the rift. The LTM 1055-3.1 mobile crane looked like a throwback to some other age. A siege engine that might have been summoned to help breach the walls of a recalcitrant fortress. It was immense but, despite weighing almost forty tons, it was still able to achieve speeds of forty miles an hour. The vehicle dwarfed the men and equipment around it and even Bannerman was taken aback by its daunting size. Mounted on six huge wheels it rumbled across the ground as easily as a tank crossing a ploughed field. The thirty-six-ton monster was heading towards the chasm, the telescopic boom it supported currently retracted but capable of reaching over thirty-five metres when extended to its full impressive length. Bannerman wondered how deep it would need to go to reach the bottom of the rift in the earth.

A Land Rover trailed the mobile crane and as it drew nearer the lieutenant could see three men apart from the driver seated in it. One he recognised instantly as Major Edward Cartwright, his commanding officer. Cartwright was an affable thin-faced man in his early fifties with bushy eyebrows and perpetually red cheeks. Like most of the men now moving about on the marshland, he had been woken from his slumbers by news of what had happened here less than an hour ago.

The Land Rover pulled up close to Bannerman who saluted sharply as his CO clambered out of the vehicle and returned the gesture. The vehicle then drove on, carrying its remaining occupants towards the chasm.

'The entire area is sealed off, sir,' Bannerman reported.

'Good,' Cartwright murmured, gazing at the huge crack in the ground. 'Now all we have to do is work out what the hell happened here.'

'That might not be so easy, sir.'

Cartwright nodded.

'What about the radiation levels?' he asked. 'You said that they were high.'

'That's the curious thing, sir. Initially they were. In fact they were dangerously high but they've been falling rapidly for the last hour or so and the most recent report is that there's no activity at all. There are not enough traces of radiation to register on a Geiger counter now.'

Cartwright frowned.

'It's as if whatever was causing the levels to rise simply disappeared,' Bannerman went on.

'Which we know is impossible,' the major said. 'Could the initial readings have been wrong?'

'It's possible, sir, but . . .' The words trailed away.

'Unlikely,' Cartwright added.

'If you don't mind me asking, sir, who are the civilians in the Land Rover?' Bannerman asked.

'Two of the research scientists from the base,' Cartwright informed him. 'They should be able to give us some clue about what's happening here.'

'You don't think this is linked to their work at the base, do you, sir?'

'Only they can tell us that, Jim.'

The two officers watched as the Land Rover pulled up about twenty yards from the chasm to allow its passengers to climb out. Both men moved towards the rim of the crack and Bannerman could see that they were both carrying Geiger counters.

'Is there any news on Private Lansing, sir?' Bannerman wanted to know. 'The soldier who was injured. Sergeant Coulson travelled back to the base hospital with him.'

'Nothing as yet,' Cartwright replied. He looked at the lieutenant. 'He was in a pretty bad way when you found him, wasn't he?'

'He had some very bad burns. But it wasn't just that – it was his mental state. He was extremely agitated, sir. Practically hysterical.'

'Shock. You've seen battlefield casualties, Jim. You know how serious wounds can affect men.'

'I know, sir, but this was different. He was absolutely terrified. He kept going on about something coming up out of the ground. Something that attacked him.'

Cartwright frowned.

'Sergeant Coulson and I tried to find out what he was talking about but he just kept saying the same thing over and over again, sir,' Bannerman went on. 'Whatever it was he saw it must have been bad because in all my time as a soldier, even under fire, I've never seen a man so frightened.'

Seven

The room was barely twelve feet square. White-painted walls and a highly polished floor reflected the cold fluorescent ceiling-mounted lights, giving the entire area an almost luminescent appearance. Everything was so white and clean. Sitting beside the one bed that occupied the centre of the room, Sergeant Michael Coulson wondered if this was what Heaven looked like. Pristine and gleaming. And so silent. It was as quiet as the grave in the room apart from the low guttural breathing of the bed's occupant.

Coulson looked at the heavily bandaged figure of Private Lansing, his attention sometimes shifting to the morphine drip and the other tubes that ran from the immobile form like clear plastic veins. There was a small cabinet on one side of the bed and an oscilloscope on the other but the volume was turned off so that the customary beeping of such a machine was absent. The only sound was Lansing's breathing. The one eye that was still visible beneath the bandages would occa-sionally open and, when it did, Coulson would gently squeeze the private's unbandaged arm as if to offer reassurance. Sometimes he would speak Lansing's name but, so far, the only response had been a widening of that single uncovered eye and a shuddering of the body for a short time until the traumatised man lapsed once again into unconsciousness. What was going on inside his tortured mind during those brief spells of lucidity Coulson could only imagine. He had been in this room with Lansing for almost two hours now, determined to stay with him despite the insistence of the medical staff who had been into the room that it was pointless. There was, though, they had said, presently no risk of contamination so it was acceptable for Coulson to remain even though they had advised against it. Coulson had ignored their advice.

He watched Lansing's face and noticed that the man's eye had opened again. He was drifting constantly in and out of unconsciousness due to his condition and also because of the amount of morphine and other chemicals that were being pumped into his system.

'Don,' the sergeant murmured as he saw Lansing's eyelid flickering. 'Don, can you hear me?'

Lansing turned his head slightly to look in the sergeant's direction but Coulson couldn't be sure whether or not he saw him.

'Don,' the NCO said again.

Lansing tried to swallow but he only succeeded in making a thick gurgling noise deep in his throat.

'Don, you're going to be all right,' Coulson told him with as much conviction as he could muster. 'Can you hear me? If you can then just move your fingers – don't try to speak.'

The fingers on Lansing's left hand stretched stiffly by way of response.

'You can hear me?' Coulson said, smiling thinly.

Again the fingers stretched, then relaxed.

'You're in hospital, back at the base. You're safe now. We brought you back from the exercise. Something happened to you out there and we need to know what it was so that we can help you. Do you think you can tell me? Move your fingers once for yes and twice for no. Do you understand?'

A single flex.

'Can you remember what happened during the exercise?' Coulson went on.

Lansing's fingers flexed once.

'Do you remember being hurt?'

One single movement.

'We saw the crater, the chasm or whatever that hole in the ground is where we found you. Did whatever hurt you come from that crater?'

Another single, jerky movement.

'Could you describe it?'

Two strained movements of the fingers.

'Was it a man?'

Two flexes of the fingers.

Coulson paused momentarily, taken aback by Lansing's response.

'Whatever hurt you wasn't a man?' he asked slowly.

The fingers flexed twice.

'Do you know what it was?'

One single movement.

Coulson's next question seemed ridiculous to him, even before he'd asked it. He swallowed hard and wondered how insane it would sound when he eventually gave voice to it. He looked down at the tortured, bandaged face of Lansing who had fixed him in the gaze of his single good eye and seemed to be waiting for him to speak again. Coulson cleared his throat and leaned closer to the injured soldier.

'Whatever attacked you,' he began softly. 'Was it human?'

Lansing stretched his fingers and held them in that rigid pose as if to reinforce the point he was trying to make. His one good eye bulged wildly in it's socket and he moved his lips convulsively, struggling to speak. But again the only sound that came out was that thick liquid gurgling.

The door of the room swung open and Coulson's attention snapped towards it.

The doctor who had swept into the room accompanied by a nurse glanced at him and then at Lansing who was trembling gently on the bed. The nurse walked around behind Coulson and checked the drip, noting on a small pad she carried how much liquid had been dispensed.

'I think it's time you left, sergeant,' the doctor said. 'There's nothing you can do for him. I told you that when he was brought in.'

'He's one of my men, sir.'

'I'm aware of that, sergeant, and your concern is admirable. But there's nothing you can do to help him. That's *our* job.'

'I was trying to get him to talk, sir. There are other men in the area where he was injured. They could be in danger too.'

'They'll be aware if there are any dangers by now, sergeant,' the doctor insisted, leaning over Lansing to shine a penlight into his one good eye. 'They've been out there long enough.'

'Were there traces of radiation in his bloodstream, sir?'

'No – why should there be?'

'The area where he was injured was showing signs of high radioactivity, sir.'

'That's impossible. If he'd been exposed to radio-activity it would have shown up in his blood and urine tests. We found nothing.'

'What about his burns, sir? Could they have been caused by radiation?'

'It would have to have been an incredibly high degree of exposure to cause burns of the extent he's suffered. The source of radiation needed to inflict burns of that severity wouldn't simply disappear. The whole area would be at risk.'

Lansing suddenly lurched violently on the bed and the doctor looked at him with an expression of alarm on his face. He glanced at the oscilloscope and noticed that the lines on the screen of the electronic monitor were rising and falling dramatically.

'What's happening?' Coulson demanded.

'His heart rate and blood pressure are going through the roof,' the doctor said. Then he turned to the nurse: 'Nurse, forty milligrams of Nembutal, IV. Quickly.'

The nurse murmured 'Yes, doctor,' and scurried from the room.

Lansing's entire body went rigid, his eye swelling so

madly that it threatened to burst from its socket. He opened his mouth as if to say something but his lips merely moved soundlessly for a moment. A foul-smelling flux of blood and pus spilled from the open orifice. Coulson took a step back, his stare fixed on Lansing's tortured features. The flesh of the man's face was pulsing and contracting, rising and falling as if there were tiny hydraulic pumps beneath it.

The nurse re-entered the room and pulled back the sheet covering Lansing, a syringe held in her hand.

As she tugged the covering away she screamed.

Even Coulson took a step backwards, his stomach somersaulting, his breath coming in ragged gasps.

The nurse dropped the syringe and backed off a couple of paces while the doctor merely stared dumb - struck at what lay before him.

On the bed, Private Lansing let out one final gurgle of agony as he died.

'Jesus Christ,' Coulson gasped, gazing at Lansing's tortured face. He thought how flat the remaining eye appeared. It seemed to have simply deflated – it now looked squashed, as if it had been trodden on. That thought made him feel even sicker and, despite himself, he bent double and retched until there was nothing left in his stomach.

Eight

The telescopic boom arm of the LTM 1055-3.1 crane could support a weight of thirty tons if necessary but, on this occasion, it was supporting far less than that.

As Lieutenant Bannerman and Major Cartwright watched, the small metal platform that the crane was holding was pulled from the yawning mouth of the chasm by the hydraulic winch with which the boom was equipped. A metallic clanking filled the night air as the platform rose into view carrying its two occupants. Even from where he was standing Bannerman could see that they were the men he'd noticed in the Land Rover earlier on. Both were civilians. One of them in his late fifties, the other a good twenty years younger. They held on to the handrail that ran around the platform as they were first raised up from inside the chasm and then deposited carefully on the wet earth. As the two men stepped off the platform Bannerman and Cartwright strode forward to meet them.

It was the younger of the two men who spoke first.

'It's incredible,' he said, shaking his head. 'I've never seen anything like it.'

'Lieutenant Bannerman, this is Doctor Peter Elliot,'

Cartwright explained and the lieutenant shook the right hand of the other man. 'And his father, Professor John Elliot.' Bannerman repeated the greeting with the older civilian. Both men smiled agreeably.

'So, what have we got?' Cartwright asked.

'As I said, it's incredible,' Peter Elliot repeated. 'For a crack of that depth to have opened I'd have to say it was due to seismic activity. But I know that's impossible.'

'An earthquake in the middle of Buckinghamshire?' Cartwright said. 'That's not likely, is it, professor?'

'It's not likely – but how else do you explain *that*?' Peter Elliot said, jabbing a finger at the chasm behind them.

'The activity needed to open a rift of this magnitude would have registered seven or eight on the Richter scale,' said John Elliot. 'They'd have felt it as far as the South Coast and beyond.'

'How deep is it?' Bannerman wanted to know.

'We couldn't reach the bottom,' the professor said. 'We got to a hundred and fifty feet down and had to come back up. We're going to try again later when a longer winch arrives.'

'How deep do you think it is?' Cartwright asked.

'Two, three hundred feet,' said the professor.

'Was there any evidence of radioactivity?' Bannerman asked.

'Not a trace,' Peter Elliot said flatly. 'Not a flicker on the Geiger counter.'

'Then how do you explain the burns that Private Lansing suffered?' the lieutenant demanded. 'And he said there were high levels of radiation detected.'

'If there were there are none now,' the professor told him.

'But how is that possible?' Bannerman persisted. 'How do you explain that?'

'At the moment, lieutenant, I can't,' the professor said almost apologetically. 'None of this adds up.' He turned to his son. 'I want Royston to see this.'

John Elliot nodded.

'Doctor Royston is working with us at the base,' the professor explained. 'He might have some theories about what happened here.'

'The American?' Cartwright asked, quietly.

'I don't think his nationality will affect his expertise, major,' the professor said, smiling.

'I wasn't implying that it would, professor,' Cartwright said, raising his eyebrows. 'I don't care who gives me answers as long as someone does. What do you suggest we do in the meantime?'

'Just what you *have* been doing,' the professor replied. 'Keep this area cordoned off. We'll do as much as we can to get you some answers, major, but we need to get to the bottom of that hole if we can.'

'Could Lansing have misread his Geiger counter, professor?' Bannerman asked. 'He said it was registering maximum. Could he have been mistaken?' 'Well, radio - active material doesn't simply disappear once it's been located,' John Elliot said.

'Except in this case, apparently,' Cartwright said flatly.

'So Lansing wasn't mistaken?' Bannerman said.

'If he was getting readings on his counter then there's

every reason to believe that he'd discovered some kind of radioactive material,' the professor explained. 'But what it was and where it is now I couldn't say.'

'There must be an explanation,' Peter Elliot assured the soldiers. 'And we'll find it.'

'You sound very sure of that,' Cartwright said.

The four men stood in silence, their attention fixed on the gaping breach in the earth that lay before them.

'This may be a stupid question,' Bannerman said. 'But could your research at the base have anything to do with what's happened here?'

Both civilians regarded him warily.

'Absolutely not,' the professor said.

'I hope you're right,' Bannerman told him. 'I could have lost a good man here tonight and I don't want to lose any more.' He turned away and headed off across the marshy ground.

'I get the feeling that Lieutenant Bannerman views us as the enemy at the moment, major,' said Peter Elliot.

Cartwright shook his head.

'He's concerned about the men under his command,' the major explained. 'That's all. He's a good officer. He cares. And, like all of us, the sooner he gets some answers the happier he'll be.'

'We'll start working on this as soon as we get back to the base,' John Elliot said. 'And if possible we'd like to speak to the soldier who was injured.'

Cartwright nodded.

Above them a Lynx helicopter cut across the sky, its spotlights illuminating the scene below it.

'That's to take you back to the base,' Cartwright said,

glancing up at the chopper. 'I'll speak to you when I get back. With luck you'll have some news for me.'

Above them, the Lynx circled and then slowly descended.

Nine

He sat up instantly when his mobile phone rang. The tone cut through the silence and drummed in his ears as he shot out a hand.

Doctor Adam Royston grabbed for the device, wanting to see who was calling but also anxious to silence the strident sound of the ringing. Once he'd done that he swung his legs out of bed, perching on the edge of the mattress.

'Royston,' he said into the mouthpiece.

At the other end of the line an agitated caller gave him details and information to which he listened intently.

'How long ago?' he muttered finally.

The voice on the line told him what he wanted to know.

'I'll be there as soon as I can,' Royston said, ending the call with a press of a button. He sat there for a moment clearing his head, rubbing his eyes with one hand to clear his vision. Then he glanced at his watch as he took it from the bedside table and strapped it on. It was 5:03 a.m. Royston stood up, shivering a little in the cold room. He wandered across to the window and closed it, shivering again. As he passed the dressing table he caught sight of his reflection in the mirror and frowned slightly as he glanced down at his midriff. He pulled at the skin around his waist. Was this the beginning of middle-aged spread he asked himself. He was approaching thirty-nine a little faster than he would have liked so did that count? Royston leaned closer to the mirror and ran a hand through his dark brown hair, checking for any signs of grey, then shook his head as he realised the stupidity of this early-morning attack of vanity. Despite his mental rebuke he cast one more glance at himself before he passed the mirror completely and, overall, he was satisfied with what he saw.

'Adam.'

The voice was heavy with sleep and came from the other side of the bed.

Royston walked back across the room and knelt down beside the source of the voice. Sandra Morgan rolled over to face him, brushing strands of her red hair from her face.

'I thought I heard the phone,' she said, softly.

'You did,' he told her. 'It was the base. I have to go.'

'Oh, Adam, not now,' she groaned. 'What time is it?'

'Just after five.'

'What's so important that you have to leave now?'

'Something's happened – they need my help.'

He leaned over and kissed her on the forehead, then began picking up his clothes from the bedroom floor, pulling them on.

'We were going to have breakfast together,' she reminded him.

'We will next time,' Royston assured her.

'You said that last time.'

'Sandi, if I could stay I would. But this is important.'

'It's always important,' Sandra Morgan grunted. She slid one shapely leg out from beneath the duvet and propped herself up on her elbows, watching Royston as he finished dressing. 'Shall I make you some coffee before you go?'

'No time.'

She pushed the duvet back, exposing her breasts.

'Anything else I can tempt you with?' she said, smiling.

'That's not fair,' Royston said, noticing her actions. 'I have to go,' he repeated. He smiled at her as she pushed down the cover even further, revealing her nakedness. Royston ran an appraising and approving stare over her slim body. She blew him a kiss, then finally climbed out of bed and padded across to him, snaking her arms around his neck.

'Maybe one time you'll stay for the whole night and we can get up together like normal people,' Sandra said. 'Instead of you rushing off like a maniac in the middle of the night.'

'It's hardly the middle of the night,' he corrected her, kissing her softly on the lips. 'It'll be light soon.'

'What's happened that's so important, anyway?'

Royston kissed her forehead, then the tip of her nose.

'You can't tell me,' she said flatly. 'It's top secret, I suppose. Like everything you do.'

'It's work,' he told her.

'How do I know you're not running off to be with another woman?' Sandra asked, trying to inject a note of mock irritation into her tone. 'You might have loads of women chasing after you on that base.'

'After a night with you I haven't got the strength for anyone else,' he said, smiling.

'I'll take that as a compliment,' she told him.

'That's how it was meant.'

Royston pulled on his jacket and headed for the bedroom door. Sandra made to follow him, pulling on a short thin dressing gown.

'No, go back to bed,' he said, touching her cheek with one hand.

'I've got to be at the hospital in two hours. I might as well have a shower, iron my uniform and get ready now. I won't be able to get back to sleep, anyway. Not now.'

He pulled her to him and kissed her, holding her tightly.

'I'll ring you later,' he said.

'No, you won't,' she replied. 'You always say that and you never do. I'll call *you*. That way I know I'll speak to you.'

Royston nodded and smiled, then hurried out of the bedroom. Sandra heard his footfalls on the stairs and then the sound of the front door opening and closing. She crossed to the window and saw him clamber into his car. He started the engine and she watched as the vehicle pulled away down the narrow street.

The sky was heavy with clouds and still coloured with the hues of night and, as she stood at the window for a moment longer, she saw the first droplets of rain spatter the glass.

Ten

The drive from the town of Broughton took Royston less than twenty minutes on roads that were still quiet in the early morning. He passed barely half a dozen other vehicles during the journey before he swung the car off the main road and guided it down the short track that led towards the main entrance of his destination.

A large white-painted sign bore the legend:

BROUGHTON GREEN MILITARY
RESEARCH FACILITY

Royston slowed down as he approached the main gate, fumbling in his jacket pocket for his ID as he saw the soldier emerge from the small brick building beside the gate. The private recognised him and waved him on good-naturedly but Royston lowered his window and presented his credentials anyway. There were certain routines and protocols that had to be followed at all times and this was one of them.

'Morning, Doctor Royston,' the private said cheerfully.

'Good morning,' Royston replied. 'How are you today?'

'I'll be better when I get relieved in an hour's time,' the soldier informed him, glancing perfunctorily at the ID that Royston presented. The young man nodded and stepped back, waving the American scientist through.

Royston took back his ID, raised a hand, then drove through the gate as it swung open.

Away to his left were the red-brick buildings which housed the troops living on the base and to his right the less generic white-painted structures designed for the civilians like him who worked at the facility. Beyond those lay the small research complex itself and the base hospital.

It was towards the hospital that Royston now turned the car.

He pulled up outside the main entrance of the three-storey construction and clambered out, passing through the set of automatic double doors and into the main entryway of the building. There was a desk to his left behind which sat another soldier who also recognised Royston. He nodded in his direction and the scientist returned the gesture.

As he moved beyond the desk and headed towards a bank of lift doors ahead of him his footsteps echoed through the high-ceilinged reception area. One of the lifts bumped to a halt as he reached it and Royston stepped in, jabbing the button marked B. It was to the basement that he needed to go because that was where the morgue was situated.

When the lift came to a halt a moment later he stepped out and made his way along the corridor until he reached the first office on his left. He knocked once, then walked in.

The doctor sitting behind the desk inside the room looked pale and a little confused. He seemed almost grateful when he looked up and saw Royston standing there.

'What happened?' Royston asked. 'Why did you call me? This isn't exactly my field of expertise.'

The doctor got to his feet and sucked in a deep breath.

'I know – but I wanted you to see it,' he announced, picking up a slim Manila file from his desk as he rose. He handed it to Royston who glanced quickly at the sheets of paper within.

Doctor Gordon Briscoe moved past him and into the corridor beyond. Royston followed close behind him.

'This is impossible,' he said as the two men walked. 'It says that when Lansing was brought in he was diagnosed with radiation burns and yet there was no trace of radiation in either his blood or urine tests. Who made a mistake like that?'

'He was exposed to radiation during an exercise he was on,' Briscoe said.

'Then why are there no traces of that in his tests?'

'I was hoping you might be able to tell me.'

'He died here at the hospital?' Royston asked, still scanning the information in the file.

Briscoe nodded. 'About an hour ago. There was nothing we could do for him.'

'He must have been exposed to incredible levels of radiation for it to kill him so quickly. Where the hell was he – in the middle of a nuclear reactor?'

'On an exercise about twenty miles from here.'

Royston was about to say something else when Briscoe pushed open the double doors ahead of them and they moved through. The temperature dropped dramatically as they entered the morgue and Royston glanced around at the three stainless steel tables that occupied the centre of the room. There were what looked like metal filing cabinets on either side of the room and Royston knew this was where bodies were kept before and after autopsy. A storehouse for sightless eyes. He could also see that there was a shape on the closest of the stainless steel slabs, covered by a thin green sheet.

Briscoe crossed to it and gripped one corner.

'Are you ready for this?' he asked.

Royston didn't answer. His gaze was fixed firmly on the sheet which the doctor now pulled back.

What lay beneath had once been a man, Royston knew that much. But it was all he could tell initially from looking at what was left of Private Lansing.

'Shit,' he said through clenched teeth, staring fixedly at the remains. He put a hand to his mouth, fearing for a second that he was going to be sick. The feeling passed and he moved a little nearer, his eyes narrowed in disbelief.

Lansing's body looked as if it had collapsed in upon itself. His flesh – that which wasn't burned black – was pale grey in colour but it lay on the slab like a shroud with nothing to support it. It was as if the bones within had merely disintegrated, leaving nothing but a husk of flesh. On the corpse's face, boils and pustules had swollen before bursting, leaving streaks of thick yellowish fluid all over the sickly grey flesh.

'Can I have some gloves, please?' Royston asked, taking a latex surgical pair from Briscoe when he handed them over. The American pulled them on, then gently used his index finger to prod the flesh of the corpse. It was pliant but so thin that it threatened to tear with the application of any more pressure. Royston lifted one of the hands that dangled before him like a lilo drained of air.

'The autopsy is scheduled for later this morning,' Briscoe said.

Royston merely nodded. 'These burns do look like radiation ones,' he conceded. 'But what caused the rest of the damage I can't begin to imagine.'

'It happened after he got to the hospital and it happened quickly.'

'It's as if the bones have just disappeared.'

Briscoe nodded.

'And this happened twenty miles from here?' Royston asked incredulously.

Again Briscoe nodded.

'I need to see where,' Royston snapped, pulling off the gloves and tossing them aside. He was already heading for the door.

Eleven

Claire Reece was numb.

There was no other word to describe the way she felt. She had walked back from the hospital to the bus stop a few hundred yards away, barely aware of her own feet making contact with the ground. Like a ghost she had seemed to glide across the pavement, unable to feel anything beneath her feet just as she was presently unable to feel anything within herself except a growing coldness.

She felt as if there was a frozen lump deep inside her belly and the chill was radiating outwards, filling her veins and vital organs. When she brushed hair from her face her fingers and hands were quivering gently. She wondered if she was in shock. Perhaps the shaking and coldness were a legacy of what she'd been told back in the quiet, well-maintained room of the Oncology Specialist at St Mary's hospital. That was one of the things that had struck her about the specialist's office: how quiet it was. Claire had felt hemmed in by that stillness, imprisoned by it, and when he had told her the results of her biopsy she had merely let out a gasp. No words had come forth. Just that small, desperate gasp. Then she had begun to shake like a Parkinson's sufferer.

Small tremors at first but they had grown more intense as the impact of what he'd said to her truly struck home.

Malignant.

The word was right up there with 'inoperable' and 'terminal'.

It was one of those words in the language that carried an impact unlike any other. When it was linked to the word 'cancer' or 'tumour' its emotional force was as unstoppable as an out-of-control train.

Malignant tumour.

The words were stuck inside her head. Stuck there as surely as the tumour was inside her breast. There had been no sign of it spreading, the specialist had said, and that was good news. Claire was sure that it was but every other piece of news had been eclipsed by the newly acquired knowledge that she had something growing inside her that could kill her. He could have told her that she'd just won the Euro Lottery jackpot but that information would not have sunk in. It would have been secondary compared with the knowledge that she had a life-threatening disease.

She could remember the specialist going on about chemotherapy and radiotherapy and mastectomy and other words that she had prayed to God she would never have to hear but what he'd said had barely pene - trated her awareness. The only words inside her mind that shone with blinding luminosity were *Malignant Tumour*. She was sure that he'd also said something about being positive and that they had caught it early and several other things intended to make her feel more upbeat about her condition but, as with everything he'd said after 'malignant tumour', the words had faded like early-morning mist when the sun rose.

Claire had tried to prepare herself for the worst before she got her results. She'd tried to persuade herself that if she expected to hear such bad news then she would be somehow braced for such a shock. The reality had been appallingly different. For a brief instant she had thought she might cry. Perhaps the explosion of emotion that accompanied the news that the specialist had given her might help to release the blockage inside her mind.

It's not going to cure the cancer in your breast, though, is it?

She couldn't look at the specialist after that. Not that she blamed him for giving her the news but she simply didn't want to make eye contact with him. She had stared blankly at his desk, listening to him as he rambled on about treatment and prognosis and other things that she no longer cared about. Had he once mentioned the possibility of her not recovering? She couldn't remember. She sat now on the bus, gazing out of the large window at the countryside and the houses that passed by, watching people out walking or seeing them in their gardens and their cars – and she hated them. She hated every single person she saw, one and all. She hated them because they weren't suffering with a disease that might kill them. She hated them because they had the happiness she might never feel again. She hated them for so many reasons. Even glancing around at the others on the bus she felt only anger and rage towards them. They were travelling home to their cosy little houses and their families and they would enjoy their evenings and they would look forward to things in the future. She couldn't. Not any more. Not when she might be dead this time next year or even sooner.

Claire Reece returned to gazing out of the bus window, her whole body now feeling as cold as if she was sitting alone in wet clothes before an open freezer. Her mouth was dry and when she tried to swallow it felt as if someone had filled her throat with chalk.

She felt helpless. Alone. And more frightened than she'd ever been in her life.

Twelve

They called it a folly.

A building constructed at the whim of a rich and sometimes eccentric landowner. A castle, a church or sometimes just a tower that had no architectural purpose or worth at all but was there simply because a wealthy man decided he wanted it to be.

The structure that bore the name Fisher's Folly was deep in the marshlands about five miles from Broughton itself. Surrounded by trees, it was approachable by a muddy and overgrown path but few ever went near the building. There was no need to. It had served no practical purpose upon its first construction and now it was nothing more than a crumbling testament to one man's vanity. It was a round tower that poked upwards from the muddy ground like an accusing finger. Surrounded on all four sides by marshland, Fisher's Folly had been built in 1745 on the orders of the landowner at the time Sir Terence Fisher. He had owned much of the village that Broughton had once been and also a sizeable amount of the land all around it, including the uncultivatable marshland where he had chosen to have the folly built.

Exactly what it had been used for no one knew. Over

the years stories had been passed down and there were even records in the vault of one of Broughton's churches mentioning the folly and its owner. But the real reason for its construction seemed to be little more than Fisher's vanity. There were the inevitable legends favoured by the children of Broughton that Fisher had been a Satanist and that he'd had the folly built as somewhere in which to act out his vile practices but there was no proof to back up this notion. It remained a fanciful story to be told on dark nights in the company of friends or a tale spun by older children to their younger siblings in the hope of inducing a few nightmares. However, older residents of Broughton had their own stories about the brick edifice and some of the things that had gone on there.

During the Second World War a German fighter plane had crashed less than a mile from the folly. Shot down during the Battle of Britain, the ME 109 had slammed into the ground and exploded but not before its pilot had managed to eject and had landed in the marshy ground close to the tower. He had made his way to the folly, presumably having spied it from the crash site and with a view perhaps to hiding inside it. No one knew. But whatever his motives had been, villagers from Broughton had seen the dogfight that had downed his plane and they had emerged from their houses to search for the invader. First they had discovered the wreckage of the plane and then they had found the foot - prints of the pilot in the mud around it. A group of about twenty of them had followed these marks through the marshes to the folly.

Stories that had been passed down from generation to generation varied concerning the exact chain of events that had followed. Some said that the German pilot had tried to hide inside Fisher's Folly to escape the mob. Those same stories told of how he had fired several shots at the men and women gathered outside who had finally managed to heroically subdue him and take him back to the village where they had held him until he was taken into captivity by British soldiers. That was the more acceptable version of the events that had happened that night. However, there were men and women still alive in Broughton who had been living in the village that night and who told a different tale.

They told how the pilot was tracked across the fields and marshes like a fox hunted by a pack of hounds. They told how a man from their village had died at Dunkirk only months earlier and that the villagers saw the German as the embodiment of the Fascist evil that the entire country was facing. A symbol of the enemy troops who had killed one of their own at Dunkirk. And they had sought retribution.

Many of those who had hunted that downed Luftwaffe pilot across the fields and marshes that night had been armed with everything from shotguns to pitchforks, scythes and knives. When they'd set off after him, they'd had no desire to capture him with a view to handing him over to the army. They had only one thought in their collective minds that night.

So they had pursued him to Fisher's Folly and they had cornered him there and, despite his attempts to surrender, they had butchered him. There had even been talk of a decapitation. Then they had disposed of the body, allowed the black water and mud to swallow it and along with it their guilt. Then they had returned to the village, feeling as if in some small way they had achieved revenge for the one of their number who had been killed at Dunkirk.

That was the story that not so many in Broughton repeated when talk of Fisher's Folly came up. Younger residents seemed more willing to speak of a more recent tragedy that had happened there. The girl's name had been Ingrid and she'd become pregnant by a man from a nearby town but, being only fifteen at the time, she hadn't dared to face her parents and family. Taunted by some who knew and without anyone to turn to for help, she had trekked out to the folly one winter night, broken into the structure, then climbed to the top and hung herself from its summit. The body had hung there for almost a week before it was discovered. Supposedly the ghost of Ingrid still haunted Fisher's Folly and the woods around it. Some even claimed to have seen the apparition stalking vengefully around the marshes and woods.

So, for most, the tower was the stuff of legend and stories. No one went near it because no one needed to. It belonged to another age and a different set of sensibilities.

The thick wooden door at its base remained closed. All the secrets it held still untold for now.

The helicopters that had passed above it that night on their way to and from Broughton Green Research Facility had picked it out with their spotlights and several of the pilots and occupants of the transports had commented on it. But it had faded quickly from their thoughts. They had more pressing matters on their minds than some decaying old tower. So they flew on above it and paid it no heed.

Why should they?

Thirteen

'At least a hundred and fifty feet deep, you say?' Adam Royston had to raise his voice considerably to make himself heard above the roar of the Lynx's rotor blades. He peered out of the side window of the chopper once again, his gaze fixed on the giant gash in the ground below.

'It's incredible,' he said, shaking his head.

The Lynx circled again and Royston ran appraising eyes over the breach in the terrain. In the early dawn light it looked even more formidable.

'And you say there was no trace of radioactivity inside it?' he went on.

'Not when we checked it,' Professor John Elliot told him. 'Whether there's any as it gets deeper I don't know.'

'And yet Lansing reported high levels of radiation in this area and he showed signs of radiation burns,' Royston said. 'But not even huge levels of overexposure to radiation would do to him what I saw.'

'So what's the answer?' Peter Elliot asked.

'To what?' Royston said. 'What caused this? This looks like seismic activity.' He pointed down towards the rip in the ground. 'Or what killed Lansing?'

'Both,' Peter Elliot said.

'My guess is that the two are linked,' Royston stated. 'It's a little coincidental otherwise, isn't it?'

'If there is a link then the other men down there could be at risk,' the professor noted.

Royston nodded, gazing down uneasily at the soldiers who were swarming over the ground around the huge rift like ants around a crack in the wall of their nest.

'We need to know how deep it goes,' he went on. 'And, if possible, we need to reach the bottom of it and take a closer look.'

'But if there is contamination the whole area could be unstable . . .' the professor began. But he allowed the sentence to trail off as he saw Royston nodding.

The American scientist leaned forward and tapped sharply on the pilot's shoulder. 'Take us down, please,' he called and the Lynx began to descend.

As it touched down gently on the muddy ground the three passengers scrambled out, ducking their heads as they moved away from the chopper which rose slowly into the air once more. Royston strode immediately to the edge of the gap in the earth and knelt beside it.

'And there was no radioactivity recorded the last time it was examined?' he asked.

'There's been nothing since the hole first opened up,' the professor told him. 'Not even deeper down inside the crevice itself.'

Two soldiers approached the trio of civilians, eyeing them suspiciously.

65

'Excuse me, sir,' said the first of them, looking at Royston. 'This area is restricted. It might be dangerous. You can't stay here.'

'It's OK,' Royston explained, producing his ID. 'We're here on official business.'

The soldier glanced at the ID and nodded.

'Where's Major Cartwright?' the professor asked.

'He's dealing with some local news people, sir,' the soldier answered. 'I don't think he's too happy about it, either.' The man smiled and so did his companion. 'He's just over that ridge.' He pointed off to the wooded rising ground ahead of them and the three men set off in that direction.

'The local police are going to have to be involved in this,' Royston noted as he and the other two men made their way across the muddy terrain and up the slope. 'If this area is contaminated or unstable then the public could be at risk.'

'Some of it's Ministry of Defence land, anyway,' Peter Elliot told him. 'It's private property, strictly speaking. No one other than designated personnel should be in this area.'

'I'm not saying that the place is going to be overrun with sightseers,' Royston went on. 'But you know what people are like: if they get wind of this they'll want to see it even if it's only to make sure that they're not in danger or that their homes aren't under threat. It's a localised problem at the moment and it's got to stay that way.'

As the three men crested the ridge they saw Major Cartwright just below them. He was standing beside a

Range Rover, faced by half a dozen civilians – one of whom was carrying an ENG video camera on his shoulder as he squinted through the eyepiece. A single uniformed policeman stood among them too, looking curiously incongruous. Royston and his companions approached slowly, standing five or six yards from the periphery of the little group whose voices were being raised occasionally. Royston glanced at each of them in turn.

'You didn't answer my question, major,' one of the journalists protested. 'Was anyone else hurt? There was a military exercise going on – were any other troops injured?'

'Will there be an official statement about what happened here?' another man asked, stepping aside to allow his cameraman a better shot of the major.

Cartwright held up a hand for silence.

'Strictly speaking,' he began, 'what happened here happened on Ministry of Defence property so the army would be perfectly entitled to withhold information should it see fit. But an official statement will be made and, in the meantime, there's very little for you to report other than that there was some minor seismic activity in the area.'

'An earthquake?' one of the men said, incredulously.

'No, not an earthquake,' Cartwright corrected him. 'We're not one hundred per cent sure what to call it at the moment but we think it was a tremor of some description. I just want to repeat that the situation is under control and there's no need for alarm.'

'Why would you want to withhold information,

major?' another journalist asked. 'Is something going on here that you feel we shouldn't know about?'

'I was making the point that there is no cover-up,' Cartwright said irritably.

'What about the soldier who was killed?' the first man persisted. 'How did it happen?'

'I'm not at liberty to say,' Cartwright announced.

'You mean you *won't* say?'

Cartwright shot the man a warning glance.

'There have been rumours that the base at Broughton Green is being used to develop chemical and biological weapons,' the second newsman interjected. 'Was the death of the soldier on the exercise linked to that?'

'As I said, there will be an official statement regarding this matter,' Cartwright said. 'As for the rumours you speak of, that is precisely what they are: rumours.'

'You wouldn't tell us if they were true, would you, major?' the first man snapped.

Cartwright ignored the comment and turned towards another of the men who was holding the microphone of a small portable tape recorder towards him.

'Have the family of the dead man been informed?' the man wanted to know.

'They will be in due course—' Cartwright said.

'Don't you think it's a little ironic, major?' the first newsman cut in. 'British troops are being killed in Afghanistan almost every day and now a man who was due to undertake his first tour of duty there in a few days has been killed before he even leaves.'

'I don't see the point you're trying to make,' the major said dismissively. 'The man died here, not in

Afghanistan. He wasn't killed as part of the exercise.'

'Will he be given a full military burial?' another man asked.

'That will be the choice of the dead man's family,' Cartwright stated. 'They will be offered all the help they need by the army – as is usual in a case like this.'

'Is there any danger to the people living in Broughton and the surrounding areas, major?' the second journalist wanted to know. 'If it was seismic activity then can we expect more?'

'As far as we can ascertain there is no danger – but, then again, I'm no geologist,' the major said. 'As I've said twice already, a formal statement will be issued.'

'What kind of chemical weapons are being manu - factured at the base, major?' the first man pressed.

Cartwright waved his hand dismissively.

'Right, gentlemen, that's it,' he said flatly. 'You'll all receive copies of the official statement when it's issued. Any other questions will have to wait. This area will be cordoned off as of 0900 this morning. Anyone found trespassing will be in direct breach of Home Office regulations and will be arrested. That's all.'

He pushed his way through the small group of newsmen and headed up the slope to where Royston, the professor and Peter were waiting.

When he reached them he glanced back to where the media men were now gathered around the uniformed policeman who was leading them away from the site, guiding and cajoling them like some kind of blue-clad sheep-dog anxious not to lose control of its flock.

'Bloody newspapers,' Cartwright muttered, watching the men as they left.

'It's only natural, major,' the professor said. 'This is a big story for this area.'

'Let's just hope it doesn't get any bigger,' Cartwright said. 'There was mention of chemical and biological weapons.'

'What did you expect?' the professor said. 'You and your men operate from a military research facility so they're bound to think the worst. They're not stupid, major.'

'Aren't they?' Cartwright said dismissively.

'You know the media, major,' Royston said. 'Always looking for a story, even if there isn't one there.'

Cartwright nodded sagely and walked on, pausing at the top of the ridge where he looked down at the rift once again.

'You're right, Doctor Royston,' he said quietly, his gaze still fixed on the split in the ground. 'But this time there *might* be a story.'

Fourteen

The ticking of the wall clock sounded thunderous in the silence of the office.

Royston glanced across almost accusingly at the timepiece, then checked it against his own watch.

1:23 p.m.

He reached for the mug of coffee on his desk and took a sip, wincing when he found that the black liquid was stone cold. He glanced at the file before him, running his gaze over its contents again just as he had been doing for the last hour or more. It was as if constantly reading and rereading the pages would somehow clarify matters for him and offer an explanation for what seemed inexplicable.

For what must have been the fifth time, Royston began to read the autopsy results on Private Donald Lansing. Halfway through he stopped once again, rubbing his forehead slowly.

Royston banged the file down on his desktop, his frustration finally boiling over.

'Jesus H. Christ,' he grunted.

'I doubt if even he'd be able to help on this one.'

Royston looked up to see that Professor Elliot was

standing in the doorway of the office, looking at him quizzically.

'I'm sorry, John, I didn't see you there. Come in,' Royston sighed, beckoning the older man to enter. 'It's the autopsy results on Lansing.'

'I know, I read them.'

'Traces of radiation in the remains,' Royston read again. 'And yet at the site where this happened there's no trace of radioactivity. It doesn't make sense. Also, the state of the body. We've all seen the effects of radiation burns and of overexposure to radioactivity but it doesn't cause the kind of damage that was done to Lansing.'

'And the rest of the autopsy findings?' the professor asked, raising an eyebrow.

'God knows,' Royston said, shaking his head. He glanced at the autopsy report and ran his index finger over one page. 'Four sizeable cancerous tumours found inside the main chest cavity, three more in the remains of the large intestine. It's as though he was eaten away from the inside by cancer but there was no trace of the disease during his last medical two months ago. These tumours seem to have grown rapidly and very recently.'

'So what's your explanation?'

'I don't have one,' Royston replied. 'I only wish I did. I did have one theory but I dismissed it as quickly as any sane and rational man would.' He smiled.

'Tell me,' the professor said.

'Lansing was killed by exposure to something highly radioactive,' Royston went on. 'A source of radio -

activity that is no longer present at the site where it was originally.'

'That would explain the burns but not the tumours.'

'An extremely high dose of concentrated radiation could have caused the cancer to develop as well but surely not in so short a space of time. The tumours inside Lansing's body look as if they've been there for months, possibly even years and yet all the medical evidence contradicts that. He was in first-class health. There was certainly no trace of disease of any kind, let alone a number of potentially fatal cancerous growths.'

The professor shrugged. 'So what are you saying?'

'There's only one explanation, John,' Royston sighed. 'The radiation he encountered caused his death – there's no disputing that – and we must assume that it also caused the unnaturally rapid growth of several cancers inside his body. But if that source of radioactivity isn't there now then it's moved – or it's *been* moved.'

'So you're telling me that Lansing was killed by a radioactive mass that is being transferred around by person or persons unknown?'

'I told you any sane or rational man would dismiss my theory.' Royston smiled grimly.

'Peter probably wouldn't,' the professor said. 'He seems to regard everything you say with something approaching awe.'

Royston frowned and sat back in his seat, watching the professor warily. 'That sounds like a slight exaggeration, John,' he said quietly.

'I know he's been doing some of your work for you.'

'He's been assisting me. There's a difference.'

'His job here is administration. I know he wants to be a scientist but there's no need for you to encourage him.'

'I thought the quest for knowledge was to be admired, not discouraged.'

'He looks up to you. He has done since you got here. You came with something of a reputation in your field. Merited, I admit, but please don't waste Peter's time.'

'I wasn't aware that I was wasting his time, John. I was trying to help him.'

'Your experiments concerning the interruption of radio waves by radioactivity were virtually completed by Peter.'

'I had more pressing matters to attend to and he was more than happy to help.'

'He would be. As I said, he looks on you with something approaching awe.'

Royston held up both hands in a pacifying gesture. 'I apologise if I've offended you in any way. That wasn't my intention.'

'And my intention isn't to sound like an over-protective father. You know how much I respect you and the work you've done, Adam,' the professor said. 'But Peter has a promising career in front of him and it's up to me to decide which direction it takes.'

'Don't you think it should be up to Peter?'

The professor regarded Royston silently for a moment, then pointed at the autopsy report lying before him. Royston could only shrug again.

'The press will be here eventually, you know,' the professor sighed.

'They'll go wherever they can to find their story.'

Royston glanced down as he felt a vibration from his mobile phone. He dug in his jacket pocket and pulled it out.

'I'll let you take care of that,' John Elliot said, getting to his feet.

'It's OK, it's just a text.' Royston smiled as he read it. 'From Sandi.'

'The woman in the town who you're sleeping with?' Royston nodded.

The professor raised one eyebrow, then turned towards the door of Royston's office.

'There's no law against me seeing her, is there, John?' the American asked. 'I'm not breaking any moral or ethical laws, am I?'

'What you do in your own time is your business, Adam.'

'She's a nurse. She works in Broughton's largest hospital.'

'That's none of my concern.' Professor Elliot smiled slightly. 'A nurse this time? Ah, well, as long as she isn't a reporter.'

'What's that supposed to mean?'

'Not long after you came to work here there were articles in the local paper, speculating about our research at Broughton Green. You were seeing a woman who worked for the local paper at the time. I'm just suggesting that perhaps you should be more careful what you say when it comes to pillow talk.'

'There's always been speculation about what we do here. It had nothing to do with my relationship with that woman. I never told her anything about our work. What the hell do you take me for, John – some green kid? I would never give details to anyone about what goes on here, let alone to a reporter.'

'Even one you were sleeping with?'

Royston shook his head. 'I don't have to justify myself to you,' he said flatly. 'Who I see and who I sleep with is my business – like you yourself just said – and it's nothing to do with my work. I'm insulted you would even insinuate that.'

'I'm just suggesting that you should take a little more care in some cases.'

Royston was about to say something else when the phone on his desk rang. He snatched it up and pressed it to his ear.

John Elliot watched him as he took the call, noticing how the expression on the American scientist's face darkened as he listened to the voice on the other end of the line. When he finally replaced the receiver he frowned and looked across the desk at the professor.

'Seven of the men who were on that same exercise as Lansing last night have been admitted to the base hos-pital in the past hour,' he said flatly. 'They're suffering from vomiting, diarrhoea, dizziness and disorientation, low blood pressure, internal bleeding and even hair loss. What does that sound like to you, John?'

'Those are the symptoms of radiation poisoning,' the professor stated quietly.

Royston was already on his feet.

Fifteen

'And all these men were admitted in the last hour?'

Royston walked slowly down the middle of the ward, glancing to his left and right at the figures lying in the beds there.

Doctor Briscoe nodded and glanced at his notes.

'They were brought from their barracks,' he said.

'And only these seven men exhibited these symptoms?' Royston asked.

'One or two others were feeling nauseous, apparently. But only these seven developed symptoms so quickly and suffered so acutely,' Briscoe replied.

Royston paused and then walked across to one of the soldiers, glancing first at the clipboard that hung at the bottom of the man's bed. The name at the top was COULSON. Royston looked down at the sergeant who was drifting in and out of consciousness.

Coulson's skin was deathly pale apart from the blotchy red marks on his face and neck. There were more of them on his arms and at the top of his chest, visible when Royston pulled back the covers slightly. Coulson's lips trembled as the American scientist ran an appraising gaze over him.

'What about temperature?' Royston asked.

'Every one of them was running a high fever when they were brought in,' Briscoe explained. 'Most seem to have stabilised now.'

'It certainly looks like radiation poisoning,' John Elliot offered.

'We're still waiting for the blood and urine tests to be completed,' Briscoe explained. 'It all happened so suddenly that it took us by surprise, to be honest.'

'Have any oncology tests been ordered?' Royston asked.

'Why would we test them for cancer?' Briscoe enquired, a look of bewilderment on his face.

'Would it be possible to do that as soon as possible?' Royston persisted.

'I can ask the lab to check their blood work for that,' Briscoe told him. 'But why?'

'Just indulge me, Doctor Briscoe,' Royston murmured, passing along to the next bed.

The man who lay there was in a similar state, his pale skin dotted with livid red marks that looked like weals or friction burns. They were concentrated around his neck and cheeks. As he turned his head Royston saw a large clump of hair come away from his scalp, leaving a bright red patch of exposed flesh.

'Hair loss doesn't usually result as rapidly as this, even in the most severe cases of exposure to radiation,' Professor Elliot commented. 'The nausea, vomiting, headaches and diarrhoea would begin fairly soon after exposure.'

'But only if these men had been exposed to severe

levels of radiation,' Royston added. 'I'm talking about between eight and ten grays or higher and even then some of the symptoms wouldn't kick in for up to a week. Not as acutely as we're seeing here.'

'So the source of radiation is even more potent than we first thought,' the professor mused.

'And yet there's no trace of it at the site of the exercise,' Royston reminded him. He shook his head and sighed. 'Signs and symptoms of radiation sickness usually appear when the entire body receives an absorbed dose of at least one gray. As I said, these men look as if they've been exposed to more than eight grays.'

Royston and the professor exchanged a look that Briscoe wasn't slow to catch.

'Meaning?' he demanded.

Royston stepped away from the beds and lowered his voice.

'Levels that high are normally untreatable,' he said quietly. 'Unless there's some improvement within the next twenty-four hours it doesn't look good for any of these men.'

'And what about those who are still out at the site?' Briscoe protested.

'Until we know the source of this threat we have no way of knowing who is and who isn't at risk,' the American told him.

'Whatever it is seems to be behaving more like a virus,' Professor Elliot offered.

'Let's pray to God it isn't,' Royston said. 'If it's communicable then I don't even want to consider the possible dangers.'

'Is that likely?' Briscoe enquired.

'No,' Royston told him. 'But just because it's unlikely doesn't mean it's impossible. Nothing that's happened around here in the past twenty-four hours has been predictable or expected but it's still happened. We have to consider every single eventuality.'

The trio of men made their way to the end of the ward where Royston paused briefly and glanced back at the men lying in the beds.

'The other men who were on that exercise last night will have to be monitored,' he said.

Briscoe nodded.

'We could run routine tests on them,' he suggested.

'That's a good idea but we don't want to cause any alarm if we can help it,' the American said.

'One man has died, seven more may well be fatally ill and there's a split in the earth out there that looks as if it's been caused by an earthquake,' the professor snapped. 'I'd say that if anything was likely to cause alarm then that is, Adam.'

The two men regarded one another warily for a moment.

'What happened out there during that exercise last night is the key to this whole thing, I'm sure of it,' Royston said. 'That split opened up and all hell broke loose.'

'Well, whatever caused that split had to have a beginning,' the professor offered.

'It had to have an end, too,' Royston told him.

'Surely the forces causing these surface rifts just disperse,' Briscoe interjected.

'Forces causing a surface rupture don't burn one man to death by radiation and poison seven others,' Royston said.

'What are you getting at?' Briscoe wanted to know. 'You said yourself that the damage Lansing suffered was nothing like the effects of radiation.'

'No effects I've ever seen before,' Royston told him. 'But that doesn't mean that radiation isn't the problem. Let's just assume that whatever caused this has something to do with that crack in the earth out there. I think that's where we should be concentrating our efforts. If we find the source of the problem then we might have some way of helping the poor bastards in here.' He looked once again at the men lying in the beds.

'And how do we determine once and for all that the seismic activity is to blame?' Briscoe asked.

'We have to get inside that breach again,' Royston told him.

'It's already been looked at,' the professor reminded him. 'Peter and I investigated it ourselves as far down as one hundred and fifty feet.'

Royston nodded. 'I know that,' he said. 'But we have to look again. We have to find the bottom and see exactly what the hell is down there.'

Sixteen

Nikki Cross hated hospitals.

She hated the smells, the sight of sick people, the ambulances roaring up to A&E carrying their latest victims and the vision of so many white-coated staff going about their business.

Many people saw hospitals as places of healing, care and eventual recovery. Not Nikki. She associated them with suffering, pain and death.

Both her parents had died in hospital when she was younger. Her father in the aftermath of a car crash and her mother of cancer. Both had arrived in an ambulance and left in a wooden box and Nikki couldn't shake that thought as she sat in the waiting room of Broughton's largest hospital, St Mary's. Admittedly she hadn't heard of too many cases of women dying while undergoing sonogram tests but, nevertheless, she shifted uncom - fortably in her seat, glancing around at the other women in the room.

Like her they were pregnant but not all of them were here for a scan as she was. In particular the woman opposite looked as if she would have been more com - fortable in the maternity unit itself rather than in antenatal because from the size of her she appeared as if she was going to have her baby at any moment. She kept getting to her feet, rubbing her bulging belly and groaning periodically. Nikki was half-expecting to hear the splash of fluid on the ground as her waters broke but, thankfully, that didn't happen.

Nikki touched her own stomach through her blouse, the memories of the pain she had felt there the previous night still fresh in her mind. She had been thankful that there had been no recurrence of the pain as the night had worn on and nothing so far today. What she had felt, however, had also left her worried. There had been a kind of warmth enveloping her belly and her pelvis for most of the morning. It wasn't an unpleasant feeling, she had to concede but it was unusual and something she hadn't read about in any of the books on pregnancy which she'd dipped into ever since she'd discovered she was carrying a child. Paul had told her not to read the books. Even a doctor and one of the midwives she'd seen had said that all pregnancies were different and that there were no hard and fast rules for what should or shouldn't be expected (apart from the obvious prob-lems like morning sickness and things of that nature). But Nikki had sought reassurance on the printed page and also on the Internet and everything bad that she'd read had stuck in her mind like a splinter.

Everything that could go wrong with the pregnancy, the birth and beyond was lodged in her consciousness, stored there in some mental filing cabinet to be drawn upon whenever she felt discomfort or stress. Pregnancy, she had heard and no doubt read, was supposed to be an almost magical time when a woman felt at her most radiant and blooming. Nikki had experienced nothing but stress and worry ever since the first day she'd discovered that she was carrying.

She wanted to enjoy the pregnancy. She wanted the positive feelings she'd read about but she couldn't shake the uncertainty. Things did go wrong, there was no point denying that, and try as she might she couldn't seem to focus her mind on anything other than the negative aspects. And now she had this warmth spreading across her pelvis and belly.

Was it a sign that the child was already dead inside her, she wondered? Strangled by its own umbilical cord? (She had read of that more than once).

Across the waiting room another woman a little younger than her flicked through one of the out-of-date magazines on offer and smiled happily to herself. Her shoulder-length brown hair was shining, her pretty face seemed to be almost glowing and when she looked up every now and then her eyes sparkled as if lit from inside by tiny lamps. That, Nikki thought, is how I'm supposed to look. 'I'm supposed to be blooming, blissfully expectant at the thought of bringing new life into the world.

She glanced down at her belly again and rubbed it, the warmth still spreading across her pelvis and now her lower back. Nikki swallowed hard, becoming more convinced by the second that there was something terribly wrong with either her, her baby or both of them.

The heavily pregnant woman was walking back and forth slowly, the weight of her belly slowing her down.

She looked like a python that had just swallowed an antelope and was waiting for the meal to digest inside her before she regained her normal grace, Nikki thought and that idea brought a smile to her lips at least for a second or two. The other woman, still glancing at the magazine on her lap, slipped off first one shoe, then the other and flexed her toes against the linoleum floor of the waiting room. Swollen feet and ankles, Nikki guessed: another unwanted by-product of pregnancy.

She herself now got to her feet and crossed to the water cooler that stood in one corner of the waiting room. She downed one paper cup of the clear liquid then refilled it and drank another before returning to her seat. She'd drunk four large glasses of water before leaving home to ensure her bladder was full as she'd been instructed and the amount of fluid she had imbibed was beginning to make her feel a little uncomfortable. The warmth she had felt across her stomach and pelvis was beginning to dissipate, she was relieved to feel. However, she hoped that wasn't a sign in itself of some catastrophic change in her body's chemistry or in the health of her growing child. Nikki was beginning to wonder if there was any state of being that would actually make her feel better. No matter how she felt physically she seemed to be in a state of anxiety about the child's health or her own.

She decided not to tell Paul about this latest episode. He would just laugh or tell her she was worrying too much as he normally did. She knew he was probably right but she just wished there was some way she could be sure once and for all that her fears and anxieties were groundless. Perhaps after the scan was completed she could relax a little more, she thought.

Nikki leaned forward and pulled a magazine from the piles on the large table in the middle of the room in a desperate attempt to occupy her mind. She flipped open the magazine and saw one of the many pointless so-called celebrities who infested its pages posing there with their latest child. Nikki scanned the headline:

MY PREGNANCY NIGHTMARE

She put the magazine back on the table and wandered over to the water cooler once more.

Barely had she finished sipping the contents of the paper cup than the door at one end of the waiting room opened and she saw a nurse emerge who looked cheerfully in Nikki's direction.

'Nikki Cross,' the nurse announced. 'Would you like to come through?'

Nikki nodded and walked through the door that the nurse was holding open for her. As she passed, Nikki saw the name badge on the nurse's tunic: Sandra Morgan.

In the centre of the room there was a couch covered in thin blue paper and surrounded by all manner of equip-ment and it was towards this that Sandra motioned her. Nikki climbed up onto it and lay back as the nurse scanned her file.

'How are you feeling, Nikki?' Sandra asked.

Tell her about the pains last night.

'Any problems?' Sandra went on. 'Anything worrying you?'

Tell her about the pains and tell her about that sensation you had in the bloody waiting room. Tell her.

'Just aches and pains,' Nikki said. 'But I suppose that's normal.'

'One of the less enjoyable parts of being pregnant,' the nurse told her, smiling. 'I used to get terrible backache when I was carrying my little girl. You forget all about that once you've had them, though.'

Nikki nodded, looking around at the equipment surrounding her.

Tell her about the pains last night.

'This is your first, isn't it?' Sandra went on. 'So everything will be new to you, anyway. But there's nothing to worry about and once this scan is done then you can relax.' She scribbled a couple of things on the sheet in front of her, then glanced at Nikki again. 'The sonographer doing the scan will be through in a minute – she's got another lady in the other room. It's like a conveyor belt in here. We're all overworked. I'm supposed to be on the children's ward, too.' She shook her head and smiled. 'You just lay back and take it easy until she gets here. You can lift your top up for me and we'll put the gel on ready for her.'

Nikki did as she was instructed, pulling her T-shirt up to expose her belly, which Sandra glanced at before reaching for a pot of clear viscous gel. Using a broad wooden spatula she began to smear it over Nikki's belly.

Nikki shuddered.

'I know it's cold – sorry about that,' Sandra said as she continued applying the clear gel. 'I'm sure you know all about these scans but I'll explain anyway.'

Nikki nodded.

'This is a real-time ultrasound scan,' the nurse told her. 'You'll be able to see the baby on the screen just there.' She pointed to a monitor next to the couch where Nikki was lying. 'Do you want to know the sex? The sonographer will be able to tell you.'

'We wanted a little girl – well, I did. I don't think Paul minds,' Nikki told her. 'Do you have to tell me whether it's a girl or a boy?'

'No. If you want it to be a surprise on the day then that's your choice. This scan will tell you the sex if you want to know and it'll tell you when the baby's going to be born so you can start planning and getting your spare room painted blue or pink, that kind of thing.' Sandra laughed.

Again Nikki nodded.

Now would be the perfect time to mention the pains, wouldn't it?

'There you go,' Sandra announced. 'I'll just nip through and check that the sonographer's ready and we'll get going.'

Alone in the room, surrounded by the equipment, Nikki felt a little more confident, her anxiety receding considerably. She looked at the clear gel on her belly and smiled, relieved that she'd had no recurrence of the discomfort or feeling of warmth she'd experienced last night or earlier in the day. The pain was gone, so why mention it? If it was serious then it would still be there, wouldn't it?

Really?

Nikki glanced at the blank monitor screen and then at her belly once more.

Sandra returned a moment later, followed by a thin-faced woman with short blonde hair who looked as if she was pursing her lips when she smiled at Nikki.

She switched on the monitor and reached for the transducer, moving it towards Nikki's belly.

'Now if you've got a full bladder – which is what we asked for – you may find this a little uncomfortable to begin with,' the sonographer said, pressing the hand-held unit against the gel and sliding it across. She glanced at Nikki, checking her reaction. Then she adjusted the contrast on the monitor. A black and white picture began to form on the screen and the sonographer now concentrated her attention on that as she moved the transducer slowly back and forth, the equipment sliding easily across Nikki's belly as it glided over the gel.

Sandra also glanced at the screen, then at Nikki, and smiled.

'And you're three months?' the sonographer said, still peering at the screen.

'Yes,' Nikki said, clearing her throat nervously.

The sonographer frowned and Nikki wasn't slow to spot the reaction. She herself glanced at the monitor but couldn't make any sense out of the mass of confused images there.

'Is something wrong?' she asked, her voice cracking.

The sonographer didn't answer; she merely pressed a little more firmly on Nikki's belly with the transducer and looked more intently at the monitor.

Sandra too was gazing at the screen now.

'The baby could be lying with its back to the camera,' she said under her breath.

'Something's wrong, isn't it?' Nikki said breathlessly, trying to sit up, craning her neck to get a clearer view of the monitor.

'Please keep still,' the sonographer said. 'I need to get a clear view.'

The image on the screen finally appeared with razor-sharp clarity.

'Oh my God,' Sandra murmured, her mouth falling open, her stare fixed on the monitor.

The sonographer said nothing but merely sat gaping at the image before her, trembling slightly.

Nikki Cross saw the vision on the screen all too clearly. Her eyes bulged wildly in their sockets and she screamed.

She was still screaming thirty seconds later.

Seventeen

'You'll bottle it. You won't do it.'

Ryan Dickinson and George Finlay stood in one corner of the playground of Simpson Junior School facing half a dozen other boys.

'You're scared,' another boy added venomously.

Even though they were all aged around ten every one of the boys facing them seemed bigger and more menacing than anyone Ryan or George had ever seen before. Neither of them could even remember being confronted like this in their last school. Their school life so far had been blissfully uneventful until their arrival at Simpson. They had found it difficult enough to settle here in Broughton and the constant harassment by some of their fellow pupils had certainly not helped the process.

They were outsiders, they knew that. New boys. And no one liked new boys. Least of all other ten-year-olds. They were viewed with suspicion by almost everyone at Simpson – but then, that was the way of children that age. Both of them had been outcasts since they had arrived. Ryan had wondered how long they had to attend the school before they could shake off that unwanted stigma but three months obviously wasn't long enough.

Many a night he had cried himself to sleep wondering why his parents had ever had to move to Broughton from their previous home. He had loved it there. Everything about it. His school, his teachers, his room (it had been bigger than the poky little one he had in their new house) and his other friends. His mum had told him that he would make new friends in Broughton but this hadn't been the case. The only friend he'd made had been George and the two of them had become closer purely and simply because they were united in their misery at being new and unaccepted.

That misery was reaching new heights now.

'We'll go,' George said defiantly, staring first at the other boys and then glancing at Ryan. 'We'll go and we'll prove to you that we've been.'

'And when we do you have to leave us alone,' Ryan offered.

'Or what? You'll tell the teacher?' one of the other boys jeered. The remaining boys laughed and the sound had a mocking edge to it.

'Even the teachers don't like you,' another boy added.

'Yeah, you're like foreigners,' said a tall gangly one. 'You weren't born in Broughton so you shouldn't be here. My dad says all foreigners should be sent home.'

'Where did you two come from, anyway?' another boy chided.

Ryan and George stood silently for a moment, wanting only respite from this ordeal. Both of them noticed a teacher on the far side of the playground, surrounded by a group of girls, but they both knew that escape was impossible and even if they reported what was going on they would only suffer more for it in the long run. Those were the rules in the world of ten-year-olds. That was how things happened.

'Did you come from Poland?' one of the boys sniggered. 'My dad says there are Poles everywhere in Broughton now.'

Some of the others laughed.

'If we're from Poland then we'd speak Poland, wouldn't we?' George said, trying to muster something like defiance in his voice but instantly regretting it when he saw the tall boy advance a step towards him.

'My mum says that your mum thinks she's better than everyone else,' another boy snapped, jabbing an accusatory finger towards Ryan.

'No, she doesn't,' Ryan protested.

'She's a right old skank, anyway, your mum,' the boy went on. 'Always walking around in her high heels with her tits hanging out. She's like a slag or something.'

The others laughed and Ryan swallowed hard as he felt tears welling up.

'My mum says that's why your dad left her,' the boy went on. 'She was shagging loads of other men so your dad left her. That's why you haven't got a dad.'

Ryan clenched his jaws together tightly, determined not to cry in front of the others but it was becoming more and more of a struggle. George looked at him and saw the emotion in his face. He spoke up quickly.

'What do you want us to do tonight?' he said, as loudly and bravely as he could.

'Do you know where Fisher's Folly is?' the tall boy demanded.

Ryan and George nodded.

'Do you even know *what* it is?' another of the little group snapped.

'It's like a castle or something,' Ryan said. 'Out in the marshes.'

'It's not a castle,' chided one of the boys. 'It's a tower. And it's haunted.'

There were murmurs from the other boys now.

'Yeah, and people get killed when they go there,' the boy said sneeringly. 'That's probably what'll happen to you two if you even dare go. My sister said someone was found there once and they'd had their head cut off.'

'They won't go,' the tall boy stated. 'If they do they might shit themselves.'

The other members of the group laughed raucously, one of them adding to the moment by blowing loud raspberries. He patted his backside and sniffed his hand.

'Ooh, Ryan and George have shit themselves,' he yelled and the remark was greeted by more laughter and jeering.

'They will if they see Old Tom,' the first of the boys offered.

'We'll go,' George said sharply.

'You have to bring back something that belongs to Old Tom,' the first boy said.

'Who's Old Tom?' Ryan wanted to know.

'You'll find out when you get there,' the boy sneered.

The little group closed in more tightly around Ryan and George.

'You get something that belongs to Old Tom,' the tall

one said. 'Bring it back and show it to us and we'll let you play with us. You can be our friends.' There was a collective mumble of approval from the others in the group. 'If you don't then you're going to get it worse. You know what I'm saying? And don't tell your mum and dad.'

Ryan and George nodded, taking a step backwards. The tall boy pushed Ryan once in the chest, then turned and ran off towards the school field, pursued by the others.

'Who's Old Tom?' Ryan murmured, watching as the group of boys raced away.

George could only shake his head.

Eighteen

'What's wrong with my baby?'

Nikki Cross repeated the words again, wiping tears from her face with a sodden tissue.

Sandra Morgan sat opposite her feeling as helpless as she'd ever felt in her life. She watched the stricken woman sitting on the couch before her, her legs drawn up beneath her in something resembling a foetal pose.

The room that they were in was small and the sparse furnishings inside it just made it feel even more cramped and overcrowded. Apart from the couch there was a wooden chair that Sandra was now seated on, a small desk and a tall metal stool that the seat covering was peeling away from. The walls were covered with shelves, each one stuffed with files and books to the point where it appeared they would collapse from the weight. The single small window was open, allowing a slight breeze to blow into the room but neither of the women noticed it as they sat facing each other. There were far more pressing things on both their minds.

Sandra handed Nikki another tissue which she took gratefully, dabbing at her puffy red eyes and then blowing her nose. She wondered how much longer she could cry for. Did the human eye have an inexhaustible amount of fluid in its tear ducts? Was it possible for this to go on much longer or would her eyes simply dry up? Such were the thoughts that tumbled through Nikki Cross's mind as she sat there but they were preferable to the others she'd had. Thoughts about her baby. About what she'd seen on the screen of the monitor? Even thinking about that almost set her off again. She sucked in a deep breath and shook her head.

'A doctor will be in to speak to you soon, Nikki,' Sandra said as softly and comfortingly as she could.

'You saw my baby,' Nikki said. 'You're a nurse. What's wrong with it?'

'I can't tell you,' Sandra said apologetically. 'A doctor will be able to explain properly, tell you what you want to know.'

'It's going to die, isn't it?'

Sandra felt like crying too and she gritted her teeth to prevent herself from doing so.

'The doctor will be in as soon as he can,' she said, reaching out to touch Nikki's arm.

Nikki pulled away sharply.

'Just tell me the truth,' she snapped. 'That's all I want. I'm not stupid. I saw the picture. I know there's something wrong with my baby. I don't need a fucking doctor to tell me that.'

'Ultrasound pictures can have a certain amount of distortion. The sonographer and the doctors know what they're looking for. If I tell you something it'll probably be wrong, anyway.' Sandra attempted a smile but it failed miserably.

'What do you think is wrong with my baby?'

Sandra swallowed hard, unable to hold the other woman's gaze. 'The sonogram picture didn't look normal,' she said reluctantly. 'I will say that much.'

'Normal?' Nikki rubbed a hand over her belly. 'I've got some kind of monster in here. Inside me. Something deformed. I saw it on the monitor and so did you.' Fresh tears began to spill down her face and this time Sandra couldn't help herself – she felt warm tears dribbling down her own cheeks. Almost angrily she wiped them away, telling herself that she had to be professional, that she had to retain her calm demeanour for the sake of the patient. But no matter how hard she tried to convince herself of that she could not shake the image she'd seen on the ultrasound monitor from her mind.

'It's going to die, isn't it?' Nikki sobbed. 'My baby is going to die.'

Sandra reached out again and gripped her hand, squeezing tightly but knowing that all the comforting touches and words in the world were useless.

The sound of Nikki Cross's sobbing filled that little room.

Nineteen

Doctor Adam Royston sat in the office of Major Cartwright, shifting in his seat, gazing at the army officer who was looking out of the window with his hands clasped behind his back.

Outside, the sky was already filled with thick banks of dark cloud, hastening the onset of the evening gloom.

Royston watched the officer for a moment longer, then cleared his throat theatrically.

'So, what's your answer going to be, major?' he said.

'I can't authorise a descent into that crevice or hole or crack or whatever you want to call it until there is some more substantial data on its nature,' Cartwright stated. 'If it was caused by seismic activity then there's no guarantee there won't be more. It's dangerous, you know that.'

'How are we supposed to collect data about the rift if you won't let us examine it, major?' Royston wanted to know.

Cartwright turned to face him, his expression dark. 'One man is already dead, seven more are on the verge of death because of that bloody thing,' he snapped. 'I won't knowingly cause the deaths of others.'

'It has to be investigated,' Royston protested. 'You might be causing the deaths of more people by preventing further examination of that crack.'

'And I'm telling you that I can't allow that. Not yet.'

'What exactly are you waiting for, major? All tests so far have shown that there are no longer traces of radioactivity present. A descent into the rift shouldn't be unduly dangerous.'

'I can't let you do that.'

'Don't tell me: you're just following orders.'

'What do you expect me to do?'

'Leave the science to the scientists, major.'

'Very funny, doctor, but science isn't the issue here. The issue is safety.'

Royston raised his hands in a despairing gesture and was about to say something else when the major spoke again. 'You may place little value on your own life, Doctor Royston,' Cartwright went on. 'But I won't allow the men under my command to be endangered further by whatever this is. I've lost too many already. And I might point out to you that you're working on a military base, for a military facility and that as an individual at such an installation you are subject to military rules where this matter is concerned.'

'That's bullshit and you know it,' snapped Royston.

'If you go anywhere near that hole without my permission you'll be arrested,' Cartwright insisted. 'For your own safety. Jesus Christ, man. Are you that anxious to end up like Lansing and the poor bastards in the hospital? God alone knows what's at the bottom of that rift.'

'And that's exactly why it has to be investigated,' Royston said, raising his voice.

'Well, you're not using men or equipment from this base to do it,' Cartwright rasped. 'Not while there's still so much we don't know about it.'

'And what about the men out there guarding it now?' Royston insisted. 'You're putting them at risk.'

'It has to be guarded to prevent anyone from going near it,' Cartwright told him. 'I don't think that simply sticking 'Keep Away' signs in the ground would be adequate, do you?' He regarded Royston evenly for a moment. 'The men out there under Lieutenant Bannerman's command are a reasonable distance from the rift with specific orders to remain clear of it and the lieutenant is more aware than most of the dangers.'

Royston got to his feet and wandered across to the large bookshelves that made up one side of Cartwright's office. He scanned the titles, then pulled out a large hardback edition of a book called *A History of Warfare*. The author was Winston Churchill.

'Would *he* have given permission, major?' Royston asked, waving the book in the air. 'Would *he* have obstructed science?'

'Very funny,' Cartwright grunted.

Royston pushed the volume back onto the shelf, then turned and faced the army officer once more. 'You understand the necessity of examining that rift?' he said, keeping his tone even and measured.

'Yes, I do. But I also understand the possible dangers involved. As long as you and your colleagues are on this base your safety is as much my concern as that of my own men.'

'I appreciate that, major. I just think that present considerations should override that kind of thinking.'

'By 'present considerations' I trust you mean the appearance of a possibly radioactive earth tremor in the middle of the Buckinghamshire countryside?'

Royston smiled. 'That's just what I mean,' he said. 'It's not exactly out of the manual, is it, major?'

'No, it isn't. But the procedures followed have to be. The MOD would have my job if they knew I'd allowed civilians onto that site now.'

'Who's going to tell them?'

Cartwright eyed the American scientist silently for a moment.

'I only need two or three men, major,' Royston continued. 'You must have that many on this base who you can trust to keep their mouths shut. And what I discover could be invaluable to everyone.'

Still Cartwright didn't speak.

Royston tapped the Churchill tome on the shelf. 'Where's your bulldog spirit, major?' he asked, smiling.

'Get out,' the officer said, trying to suppress a grin. 'Bloody Yanks.'

Royston paused at the door and offered a mock salute.

'Just two or three men?' the major called.

Royston nodded.

'Let me think about it,' Cartwright said.

Royston closed the door quietly behind him.

Twenty

'Could it be genetic?'

The words were spoken quietly, almost reverentially within the confines of the room.

Sandra Morgan looked again at the ultrasound photograph, shaking her head as she ran her gaze over the image on the flimsy black and white picture.

'There were no traces of anything like this during her first scan,' the sonographer said, her own attention still fixed on the monitor. 'If it had been genetic we'd have seen something then.'

'What did the doctors say?'

The sonographer shook her head gently.

'They recommended termination,' she said finally. 'Because of the level of . . .' She struggled to find the word. 'Of infection. I think the patient has been advised of that.'

Sandra looked again at the ultrasound picture. Then she ran a hand through her hair and exhaled wearily.

'But I don't understand why this didn't show up during the first scan,' the sonographer went on. 'Even at eight weeks there should have been something to alert us. Some clue that this was going to develop.' She touched the photograph with one index finger, then quickly withdrew it as if the image itself was toxic. Her hand was shaking slightly as she pulled it away.

'What could have caused it?' Sandra asked.

Again the sonographer could only shake her head.

Both of them looked at the picture as if hypnotised by the image there.

'I've never seen anything like this,' the sonographer said finally.

'Do you think there's brain damage as well as the physical problems?'

'It's difficult to tell just from the scan. One of the doctors I showed this to said that it wasn't definite, though. Mentally it could be perfectly normal. Which makes things worse when you think about it.'

'So they're encouraging her to have it terminated?'

'Do you blame them?'

'And nothing can be done?'

The words hung in the air like stale smoke.

'That poor girl,' the sonographer murmured. 'I don't think I'll ever forget the look on her face.'

'I don't know what I would have done in her place,' Sandra confessed.

'If she's got any sense she'll listen to the advice the doctors give her.'

'It might not be as easy for her as that. It's still her child.'

'God help her.'

The two women remained silent for a moment. Then Sandra spoke again.

'What about the others?' she asked, hesitantly.

There were three more ultrasound pictures arranged

on the desk, all marked with the names of the women carrying the children.

'Four women, all pregnant and each one carrying a child riddled with cancer,' the sonographer murmured. 'At least two cases so badly infected that it's caused deformity.'

'Do you think any of them could survive?' Sandra wanted to know.

'Not with tumours so far advanced.'

The sonographer sat back in her seat and exhaled wearily. 'And all these have appeared in the last week,' she breathed. 'None of the previous scans showed anything abnormal. It's as if these cancers have just appeared out of thin air.'

'Isn't it a little strange that none of the mothers are infected too?'

The sonographer nodded. 'It's as if the disease has just targeted the children,' she said.

She stared blankly at the monitor before her, then at the ultrasound pictures again, once more touching them with a shaking hand – like a faith healer who hopes that a simple and desperate gesture will somehow rectify the damage shown in photographs of sufferers.

Sandra felt a single tear run down her cheek.

She didn't bother to wipe it away.

Twenty-One

'If my dad finds out about this he'll kill me.'

George Finlay stood among the trees, gazing across the marshy ground before him, his breath clouding in the chilly night air.

'We've got to do it,' Ryan Dickinson reminded him, slipping his hood up to cover his head. 'If we take something back from inside the tower and show it to those other boys at school then they'll leave us alone.'

George nodded, still glancing around the woods where they waited.

'Come on,' Ryan urged and he stepped out from behind the trees, motioning George to follow him.

The journey from Broughton had taken them about thirty minutes, walking along the side of the roads where they could before they finally had to take a detour, first across open fields and then the marshland that they now found themselves in. As they'd got closer to the outskirts of the town the houses and other buildings had become less numerous. It was as if the town just seemed to fade away as they reached the countryside surrounding it. As the houses receded behind them so too did their main source of light. The illuminated windows of the houses that they had passed had reassured them and given them strength in the darkness. But there were no street lights out in the fields and woods. No welcoming glows from living-room windows to comfort them as they advanced further into the countryside and away from the populated areas. There was a weak and watery moon that night but it was covered by thick grey cloud for the most part and offered them only partial illu-mination. The chill white light in which it occasionally bathed the landscape was far from comforting, though. It just made everything look colder and caused both boys to be even more acutely aware that they were so far away from the warmth and safety of their own houses.

'Did you bring something to carry it in?' Ryan asked, picking his way as best he could over the sodden ground.

'Carry what in?' George wanted to know, grunting when he slipped and slid into a puddle of reeking water that covered his trainers.

'Whatever we take back from the tower. We've got to take something back that belongs to Old Tom haven't we?'

George nodded and dug a hand into his pocket. He pulled out a plastic Tesco bag and waved it around for Ryan to see.

Ryan nodded and George pushed the bag back inside his sweatshirt.

'What sort of thing are we going to get?' George wanted to know.

'I don't know.'

'They probably won't even believe us when we show them what we found.'

'Yes, they will. That's why we've got to get something and take it back.'

The two boys moved on, up a slight incline and through a copse. Ryan hissed as the lower branch of one tree snagged his jacket. He pulled free and inspected the material for damage, relieved that there was none.

'Who is Old Tom, anyway?' George asked, ducking his head to avoid more low-hanging twigs.

'I don't know,' Ryan answered. 'He's probably not real. They're just trying to scare us by saying he lives in the tower. I mean, how could anyone live out here?'

Both boys looked around them. High above, the moon broke free of the enveloping cloud and, for a brief moment, the entire landscape was bathed in its light.

In that moment they both saw the unmistakeable shape of the folly a hundred or so yards ahead of them.

Ryan pointed at the structure but George had already seen it and he merely nodded. They pressed on.

The ground sloped down quite sharply and both boys had to concentrate to keep their balance on the slippery incline, both of them using the trees to support them and prevent them falling on the glutinous mud. When the slope finally leveled out, however, it was onto ground that was almost liquid beneath them.

'How am I going to tell my mum about all this mud?' George protested. 'She's going to want to know how my trainers got so dirty.'

'Tell her we were playing football in my garden,' Ryan offered.

'In the middle of the night? She's not stupid. She's going to find out where we've been.'

'She'll only find out if you tell her,' Ryan snapped, glaring at his friend.

The two boys stood motionless for a moment. Then Ryan turned, ready to lead the way once again. His own heart was thudding hard against his ribs now but he had no intention of stopping before he reached the folly. They were too close. There was no way he was going back empty-handed.

Above them something moved.

Both boys spun around and looked up in the direction of the sound.

George tried to swallow but his throat was dry.

'What was that?' he gasped.

'It must have been a bird,' Ryan told him. 'An owl or something.'

There was more movement, this time ahead of them. They both saw bushes moving and there was a crack of breaking twigs.

A hedgehog ambled into view, holding a worm in its jaws. It scuttled away out of sight when it saw the two boys, both of whom let out sighs of relief as the little creature retreated back into the gloom.

They moved on.

Ryan almost stumbled more than once in the gloom and he muttered under his breath when one of his feet sank into a puddle of mud. With the moon hidden once more behind thick cloud it was difficult to see more than a few feet ahead. He held onto a nearby sapling and glanced up at the sky as if willing the moon to emerge once again and light their way. Behind him, George found that he was sweating despite the chill in the air.

'Let's go back,' he hissed.

'No. We've come all this way,' Ryan told him. 'We'll get something from the tower, then we'll go.'

'Come on, Ryan,' George insisted. 'This is stupid.'

The moon emerged from behind cloud once again.

'There it is,' Ryan said quietly, pointing ahead of them. 'That's the tower.'

The folly was no more than twenty yards ahead of them now. They could make out the shape and every detail of the building. Windows set at various points in the structure looked like black eyes watching them. At the base of the construction lay the large wooden door.

'Come on,' Ryan said, striding forward.

'You go,' George told him, his voice cracking. 'I'm going to wait here.'

'I'm not going in there on my own,' Ryan protested.

'I'll wait here and keep watch, see if anyone comes.' George looked imploringly at Ryan. 'Please. I'll wait here until you get back.'

'You'd better not go without me,' Ryan snapped.

George shook his head.

Ryan hesitated for a moment, then moved cautiously beyond the trees towards Fisher's Folly.

Twenty-Two

As he advanced across the tree-covered patch of land that marked the approach to the folly, Ryan glanced back to where George was standing.

He did this several times to reassure himself that his friend was still where he had promised to stay until their task here tonight was over. Ryan's primary emotion was one of anger. He was mad with George for not coming into Fisher's Folly with him and that irritation fortified him as he made his way nearer and nearer to the tower. However, as he drew to within ten yards of the structure he felt a different and more familiar feeling sweep through him: he recognised it all too easily as fear.

From where he stood he could see the door of the tower. A huge metal-braced wooden rectangle that time and the elements had battered so that the material from which it was made looked almost black. There was no light from inside the folly itself despite the fact that there were at least six windows in the brickwork reaching nearly as far as the battlements at the top. Bushes grew thickly around the base of the folly except at the door and Ryan could see that there was what appeared to be a muddy path leading away from this. Marked out by the feet of Old Tom? he wondered.

What he also wondered was: who exactly was Old Tom? Was he a figure invented by the local kids to frighten others? Or did he really exist and was he sitting in the tower now? Sitting and waiting for anyone who would dare to trespass on his territory. Ryan shuddered at that thought but the idea that entered his mind next was even more unsettling. What if Old Tom wasn't even a man? What if he was some kind of spirit or ghost or monster?

Ryan hesitated, standing still where he was and looking fixedly at the door of the folly.

Perhaps Old Tom was watching him even now. Perched up there on the battlements like some monstrous bird of prey, just watching as his latest victim wandered helplessly towards him as surely as a fly steps into a spider's web. Ryan glanced up towards the summit of the tower, squinting in the gloom in his efforts to see if anyone or anything was watching him. He could see nothing in the blackness but, he told himself, that didn't mean that no one was there. If Old Tom was some sort of monster then the night would be his friend – he would welcome the darkness. Monsters liked the dark, Ryan reminded himself. In horror films and horror stories they always came out at night and prowled around looking for victims. The night was their domain. He swallowed hard, trying to force these thoughts from his mind, forcing himself to fight back the overwhelming urge to simply turn and run from this place.

If he did, then he and George would have to face the wrath of the boys at school who had dared them to undertake this task. But were their bullying and hurtful comments worse than what might happen to him if he stepped inside Fisher's Folly? What could they do to him that they hadn't already? What insults could they throw at him that they hadn't already subjected him to? How much more pain could they inflict? Ryan decided that the answer was more than he wanted to take. He had discovered over these past few months that bullies like the boys at school seemed to have limitless imaginations when it came to causing upset and hurt. They never seemed to tire of their self-appointed mission to inflict misery on George and himself. Perhaps if the two of them did return with something from Old Tom's place then the bullies would find different targets. He nodded to himself, satisfied that he had but one course of action open to him. He had to get inside the tower and find something belonging to Old Tom. No matter what.

He was about to advance towards the main door when he heard something away to his right.

Ryan spun around, hoping that George had decided not to wait alone for him among the trees but to join him. He scanned the wooded area for any sign of his companion but saw nothing. Ryan considered calling the other boy's name but then decided that any sound might alert an occupant of the tower to his presence. Silence was the best ally here. He clenched his fists, steeling himself for his approach to the door. He was about to move towards it again when he heard some - thing else that caused him to hesitate.

His breath coming in rapid gasps now, Ryan turned towards the source of the sound, eyes watchful for even the slightest sign of movement. Could it be another animal? he wondered. A fox or a badger or something bigger? Could it be Old Tom himself?

He felt his body beginning to shake slightly.

Again he heard a sound but it wasn't breaking twigs or sucking mud or the noise that an animal would make. It was a low crackling sound.

Ryan turned his back on the tower, now more intent on discovering what was making that noise. Whatever it was he realised it was coming closer. The crackling had now transformed into a low hiss. He looked around frantically for what was making it, standing still on a patch of open ground as the sound grew louder. It seemed to be coming from a ditch ten or twelve feet ahead of him.

For a few fanciful seconds he wondered if some huge monstrous snake was loose in the marshes around the folly and that it was the source of the hissing. But then, as he stared with bulging eyes towards the ditch, he saw that his theory was wrong. It wasn't a massive snake that rose from the ground ahead of him. Perhaps it would have been better if it had been.

Exactly what it was he had no idea. Nothing in his young life had prepared him for such a sight. In fact, even if he had been many years older it would have been doubtful if he could have found the words to describe appropriately what rose from the ditch.

Ryan finally found the strength to turn and run.

He ran as he'd never run in his life, not daring to turn

and look over his shoulder, not caring that branches and twigs slashed at his face and hands as he raced madly across the marshland. Even when a sharp skeletal branch cut his left cheek and sent blood spilling hotly over his skin he didn't stop running.

When he saw George just up ahead of him he ran on, wanting to scream but not finding the voice for it.

He ran straight past George who watched him for a second, startled and unnerved by the horrified look on his friend's face.

George called the other boy's name, shouting after the fleeing figure. But Ryan Dickinson ran on, tears now coursing down his cheeks to mingle with the blood that was already there.

George waited a split second, then bolted after his friend, the two boys hurtling across the marshland with a speed born of absolute terror.

Twenty-Three

The house was in darkness when he walked in.

Even from the street as he'd approached the house he'd thought it was strange that there were no lights on and stranger still that the glow of the television couldn't be seen in the living room. Paul Coleman smiled to himself. Nikki always had the TV on, no matter what she was doing. Even if she wasn't in the room at the time or even if she was sitting there reading the set would still be switched on. She said it was company for her, especially when he wasn't there. But now, as he fumbled in his jacket for his keys, he wondered why there were no lights at all on inside the house – let alone in the main room of the building.

He let himself in, waving to one of their neighbours in the process before closing the door behind him.

'Nikki,' he called as he hung up his coat on the rack just inside the small hallway.

There was no answer.

'Sorry I'm late,' he said. 'There was all sorts of shit going on at work. I couldn't get away any earlier. We can get a pizza or something if you don't want to cook.'

Coleman stood in the hallway for a moment longer, glancing up the stairs.

No lights up there, either. He wondered for a moment if she had gone to bed but it was barely ten o'clock: she wouldn't have gone up that early, not without letting him know at least. She'd have texted or phoned or something. He had a sudden thought and it frightened him.

What if there was something wrong? What if she was ill? What if there'd been bad news?

The speculation ceased as he pushed open the living-room door and saw her sitting on one end of the sofa.

'I called you,' he said, reaching out to turn on the light.

'Leave the light off,' Nikki told him, her voice wavering.

Coleman hesitated for a moment, then took his hand away. The room remained in darkness. He moved across to the sofa and sat down at the other end. Even in the dark he could see that her cheeks were moist with tears and she gripped a tissue in one hand.

'What is it, Nik?' he asked falteringly. 'I rang earlier but it went straight to voicemail. You didn't return my texts.'

He moved a little closer to her.

She sniffed back some tears and the realisation hit him hard.

'Oh, God – is it the baby?' he asked.

'They want me to have it aborted,' she blurted.

'Why?' Coleman asked, slipping an arm around her shoulder. He could feel her body shuddering against him.

'There's something wrong with it, Paul. It's . . . it's disfigured. It's a freak. And it's ill.'

Coleman felt a cold feeling in the pit of his stomach.

'They think it's got cancer,' Nikki went on. 'There are growths all over its face.' Her words dissolved away into a fit of sobs.

Coleman held her tighter.

'Are they sure?' he wanted to know.

'I'm not going to get rid of it. I won't kill my baby and I won't let them take it away. I don't care if it's sick. I don't care what it looks like. I'm not going to let them do it.'

'Nikki, did they tell you to have an abortion?'

She nodded. 'I'm not doing it, Paul,' she whimpered. 'I won't have the abortion. I don't care what they say.'

'We need to talk about this when you're feeling better.'

'I won't be feeling better,' she snapped. 'I've got a deformed baby inside me that the doctors say I should have aborted.' She got to her feet and blundered towards the living-room door. 'The baby won't get better and I'm not going to let them kill it.' She pulled the door open and Coleman heard her footsteps thumping up the stairs.

He thought about following her but then just slumped back helplessly on the sofa. He sat there in the darkness. Upstairs he could hear her crying and he knew that he should go to her although what the hell he was going to say he had no idea.

It was a long time before he moved.

Twenty-Four

Doctor Adam Royston smiled briefly when Sandra Morgan entered the room, carrying a clear plastic drip bag. The nurse returned the gesture before crossing to the bed beside which the American stood.

On the other side of it Doctor Martin Kelly stood looking down at the bed's occupant.

Ryan Dickinson lay immobile before him, a thin sheen of sweat on his face and neck.

'His temperature has been high ever since he was brought in,' Kelly announced, pulling back the sheet that covered the boy and easing it down as far as his chest. 'Despite the drugs we've given him.'

Sandra attached a fresh drip, hanging it on the metal stand beside the bed, adjusting the flow of the clear liquid within.

'What is that?' Royston asked, nodding in the direction of the drip.

'We had him on saline to begin with but he was in so much pain we've had to add morphine too,' Kelly explained. As he spoke, he leaned forward and gently opened the front of Ryan's pyjama jacket to expose the flesh beneath.

Royston frowned as he looked down at the boy's chest.

The flesh there was red and blotchy but the most striking thing were the dark and angry-looking burns. The more severe had been dressed and Royston could see a mixture of pus and blood seeping through the gauze that covered them.

'I only changed the dressings half an hour ago,' Sandra exclaimed.

Royston glanced at her and then returned his attention to the boy.

'First-degree radiation burns,' he said softly.

'That's what I thought. That was why I called you in,' Kelly said.

Royston looked more intently at the boy's injuries. 'When was he brought in?' he asked.

'About two hours ago,' Kelly said. He let out a deep sigh. 'Listen, Royston, it's not just the burns.'

'What do you mean?' the American enquired.

'Naturally, we ran tests when he was admitted,' the doctor went on. 'There are several large tumours in his lungs and stomach. From the size of them they must have been present for months and yet he's displayed no outward symptoms of cancer. His mother said he hasn't even been to a doctor for almost a year, that he's a healthy boy. She might not agree if she'd seen the X-rays we took.'

'His mother knows about the cancer?'

'I haven't told her everything yet – I thought she had enough to cope with. And to be honest, I'm not even sure what I'm going to say to her. Tumours of the size this boy is infected with would have manifested symptoms long before now. I don't understand it.'

'You mean it's as if they appeared very recently?' Royston asked.

'Yes, but their size makes that impossible. I've seen cancer more times than I care to remember but nothing as virulent as this.'

'And there've been other cases too,' Sandra said. 'Among unborn children.'

'Thank you, nurse,' Kelly snapped, shooting her an angry look. 'That will be all.'

'I thought it was relevant, doctor,' she protested.

'Unborn children?' Royston murmured.

'We've had a number of them, all aged from three to eight months and all with recent and extremely aggressive cancers,' Kelly sighed. 'Some internal and some external. There was a case yesterday where most of the child's head was covered by growths. I've never seen anything like it.'

'There've been cases at the bases too,' Royston admitted. 'But all those men were exposed to high levels of radiation. That might explain why they've developed tumours. Were the mothers of the children somehow exposed?'

'We don't know,' Kelly confessed. 'Just like we don't know how this boy came to be in contact with radio - active material. We're hoping his mother can tell us. She's outside if you'd like to speak to her.'

The American nodded and the two men moved towards the door of the room. As he reached it, Kelly turned and looked at Sandra.

'Change the dressings, please, nurse,' he told her.

'Yes, doctor,' she said, smiling one last time at Royston before he stepped out of the room. She mouthed the words 'See you later' at him. Royston smiled and nodded before closing the door behind him.

As he stepped out into the corridor he saw a woman with long dark hair sitting on one of the plastic chairs in the area outside the room. She was gazing blankly at the floor but as the two men moved into view she raised her head and got to her feet. She looked pale, her eyes red-rimmed and puffy.

'This is Mrs Dickinson,' Kelly announced.

'What's wrong with him, doctor?' Lauren Dickinson asked urgently.

'There's not too much I can tell you at the moment,' Kelly said apologetically. 'There are still a number of tests we have to complete.'

'You must be able to tell me *something*,' Lauren protested.

'Your son was burned,' Royston said.

'By what?' Lauren wanted to know.

'We don't know yet,' Royston replied 'That's what we're trying to find out. When did you first notice anything?'

'When I went into his room this morning to wake him up for school,' Lauren said. She wiped a tear from her face. 'He was lying there with those horrible marks all over his chest and neck.'

Royston placed a comforting arm around her shoulder. 'Have you any idea where he might have been to sustain injuries like that?' he asked.

Lauren shook her head.

'Where did he go yesterday?' the American.

'He went out to play with a friend of his after school but he was back for his dinner. He didn't go out again after that and I found him in bed this morning, as I told you. I brought him straight down here when I saw him. I knew it was serious.'

'And you've got no idea where he might have gone?' Royston persisted.

Again Lauren shook her head.

'What about his friend, the one he was playing with?' Royston asked. 'Is he all right?'

'I don't know,' Lauren said, wiping more tears away. She looked imploringly at Kelly. 'Please make him better. He's all I've got.'

'What was the name of this friend he was playing with?' Royston asked.

'George Finlay,' she told him. 'He's Ryan's only friend. He's had trouble making friends since we moved here. George is the only one he took to. They both go to Simpson Junior School here in Broughton.'

'I should speak to the other boy,' Royston said and Kelly nodded.

'Is Ryan going to be all right?' Lauren asked again, her voice cracking.

'We're going to do our best for him, Mrs Dickinson,' Kelly told her. 'Perhaps you'd like to come through and see him, sit with him for a little while.'

'I'll speak to you later,' Royston called to Kelly as he turned to leave.

He headed up the corridor towards the main entrance

of the hospital and then out into the car park beyond. An ambulance was hurtling away from St Mary's with its blue lights spinning and siren wailing. Royston glanced at the emergency vehicle, wondering where it was heading. Then he slid behind the wheel of his own vehicle and started the engine.

As he prepared to pull away his mobile phone rang.

Twenty-Five

Claire Reece heard the words but they didn't really register.

As she stood beside the main gate of Simpson Junior School she was aware of two other women standing close to her and she was also sure that they had been directing some of their questions towards her. But exactly what they had said she couldn't be sure. Her mind was elsewhere. She was preoccupied. Unable to think about anything except her own condition. She glanced down and pulled her blouse more tightly across her chest as if that simple action would prevent her thinking about the cancer beneath.

Claire had watched as her two children had hurried off into the school, waving at her as they did. And she had waved back, forcing a smile but also fighting to keep back the tears she had felt welling up on more than one occasion. Each time she looked at her children she felt a stab of fear. What if she never saw them again? What if the cancer was so aggressive that it took her life in the next few months? How was she going to tell them that she was ill? How did anyone tell their children that they might be losing their mother to a disease so vile and unstoppable? She had tried to think positively but when all was said and done she knew that the power of positive thought alone could not help her. Neither could the love of her family. She had read in the past of people who had beaten cancer and who attributed their victory as much to their state of mind as to their treatment and she had marvelled at their fortitude and courage. But now, put in that place herself, Claire could not find the strength she knew she needed. She was overcome with fear and there seemed no way to banish that steadily growing emotion, even if it was only for a few minutes here and there.

It consumed her. It filled her every waking moment. The fear of death. Of leaving her children without their mother and her husband without his wife. On a number of occasions Claire had scolded herself out loud, convincing herself not only that she was going to fight this disease but that she was going to beat it. But then, in a quiet moment, all the fear and dread came sweeping back over her like a tidal wave. The enormity of her situation and its possible outcome was too terrible to contemplate. The knowledge that she was helpless against the disease devastated her. Whatever she did couldn't help. She was completely at the mercy of the doctors treating her and even then, with the most advanced treatment available, she might still succumb.

These thoughts crowded in on her now, just as they did at any given moment. She wore her fake smile when she needed it and she kept her secret to herself because she saw no point in telling others. What could these other women do to help her? What good would talking about her disease do? Explaining it and discussing its nature wasn't going to cure her, was it? And, ultimately, no one but those close to her cared anyway, she reasoned. They would tell her how sorry they were and how they would do anything they could to help her if they could but all they would really be thinking would be 'Thank God it's her and not me.' The only thing that would help was a cure.

And, as she had done with so many other people, she now looked at these other women around her with something approaching hatred.

They went about their lives with their trivial little concerns and they complained about the most insignificant of things. But at least they had things to look forward to. They *could* look forward. Claire Reece didn't even know if she had a future beyond the next few months. She was like a prisoner on Death Row waiting for the order to come through that would send her to the electric chair. The main difference was that her own death would be longer, more painful and more drawn out than a seat in the executioner's chamber.

She sucked in a deep breath and tried to force the thoughts aside, tried to focus on what the other women were saying to her. But her responses when they came were mechanical. Still, they helped keep up the façade, the necessary façade that everything was fine. She didn't want anyone to know the physical or psycho-logical pain she was going through and that wasn't out of a misguided desire to appear like some kind of hero. She just couldn't see the point of telling anyone else. Let them live their untroubled lives, she thought, and let her own unfold however it might.

Perhaps, she thought, there would come a time when she would just resign herself to her fate and that would be an end to it. Or they would cure her. But at the moment she dared not even cling to that faint hope for if it was dashed she knew she couldn't cope with the inevitable outcome. Better to think the worst and then anything else would be a bonus. Better a life of torment and pain than no life at all.

Claire looked at the women around her and she smiled her practised smile and for now it worked.

Twenty-Six

Some of the children who passed him smiled at him. Others looked at him with ill-disguised suspicion. But every single one who walked by looked with interest at Adam Royston.

He was seated in the outer office of the head-mistress's room in Simpson Junior School, the largest of Broughton's educational establishments for children aged from five to eleven years. There was a door of bevelled glass leading into the outer office but the area itself was open to the view of those who passed due to the fact that it had two large plate-glass panels separating it from the main entryway of the school. Despite the constant coming and going of the blue-uniformed pupils, the noise levels inside the outer office were negligible and Royston gazed out at those who passed, feeling a little like a goldfish in a bowl.

An officious-looking woman with greying hair and too much make-up sat behind the wooden desk in the outer office tapping feverishly away at her computer keyboard when she wasn't taking what seemed like a seemingly never-ending stream of phone calls, all of which she received via a console on one side of her desk. She answered each one in the same impeccable if slightly cold tone. There was too, Royston felt, a certain iciness in the looks she gave him as he walked back and forth in the room, glancing at the pictures on the green-painted walls there. They had been done by pupils at the school, each one bearing the artist's signature somewhere on it. One, he noticed, bore the name of Ryan Dickinson.

He was still gazing at the painting when the outer office door opened and, along with some extraneous noise from a group of passing children, the headmistress herself entered, ushering a young boy in before her. The boy looked at Royston briefly, then dropped his gaze.

'This is Doctor Royston, George,' she said cheerily. Then to the American scientist: 'Doctor Royston, this is George Finlay. This is who you want to speak to.'

Royston was about to say hello when the headmistress ushered both himself and the boy through into her somewhat smaller office that was reached by the door to their right.

'Can you tell anyone who wants me that I'm in a meeting for the next half-hour, please, Alison?' the headmistress asked, holding the door open for Royston and the boy as they passed through. On that door was a plastic plaque bearing the legend MRS J. WAGSTAFF.

She closed the door behind them, then sat down on the seat behind her desk.

'Please sit down,' she said brightly. 'Both of you.'

George looked around nervously and perched on the edge of the leather sofa on one side of the room. Royston sat next to him and tried to look as child-friendly as he could.

'There's nothing to worry about, George,' the headmistress said. 'You're not in trouble. Doctor Royston just wants to ask you some questions.'

'Hello, George,' Royston began, extending his right hand.

The boy regarded him with even more suspicion when he heard his American accent but he shook the offered hand nervously. Then he shuffled a little further away from Royston, as far as the small leather sofa would allow.

'I wanted to ask you about your friend Ryan Dickinson,' Royston began.

George nodded.

'Do you know why he's not at school today?' Royston went on.

George shook his head.

'I've just come from the hospital,' Royston continued. 'I've been visiting him. He's not very well, George.'

'What's wrong with him?' George asked.

'You and he were out playing last night, weren't you?'

George swallowed hard, then looked at Mrs Wagstaff as if seeking permission to answer.

'It's all right, George,' she said softly.

The boy nodded.

'Something must have happened to him while you two were out,' Royston said. 'What was it, George? What happened to Ryan?'

George shook his head and refused to meet Royston's searching gaze.

'Where were you, George?' Royston asked. 'Where were you playing? Where was it?'

'I can't tell you,' George protested.

'Why not?' Royston asked.

'You're not in trouble, George,' Mrs Wagstaff added. 'The doctor just wants to help Ryan.'

Still the boy hesitated.

'Where were you when Ryan was hurt, George?' Royston went on as calmly as he could.

'We promised we wouldn't tell anyone,' George blurted.

Royston looked at the headmistress and then at the boy again. 'Where were you?' he repeated.

George looked at the books on the shelves that lined the walls, then down at his scuffed shoes and even at Miss Wagstaff. But he wouldn't look at Royston.

'Ryan's sick,' the American said. 'He's very sick, George.'

'They made us promise we wouldn't tell where we were going,' George said, his voice shaky.

'Who made you promise?' Mrs Wagstaff interjected.

'Some of the other boys in our class,' George confessed.

'Well, they're not the ones who are sick, are they, George? Your friend Ryan is sick and you can help him by telling me where you two went last night,' Royston said, trying to keep his tone as even as possible. 'Ryan would want you to tell me what happened. He's the one who needs your help, George, not these other boys.'

George swallowed hard, his face pale. He had his hands clenched together and he kept moving his fingers agitatedly, stretching then curling them as if that simple gesture would somehow help him. Royston put what he hoped would be a comforting hand on the boy's shoulder, relieved when George didn't bolt from his seat.

'I want Ryan to get better,' he said weakly.

'Then tell me where you were,' Royston insisted. 'That's the only way you can help your friend now.'

'We went out to the tower in the marshes,' George said, clearing his throat.

'Fisher's Folly?' Mrs Wagstaff said, frowning. 'What were you doing out there?'

Royston looked at her for clarification.

'It's an old building,' she explained. 'It's been there for centuries. No one goes near it.'

'It was really creepy,' George said. 'We went there to get something that belonged to Old Tom, to prove to the other boys that we weren't scared – so they'd let us play with them.'

'Who's Old Tom?' Royston wanted to know.

Mrs Wagstaff got to her feet and moved around to the sofa where she stroked George's hair gently. He was shaking and she could see that he was fighting back tears as he spoke.

'Do you want me to call your mum, George?' she asked. 'She can take you home if you like.'

'No,' George snapped. 'I don't want my mum to know where we were – she'll go mad.'

'Who's Old Tom?' Royston asked again.

'It's a local legend, Doctor Royston,' the head-mistress said. 'He was supposedly a gamekeeper on the estate where the tower was built. One night he was out looking for poachers and he got caught in one of his own mantraps. It cut off both his legs. He crawled to the tower and bled to death there. That's the story that people tell. His ghost is supposed to haunt the marshes.'

'And you and Ryan were out in the marshes last night looking for Old Tom?' Royston asked George.

'The other boys said we had to go inside the tower and get something that belonged to him,' George told him.

'It must have been some kind of stupid dare,' Mrs Wagstaff said irritably.

'And that's where Ryan was hurt?' Royston asked.

'I didn't go with him,' George admitted. 'I was really scared. He went on his own. I waited for him but when he came back he was running. I just ran after him.'

'Did he say what happened, George? Did he tell you how he hurt himself?'

'He just said he'd seen something,' George insisted. 'He didn't say what it was. He was crying and he was really scared.'

George finally lost his battle to retain his composure. Tears began to course down both his cheeks.

Mrs Wagstaff put her arms around him and held him comfortingly.

'How do I reach this place?' Royston wanted to know.

'A dirt track runs through the marshes quite close to it,' the headmistress told him. 'You can't miss it.'

Royston nodded. 'Thank you,' he said. 'And thank you for your help, George.'

The boy was still crying.

'What are you expecting to find, Doctor Royston?' the headmistress called after him as he pulled open the office door and stepped through.

'I don't know,' he told her, hesitating a moment. 'I really don't know.'

Twenty-Seven

Even in daylight the area around Fisher's Folly looked pretty forbidding, Royston thought as he drove along the track leading through the marshes. He could only begin to imagine how frightening it must have been to the two boys who had been there the previous night. However, there was a world of difference between 'frightening' and 'dangerous' he told himself. In the dull light of the overcast day there was certainly nothing he'd seen so far that might have caused the kind of injuries suffered by Ryan Dickinson.

On one side of the track the ground sloped up sharply but on the other it fell away gradually from the rudimentary road for about thirty feet before rising less steeply once again. The surface he was driving on wasn't tarmacked and, from the number of weeds growing along its length, it obviously wasn't main - tained. It had simply been informally marked out during the course of many years, perhaps by horses and carts at the beginning and then by the tyres of the earliest motor vehicles. Now it served as a kind of short cut – for those aware of its existence – between Broughton and the road leading to the neighbouring town of Monkston.

The entire area was thickly wooded, some of the low-hanging branches actually scraping against the roof of Royston's car as he drove. There were puddles of rancid water both on the track and also among the trees. As he drove Royston looked to his left and right, trying to pick out the shape of the building he sought.

He drove another two hundred yards before he saw it.

Royston stepped on his brake and brought the car to a halt as far to the right-hand side of the track as he could – not that he would have to worry about any oncoming traffic hitting him, he reasoned. Nevertheless he turned the wheel to lock it, then clambered out of the car, peering in the direction of Fisher's Folly. He wondered what could have possessed two ten-year-olds to come to a place like this for the sake of some stupid schoolboy dare. He shook his head and moved quickly to the boot of his vehicle. He took out the Geiger counter that lay among the other items and flicked it on, moving the probe back and forth before him both to check that it was working and also to test if there was any faint trace of radiation showing. After all, Ryan Dickinson had received very severe radiation burns somewhere in this area the previous night; it was safe to assume that the source of those burns was still present. Royston moved towards the tower, the detecting device pointed ahead of him.

Nothing came from the machine as he walked, picking his way over fallen branches and moving between the trees. There were no crackling sounds to warn him of a radioactive source, just the silence that seemed to crowd around him from all sides. Indeed, he stood still for a moment to listen more intently and only then did it strike him. There wasn't even the sound of birdsong in the air. Royston looked up at the tower, peering towards it's top, but despite the fact that it would have provided a perfect nesting spot there was still no evidence of birds. The silence was oppressive. He moved closer to the tower, aware of nothing now but his own breathing. He glanced down at the muddy ground not even sure what he was looking for. There were no footprints in the dirt, no sign that Ryan Dickinson had been this close to the structure the previous night.

The Geiger counter was still silent.

Royston looked at the folly, taking in the details of the building. From the look of the fragments of red brick piled up around and on both sides of the entrance, it had been part of a larger structure at one time. There were several embrasures cut into the stonework higher up the tower that served as windows and at its summit he could see broken battlements. Facing him was a heavy steel-braced wooden door. The metal was rusted and in a number of places had merely crumbled away due to the passage of time. The lock, however, still looked quite sturdy. Royston aimed the Geiger counter at the tower's entrance, not sure whether to feel relieved or puzzled when the machine still emitted no sound.

He pushed the door with one hand, surprised when it swung open.

The hinges creaked loudly.

Royston hesitated for a moment, then stepped across

the threshold, wiping some fresh cobwebs from his face as he passed through. He brushed the gossamer threads away and moved into the tower itself.

The overwhelming stench was one of damp. The walls of the folly were patchy with dark mould and yet curiously enough the flagstone-covered floor was relatively untouched by the fungus. Puzzled by this, Royston put the flat of his hand to the stone and was surprised to find that it wasn't as bone-chillingly cold as he'd expected. Was there some source of warmth beneath the flags or even beneath the ground that was preventing the infestation of mould that had dotted the walls? He frowned thoughtfully, deciding that this was a ludicrously fanciful supposition, and glanced around more intently. In every corner dust-covered thick spiderwebs looked as if they were holding the building together. A particularly large spider suddenly scuttled across the floor and despite himself Royston took a hasty step back, his heart thudding a little harder against his ribs. He shook his head, administering a swift mental rebuke to himself for his reaction.

Calm down. It's only a spider, even if it is as big as your hand.

The eight-legged creature disappeared into one of the dark corners out of sight and Royston glanced around again at the interior of the tower. The room he was in was about ten feet square. Dust filled the air when he moved and he could see the motes turning slowly in the shafts of weak light that cut through the gloom.

There was a sound just ahead of him, a steady dripping noise. He moved towards it, dropping to one knee to see that there was indeed a puddle of fluid in the centre of the room. As he watched he saw several droplets fall into it. Royston aimed the Geiger counter at this small pool but still the machine was silent. He pulled a handkerchief from his pocket and dipped one corner into the liquid seeing the linen turn darker as it became damp. However, that was the only reaction and Royston concluded that whatever the fluid was it wasn't corrosive. It certainly wasn't exposure to this that had burned Ryan Dickinson so badly. He sniffed the corner of his handkerchief and detected an acrid odour where the liquid had soaked into the material.

Behind him there was a doorway with steps leading up to what he assumed must be the next level of the tower. It was from there that the liquid was dripping – he could see it coming through a small hole in the ceiling. The American pushed the probe of the Geiger counter ahead of him and slowly began to climb the stone steps.

He was on the third step when he noticed that the thick dust there had been disturbed.

Someone had been up these stairs before him – and recently, by the look of it.

He wondered if Ryan Dickinson had wandered into the tower the previous night and got this far. If he had then whatever had burned him might well be just ahead. Royston gripped the probe more tightly and moved higher, alert for the slightest sound or movement.

The stone steps opened out onto a kind of landing that led into another chamber on the first floor of the tower. Royston glanced down at the Geiger counter but not only was it making no sound, there was not even a flicker of movement from its dials. Royston stepped into the next chamber, frowning in puzzlement.

There was a large metal drum that had several pipes leading from it in the centre of the room. As Royston looked he could see that there was steam rising gently from the drum. There was clear liquid dripping from one side of the cylindrical object. Most of it had collected in two or three glass containers beneath but the remainder of the fluid was puddling on the stone floor, some of it seeping through a large crack in the flag-stones. It was this, he reasoned, that had been dripping through into the ground-floor chamber. There was a sour smell and also a more acrid aroma that he thought he recognised.

Royston paused for a moment, glancing around the room, surprised to see that there were several rudimentary wooden shelves attached to the far wall and upon these there were tin cans, more of the glass containers like those on the floor, some cups and several small flowerpots. On the floor beneath were what looked like half-used paint tins. Royston drew a deep breath and felt it stick in his throat when he spotted the rough wooden bed close by.

There was a figure lying on it.

Twenty-Eight

Covered by a thick overcoat and also by a dirty blanket, the figure was turned away from Royston, facing the stone wall.

He advanced towards it, realising that the smell he'd detected and thought he recognised was the stink of dried perspiration. The smell became stronger as he drew closer to the immobile shape.

Royston steadied himself, then reached out a hand, closed it on the shoulder of the figure and shook it. 'Hey,' he said loudly, still shaking. 'Hey, you.'

The figure rolled over onto its back, coughing and spluttering. Then Royston watched as the man he'd awoken sat up.

'What are you doing?' the man snapped, shaking his head and trying to clear his vision as he stared up in bewilderment at Royston. 'What are you doing here?'

'Wake up,' Royston said, taking a step backwards.

'I'm awake,' the man rasped. 'You just woke me up, didn't you?' He coughed again, hawked loudly and spat on the floor next to the bed. He sat on the edge of the wooden bed and filthy mattress, his head bowed.

Royston regarded him appraisingly and realised that

the man was in his fifties, perhaps older. His face was covered by a thick grey beard, his skin leathery beneath it and around his eyes. There were several scars on the top of his bald head and his left eye was rheumy and puffy. He wiped his nose with the back of one hand and got to his feet.

'Coming into a man's home and disturbing him,' he grunted. 'Who are you, anyway? Are you with the police?'

Royston shook his head.

'If you are you have to say, you know – you can't just walk in here like this.'

'I'm not with the police,' Royston told him, watching the other man as he got to his feet a little uncertainly. The American set the Geiger counter down on the stone floor.

'Do you know what this is?' the man asked, jabbing a finger at the metal container in the middle of the room.

'It's a still,' Royston replied. 'I know what it's for. Brewing up a little illegal hooch out here?'

The man crossed to the container and then dropped to his knees, picking up one of the overflowing glass receptacles. He lifted it to his mouth and took a sip, wincing when he swallowed.

'It's good stuff,' he growled, pushing the container towards Royston. 'Have some.'

Royston shook his head.

'Are you sure you're not with the police?' the man asked again.

'I'm a scientist.'

'So what do you want here? You don't look like a

scientist. Why come in here disturbing me?' He pointed at the Geiger counter. 'What's that thing for?'

'It's a Geiger counter. It measures radioactivity.'

'I'll swap it for three jars of my brew.'

Again, Royston shook his head. 'I need to talk to you,' he said earnestly.

'What about?'

'Were you here last night?'

'I'm here every night unless I go into Broughton or Monkston to do a bit of business, if you know what I mean.' The still operator nudged Royston. 'I sell this stuff to people cheap.' He took another sip. He smiled, then broke into a paroxysm of coughing, finally sucking in a deep breath and wiping his chin with one hand. 'It's good.'

'You told me.'

'So many people are out of work now – they can't afford the stuff that pubs and off-licences sell, so they take this off me. It's cheaper and it works quicker.' The man grinned and sipped some more of the liquid.

'Did you see anyone around here last night, out in the marshes? Some young boys?'

The man regarded him suspiciously.

'A young boy was hurt out here last night,' Royston went on. 'Near to this place, by all accounts. Did you see anything?'

'Are you trying to say I had something to do with it? I'm not interested in little boys. What do you think I am, some kind of paedophile? I wouldn't touch a kid and I'd certainly never hurt one.'

'That's not what I'm saying. I'm just asking if you saw

any young boys around this area last night.'

The man shook his head and turned towards the shelves on the far wall. 'I live here because I've got nowhere else to go,' he grunted. 'Do you think I want to live like this? If I had a house and money I wouldn't have to be here. And now you come here accusing me of molesting some kid.'

'I didn't say that,' Royston corrected him.

'I went into Broughton last night to try and sell some of this,' the man said. He raised one of the containers of liquor. 'I got back here late. There was no one around. No kids. Nobody. No one ever comes out here.' He turned and glared at Royston. 'Except you.'

'Have you seen anything strange out here in the last few days?'

'Like what?' the man wanted to know.

Royston could only shrug.

'There've been lots of dead animals in the marshes,' the man told him. 'Badgers, foxes, rabbits. Even birds. I've found lots of them. More than usual.'

'Around here? Around the tower?'

'All over the marshes.'

The man moved some chipped cups to make a space for the container of clear liquid and, as he did, Royston stepped forward, his stare suddenly fixed on a small metal cylinder that had previously been hidden from view. The man was about to pick it up when Royston grabbed his arm.

'What are you doing?' the man protested, trying to shake loose. Several cups fell to the floor, one of them shattering on the stone.

'Don't touch that,' Royston snapped.

Again the man tried to pull away from his grip. 'Get off me,' he snarled.

'You touch that and it may kill you,' Royston snapped. 'Where the hell did you get it?'

The man looked in bewilderment at the American and then at the small cylinder on the shelf. 'I found it out there in the marshes,' he said quietly, the anger now disappearing from his tone to be replaced by concern. 'What is it?'

Royston retrieved the Geiger counter and pointed the probe towards the small cylinder, waiting for the clicking of the machine to begin in earnest.

There was only silence.

'What is that thing?' the man persisted. 'What's in it? You said it could kill me.'

Royston didn't answer; he was still gazing fixedly at the cylinder. 'This container is mine,' he said finally. 'It was stolen from my laboratory.'

'I never stole it. I wouldn't do that.'

'Well, someone has – and I need to know who and why.'

Twenty-Nine

'I was expecting you earlier,' Peter Elliot said as Royston stood in the centre of the laboratory gazing around him in disbelief. 'When I rang you and said there'd been a break-in here I thought you would have come back straight away.'

'I didn't think there was anything I could do,' Royston said distractedly, his brow furrowed. 'Besides, I had other things to take care of. I knew that you and your father would be able to cope here.'

'The military police wanted to seal off the entire base but the civil authorities insisted that they be allowed to inspect the scene first,' Peter told him.

Royston shook his head again as he surveyed the damage.

The laboratory was a wreck. Shattered glass was spread all over the floor like crystal confetti. Instruments had been smashed beyond repair.

'How the hell did anyone get in here to cause this kind of damage?' Royston said. 'How did anyone with-out authority get onto the base in the first place? Let alone in here.'

'To say that this incident has caused embarrass-ment here would be an understatement,' Peter said. 'A top-secret military research facility broken into by person or persons unknown. Someone's going to suffer, I suspect.' He managed a thin smile.

'Was this the only part of the complex that was broken into?'

'As far as we can tell.'

Royston picked up a large lump of battered metal. It had been square once but now it was bent and twisted out of shape. It was hard to believe that the metal had only recently formed one wall of a safe-like construction designed to withstand even the most powerful of impacts. Whoever had damaged the metal had done so as easily as if they were crushing tin foil.

'This is lead,' the American scientist muttered. 'Two inches thick.'

'You mean it *was*.'

'What about the samples that were inside?'

'Still here,' Peter told him, gesturing to several small cylindrical containers standing on a bench nearby. 'That's what makes it even stranger. There's been a break-in but nothing seems to have been taken.'

'So equipment's been destroyed but not stolen?'

'And I took a radiation reading from the containers and there was nothing. Not a flicker. They're not radioactive any more.'

'That lead safe was full of triennium. Do you know how long it retains its radioactivity?'

'It's not a very stable compound,' Peter commented. 'Thirty years?'

'Twenty-eight actually. The point is that those

samples were giving off danger-point radiation readings yesterday. Now it's nothing.'

'But that's impossible.' Pete swallowed hard. 'Isn't it?'

'Yesterday I would have said yes but the fact is that the energy that was in that triennium has been sucked right out of it.'

'By what?'

'I wish I knew,' Royston exclaimed. 'Does it remind you of anything?'

Peter Elliot looked vague.

'When we first investigated that chasm that opened up during the army exercise there was no trace of radioactivity and yet seven men were either burned or suffered radioactive poisoning because they were close to it,' Royston explained. 'When we checked the location with Geiger counters we found no trace of radioactivity.'

'That's right,' Peter said.

'It was the same at the tower in the marshes,' Royston went on. 'A boy was badly burned in that area last night and yet when I went out there earlier there were no traces of radioactivity, no sign of anything that might have given him first-degree radiation burns. It's as if the source of the radiation appeared suddenly and then simply vanished later.' He shook his head. 'Which we all know by every law of science is impossible.'

Peter Elliot regarded his senior colleague blankly.

'And what the hell is this?' Royston commented. He was pointing to a white powder that covered the nearest worktop. 'Some kind of residue?' It looked a little like thin talcum powder or flour. He could see that it had coated other objects inside the room, too.

'It seems harmless, whatever it is,' Peter told him. 'It vanishes after an hour or two.'

'I saw dust like this in that tower on the marshes,' Royston said.

'What were you doing out there?'

'I told you, a young boy was injured in that area last night. I went out there to see what might have caused it. This white residue was inside that tower.'

Royston took a couple of steps back and saw that the white dust covered a fair proportion of the laboratory floor and also that there was some on one of the walls that led away from a large air vent. He put one index finger lightly in the coating and then rolled the soft particles together between his thumb and finger, sniffing lightly to try and detect some kind of odour that might help him discern what the material was. 'Odourless,' he murmured.

'And non-corrosive, fortunately,' Peter added.

'And you say it disappears after an hour or two?'

Peter nodded.

Royston shook his head.

'There's no way onto this base without the required authorisation,' he sighed. 'The doors and windows of this complex were locked from the inside and still are now. The whole place is alarmed and yet someone managed to slip in and out without even stealing any - thing. This place is locked down so tightly we'd know it if the Holy Ghost himself got in – and yet someone managed to breach security easily enough to destroy this laboratory and the samples inside it.' He stroked his chin thoughtfully. 'Who the hell got inside here, Peter?' The words hung in the air like a bad smell.

Thirty

Leo McGill was a small, rotund man with curly black hair and jowls that some had said made him look like a relative of a beagle. McGill didn't mind the comparison – in fact it amused him. He'd always admired that breed of dog for its fortitude and determination and he liked to feel that he possessed those qualities himself. His doggedness and obsessive attention to detail were two of the things that had helped him to advance within his department of the Home Office. McGill saw himself as much more than just a civil servant. He felt little affinity with some of his colleagues back in London, not merely because he was a younger man (he was yet to reach his fortieth birthday) but because he seemed to carry out his work with a zeal that others in his department lacked. He'd always found that difficult to understand: if one was given a job then one should perform the duties expected to the best of one's ability. He had been told that on his first day in his department and it was a credo he had stuck to all his working life. Those who didn't apply themselves fully to their work were looked upon with something approaching contempt by McGill.

Now he sat on one of the chairs in Professor John

Elliot's office, running his appraising gaze over the surroundings and indeed over the professor himself. The older man was standing behind his desk holding several sheets of paper, glancing from them to McGill and then back again as he spoke. McGill listened with the requisite amount of respect and retained what he liked to call his professional smile as the professor went on. McGill couldn't help but feel that the professor's round glasses gave him the appearance of either an owl or a Nazi war criminal. At the moment he couldn't decide which it was.

'To be honest, Inspector McGill—' Professor Elliot said.

The younger man held up an index finger and cut across him. '*Mister* McGill,' he corrected.

'I'm sorry, but the whole thing's quite ridiculous,' Elliot continued. 'I never thought that anyone would call you people in on this.'

'The local police called us,' McGill informed him. 'As you know, any crime, however small, connected with this facility comes through to us. There are certain procedures that must be followed. You appreciate that. It's bad enough when there's crime anywhere but when it occurs at a top-secret military research facility then there are factors to be considered that wouldn't normally arise.'

'Obviously, and I accept that you have to investigate. But this crime, if you want to call it that—'

Again McGill cut across the older man. 'What would *you* call it, sir?' he asked. 'Breaking and entering has always been a crime as far as I'm concerned.'

'But nothing was taken from Doctor Royston's laboratory. How can that be a crime?'

'Someone broke in and wrecked it,' McGill reminded the older man.

'Yes, they did, but I would have thought the local police were well able to take care of an investigation like that without any outside help from Whitehall.'

McGill smiled sagely. 'Well, that's what I was sent here to find out, sir,' he said. 'As I mentioned before, this isn't a normal army base, is it? The work here is delicate – to put it mildly.'

'What do you mean?'

'If the media become aware of this break-in the story will spread like wildfire and if they can't get a story that suits them then they'll make one up. There have already been rumblings back in London about what happened during the exercise out on the moor – the last thing the department needs is more adverse publicity.'

'What kind of rumblings?' Elliot asked defensively.

'From a lot higher up the food chain than myself, sir,' McGill said gravely. 'Cabinet level.'

Elliot regarded the other man warily for a moment. Then he drew a deep breath. 'Well, I spoke to Doctor Royston about the break-in and the local police were quite satisfied with his cooperation too,' the professor said. 'To be honest, I don't want to hear any more of the matter.'

'Well, *I* do, sir,' McGill said, his tone turning a little darker. 'So perhaps you can tell me where I can find Doctor Royston.'

'I'm not sure I like your tone, Inspector . . . sorry, Mr McGill,' Elliot announced.

'I apologise if I come across as a little brusque, sir, but I've been sent up here to pursue an investigation and no one is going to stop me from doing that.'

The two men locked stares and Elliot saw a determination in the other man's eyes that was matched by the steeliness of his voice.

'Now I'll ask you again,' McGill said flatly. 'Where can I find Doctor Royston?'

Thirty-One

The public bar of The Three Horseshoes pub was always crowded. At least, that was how it seemed to Adam Royston. The pub was a short drive from Broughton town centre and there were a number of office buildings in the vicinity too that provided it with customers. It was popular with residents of the town and visitors alike, from the time it opened until eleven at night when it took its final orders.

Royston sat at a small table in one corner of the bar, close to the large open but unlit fireplace, beneath some of the horse brasses and paintings that decorated the walls. There were people standing at the bar and also seated at most of the tables and booths. A group of customers were playing darts on the far side of the bar, watched by three old men who were muttering either encouragement or insults as each player threw. There was a pleasant hum of chatter throughout the pub – Royston didn't find it a distraction as he scribbled on his notepad and compared some of the figures he'd already written there. He reached for his sandwich and took a bite, glancing again at the words and numbers he'd committed to paper. Chemical formulae, atomic numbers, names from the periodic table vied for space with the names he had also written there.

RYAN DICKINSON.

LANSING. COULSON. DAWSON.

He washed down the fragment of sandwich with a swallow of beer.

'Don't you chaps even stop to eat?'

The voice startled him, coming as it did from right beside him. Royston looked up and saw a small rotund man with curly black hair looking down at him.

'My name's McGill,' the man told him. 'Do you mind if I sit down?'

'Have we met?' Royston asked, watching as the man seated himself in the chair opposite. 'My memory isn't so good these days.'

McGill pulled out a small leather wallet, flipped it open and handed it to Royston who scanned the photograph and the information on the ID.

'Leo McGill, Atomic Energy Commission Internal Security Division,' he read. 'It sounds very impressive.' He handed the ID back to the other man.

'Impressive, yes,' McGill said, smiling. 'But not on paydays.'

'Can I get you a drink?' Royston asked.

'Thanks, but not while I'm working,' McGill told him.

'Well, Inspector McGill, what can I—'

McGill held up a hand and interjected. '*Mister* McGill,' he said. 'My friends call me Mac. Or they would if I had any.'

'Is it that bad?' Royston said, grinning.

'Men like me in official positions are usually seen as bringers of bad news.'

'It sounds like someone wants to shoot the messenger. Is it bad news you're bringing me?'

'I hope not, doctor. I need your expertise.'

'OK, Mac, what can I help you with?'

'It's about that child who was burned.'

'Ryan Dickinson. How did you hear about him?'

'Let's just say I have sources. Have you any idea how it happened?'

'Well, he was exhibiting the signs of radiation burns.'

'Like the soldiers in the base hospital at Broughton Green?'

'You know one man was killed during an exercise out on the moor?'

'I'm aware of that. I'm also aware that seven others seem to be suffering from radiation sickness. Do you think the boy and the soldiers were exposed to the same radioactive source?'

'It's possible but . . .'

'Unlikely.'

'Well, all the injuries happened within five miles of each other. But the boy might have been burned when he handled a sample container . . .'

'The case of the missing radiation. Yes, I've heard that one already. I know all about the break-in at the base.'

'From the professor?'

'Yes, I spoke to him earlier. There's no doubt as to his opinion on the matter.'

'What about yours?' Royston asked.

'I'm not entitled to have any opinions,' McGill said, smiling. 'I'm only interested in facts. I spoke to that old man, too, the one who lives in the tower near where the child was injured.'

'Colourful, isn't he?'

'He couldn't tell me anything useful. He said that someone else had been out there to speak to him, though.'

'I went to the tower to see if I could find out what burned that boy.'

'Nothing inside that building or in the vicinity?'

'Nothing that's there now. I took a Geiger counter with me when I went. There's no trace of radioactivity anywhere around that place.'

'Well, *something* burned that boy and I'd like you to help me find out what it was.'

Royston nodded and was about to speak again when his mobile phone went off. He reached for it and saw that the message was from Sandra Morgan. 'Excuse me while I just check this,' he said.

McGill nodded, watching as the American pressed various buttons on the phone to read the message.

Royston's expression darkened noticeably. 'It's from a friend of mine,' he said finally. 'A nurse at the hospital where they took the boy. She says he's deteriorating fast. His condition is critical. They don't think he'll last an hour.'

McGill was already on his feet. 'We'd better get to the hospital,' he said.

Thirty-Two

In all his years of practising medicine Doctor Martin Kelly had never found an easy way to speak the words he knew he would have to say to Lauren Dickinson.

Conveying news of the death of a loved one was the most intolerable aspect of his profession.

He stood next to the bed where her son lay and gazed down helplessly at the boy. Kelly was enveloped by an overwhelming feeling of weariness, as if part of him had been drained by what he'd seen and what he must soon say. And he felt anger, too. Anger that he hadn't been able to do more to help the boy.

He experienced that feeling every single time he lost a patient.

When it was a child or someone particularly young the feeling was even more acute. Of course he felt the pain when an older patient died but there was a kind of inevitability about the death of an octogenarian that made the loss somehow easier to cope with. As a doctor he had tried to steel himself against the feelings he experienced in situations such as these. However, no matter how long he worked in the medical profession, he told himself he'd never be able to fully insulate himself against such occurrences. And the death of a child distressed him as much every time.

He looked at the face of Ryan Dickinson and, as so often happened when someone had died, he thought that there was a peacefulness to the boy's features. At least all his pain and suffering was over now and that was mirrored on the dead countenance. But now the suffering would be transferred to those who had loved him, Kelly thought.

He took the edge of the sheet and pulled it gently over the boy, covering his face. Behind him he heard the sound of weeping and when he turned he saw that Lauren Dickinson was standing shakily on the other side of the room, supported by Sandra Morgan. The nurse had one arm around the woman's shoulder in a futile attempt to comfort her.

Kelly released his grip on the sheet, knowing that he would have to turn and face Mrs Dickinson but wanting to delay the moment as long as he could. It was as if the boy were still alive until Kelly himself spoke the words that announced his passing. The doctor drew a deep, almost painful breath, then turned to face Lauren Dickinson.

'I'm so sorry,' he said finally.

Lauren nodded, tears pouring down her cheeks. 'Was he in a lot of pain?' she asked breathlessly.

'No,' Kelly told her gently. 'He never woke. He wouldn't have felt anything.' He watched as Sandra guided the woman towards the door of the room, helping her through.

As Mrs Dickinson reached the threshold she turned back towards the bed. 'Ryan,' she said helplessly.

'If you'd like to sit down for a little while you can use my room,' Kelly told her. 'The nurse will sit with you.'

'Come on, Lauren,' Sandra whispered, again helping the stricken woman out of the room.

They had barely emerged into the corridor when Sandra glanced up and saw two figures at the far end. One she recognised immediately as Royston but she didn't know the smaller, rotund man he was with. She nodded towards Royston, then helped Lauren Dickinson into the room that Kelly indicated.

Royston slowed his pace as Kelly approached him.

'Is the boy dead?' Royston asked.

'He never regained consciousness,' Kelly said quietly. The knot of muscles at the side of his jaw pulsed. 'Adam, we've got to find out how this happened.'

'That's what we're trying to do, Doctor . . .?' McGill said.

'Kelly,' the doctor told him, looking quizzically at the smaller man. 'Doctor Martin Kelly.'

'My name's McGill. I'm with the Atomic Energy Commission,' he explained, extending his right hand which Kelly shook. 'That's why we came to see the boy, to find if he could tell us anything.'

'He won't be telling anyone anything now,' Kelly said quietly.

'Could we look at the body before it's removed?' McGill asked.

Kelly hesitated for a moment, then nodded and indi-cated the door to the room where Ryan Dickinson lay.

The three men were about to enter when Lauren Dickinson emerged from Kelly's room, her eyes red and puffy and her mascara smeared. She looked straight at Royston and walked towards him, her upper lip quivering. Close behind her, Sandra Morgan followed, looking agitatedly between the stricken woman and the American scientist.

Royston gave the women a consoling smile but he knew that it was a wasted and woefully inadequate token.

'Doctor Royston,' Lauren Dickinson said.

'Mrs Dickinson,' Royston began weakly. 'If there's anything at all . . .'

She cut him short. 'There's nothing you can say or do that would help now,' Lauren said tearfully. 'Nothing you can say or do that would bring my Ryan back.' She wiped some tears away with an already sodden tissue. 'He was everything to me. All I had. And now he's gone. He's gone because of you and people like you.'

Royston opened his mouth to speak but the woman continued.

'I know who you are, Doctor Royston,' she went on. 'You're a scientist, not a doctor. You don't cure people – you invent things that kill them. Just like they killed my Ryan. I've heard about the kind of thing that goes on at that research base where you work.'

Sandra stepped forward and attempted to pull the crying woman away but she shook loose and continued glaring at Royston.

'You should be locked up, you and those like you,' Lauren blurted. 'So no more innocent people like my

Ryan have to die while you do your experiments out there behind those fences, in those laboratories.' She sniffed back more tears. 'Was it something you made that killed him? Some kind of disease that you created?'

'Mrs Dickinson, your son was killed by a high dose of radiation,' Royston explained.

'Radiation – or something else you can't control?' she snarled. 'You're not safe. You're a murderer.'

'Mrs Dickinson, please,' Kelly said gently.

'It's all right,' Lauren Dickinson said, her stare still fixed on Royston. 'I've finished. I don't want to look at him any longer.' She turned and walked hurriedly off down the corridor.

'Go with her, nurse,' Kelly instructed. Sandra ran off after the crying woman, holding her arm and murmuring softly to her as they walked.

Royston watched them go, his face pale.

'She's wrong, Adam,' said McGill.

'Is she?' Royston murmured.

'You were no more responsible for that boy's death than I was,' McGill told him.

'Perhaps we're both to blame in some way, Mac,' Royston said. 'The industry we work in . . .' He allowed the sentence to trail off.

'We can help her now by finding out what killed her boy,' McGill insisted. He turned towards the door behind them and allowed Kelly to push it open. The three men stepped inside and the doctor pulled back the sheet that covered Ryan Dickinson's body.

'My God,' McGill exclaimed, looking at the angry red burns that covered the boy's torso and neck.

'That's not all,' Royston said. 'He was riddled with cancer that seems to have been induced by the same dose of radiation that killed him.'

'It grew incredibly fast and infected most of the vital organs of his body,' Kelly added.

'The soldiers in the hospital up at Broughton Green are also infected with the same kind of highly aggressive cancer,' Royston said.

'And you think it was brought about by exposure to radiation?' McGill asked.

'Cancer can be a long-term product of exposure to high concentrations of radiation,' Royston told him. 'Those soldiers and this boy and some unborn children have also been infected with a fast-growing form of cancer. I think the only conclusion is that they were all exposed to the same source. It was the radiation that killed them or infected them. We have to find the radiation source.'

'But what about the other men on the army exercise?' McGill asked. 'Not all of them were affected, were they?'

'Just the ones who were close to that crack in the ground that opened up,' Royston told him. 'All these incidents began to happen after that appeared.'

'But this boy was miles away from that when he was burned,' Kelly said.

'What about the men out there now?' McGill asked. 'Surely they're in danger too.'

'Until we discover what's causing deaths like these,' Royston said, his gaze fixed on the boy's corpse, 'anyone could be in danger.'

Thirty-Three

Claire Reece usually saw the same faces at every session of radiotherapy. Two or three other patients who had appointments around the same time as she did. There was a man in his sixties who was impeccably dressed and groomed and who made a point of nodding politely to her if he saw her. The others were a woman in her forties with glasses and short hair who always carried the same battered brown handbag and a young woman who Claire guessed couldn't be much more than twenty. She sometimes had a friend with her, but not today. Claire had seen her leaving as she herself entered St Mary's radiotherapy department and, as usual, the two of them had exchanged smiles and waves.

The other members of the Cancer Club, as Claire liked to think of them, were seated in the waiting room when she walked in. The well-dressed older man nodded in his usual manner and the woman with the glasses attempted a smile, as was her way. Claire seated herself, took a magazine from the pile on the table in the middle of the room and glanced at the pages open before her. As she peered distractedly at the magazine she wondered, as she usually did, what kind of treatment the other members of the club were receiving. Was the old man being helped through prostate cancer? The woman treated for breast cancer like herself? Never, during any of her visits, had she exchanged one single word with her fellow sufferers. It wasn't really the kind of conversation to strike up in the waiting room of a radiotherapy unit. Comparing the size and nature of tumours or the progress of treatment to destroy them really wasn't the stuff of polite discussion, Claire had decided. She assumed that the other members of the club would have similar questions about her. The nature of her cancer and the progress of her treatment might well have been important to them but she guessed that their own problems were uppermost in their minds, as her own were in hers.

Nevertheless, she couldn't help but wonder if the other members of the Cancer Club had pondered the same kind of questions she had over the past days and weeks. What if the treatment didn't work? What if the cancer wasn't destroyed? What if it spread to another part of the body? All these thoughts tumbled through her mind and, she was sure, through the minds of the other members of the club at any time of the day or night. Claire usually found that these obsessions and fears surfaced most strongly first thing in the morning and when she was alone with too much time to think. If she had quiet times during the day then these dreads would crowd in upon her to the point where she felt that her head would explode. What if the final outcome of the treatment wasn't successful? She shook her head quickly, deciding that particular line of speculation wasn't to be followed. God knew the thoughts came to her often enough during the night if she woke. Lying there in the blackness with her fears gnawing away at her was almost intolerable.

She had Stephen to talk to and she was grateful for that but no matter how much she talked it still didn't help. All the talking, all the sympathy in the world wasn't going to cure her, was it?

When she heard the door of the radiotherapy room open she looked up and saw the all too familiar face of the radiographer looking out at her.

'Claire,' he said, good-naturedly. 'Would you like to come through?'

Not really, but if I don't have the treatment I'll die, won't I?

She dropped the magazine back onto the table and headed through into the larger room beyond, closing the door behind her.

'How have you been feeling?' the radiographer asked, ushering her towards the black couch in the centre of the room. 'Any side effects from the treatment?'

'I've felt a little bit sick sometimes,' Claire explained. 'Especially just after the treatment. Some of my joints have been a bit stiff, too, but otherwise nothing much.'

'That's to be expected,' the radiographer told her. 'You might find that the skin around the area being treated sometimes becomes a bit red and blotchy too but there's cream we can prescribe for that if it becomes too severe.'

Claire nodded and seated herself on the couch close

to the linear accelerator machine. She looked at it with a combination of fear and hope. The same emotions were in her expression as she regarded the radiographer himself. He crossed to the control panel of the machine, seemingly engrossed in his own thoughts and she watched as he flicked a couple of switches. There was a low buzzing sound in the room that increased in volume once the switches had been pressed.

'If you want to get yourself comfortable on the couch,' the technician told her, 'we'll get your treatment underway.'

Claire pulled off her shoes and placed them under the couch. Then she lay down, shuffling backwards until her head was on the pillow at the far end.

The radiographer was still standing beside the control panel near her, pressing more switches and checking readings. She wondered why he was frowning.

'Is something wrong?' Claire asked.

The man didn't answer at first; he was too pre-occupied with the electrical panel before him. Lights were blinking and flashing and the low hum filling the room was growing louder by the minute. Claire sat up and looked around her, a crackling noise now becoming audible too.

'It's some kind of power surge,' the technician said, jabbing at switches all over the control panel now.

There was a loud bang.

He jumped back sharply as one portion of the panel exploded. Small fragments of plastic and metal spun into the air, propelled on a ribbon of white sparks.

'Jesus Christ,' he hissed, backing off further.

The crackling noise was now much louder and seemed to be coming from every side of the room.

Claire swung herself off the couch, her gaze darting around the room as if to locate the source of the sound. She winced and put a hand to her ear as it became almost deafening.

'What is it?' she called, seeing that the radiographer was now staring fixedly at something below the control panel. Claire saw a ventilator grille there and realised it was that he was looking at.

He suddenly dropped to his knees, his face contorted with pain and she could see the flesh there rising and falling as if controlled from beneath by dozens of miniature pumps. A blister rose with incredible speed on his forehead, swelling and ripening like some vile fruit. It burst just as quickly and thick yellow pus spilled down his face. More of the pustules erupted on his cheeks and neck and, when he raised his hand helplessly before him, she could see that the fingers were swollen and bloated. She saw the nail of the index finger peel backwards and then drop off, clear fluid spurting from the end of the digit.

Claire stood frozen to the spot, not sure whether to try and help the radiographer or run for the door and possible safety.

As it was she did neither.

The radiographer screamed in agony and fell forward, his body shaking uncontrollably, and Claire finally saw what he had been staring at.

Then she too screamed.

Thirty-Four

As he passed through the door Royston glanced at the sign upon it.

DANGER: RADIATION.

That word radiation again.

It seemed to be the dominant word in his life recently. Uppermost in his mind for so many different reasons, each one seemingly without a suitable explanation.

He glanced around the radiotherapy room as he entered, shaking his head at what he saw. Beside him, McGill looked similarly bemused. Doctor Martin Kelly walked ahead of them, gesturing towards a metal container set into the far wall of the room.

'That's where we store the radium,' Kelly announced, indicating the remains of the thick metal door that had been blasted open to reveal a safe-like box about two feet square. 'Or should I say *stored*?'

Royston sighed heavily as he surveyed the destruction before him. It looked as if someone had fired a cannon shell at the wall from incredibly close range. There was a large hole in the centre of the metal door and all around it the walls were blackened and charred as if they had been subjected to some incredible impact. Globules of molten metal had dripped to the floor and formed gleaming puddles and the door of the large container itself was so twisted and mangled out of shape that had Royston not known better he would have thought that several dozen blowtorches had been trained on it for hours on end. The metal had been melted as easily as candle wax. By what he could only begin to imagine. As he glanced down at the floor, some of which had also melted, he winced in disgust when he saw that there were several fragments of blackened human flesh mixed in with the other debris. It looked like a bomb site in that small room and as he stood there he became aware of a thick and noxious odour that he recognised all too quickly as that of seared human flesh.

The black leather couch had also been burned as had some of the worktops and part of the radiotherapy machine itself. But nowhere was the damage so severe as that which had been inflicted on the radium container set into the wall.

'Obviously the radium was the target,' Royston said.

'Obviously,' Kelly echoed. 'The radiographer just got in the way.'

'Is his body in the morgue?' McGill wanted to know.

'What's left of it,' Kelly told him. 'He must have been badly exposed to the source of heat used to cut through the safe door.'

'That safe proved no obstacle at all,' Royston went on, his gaze still fixed on the remains of the obliterated container on the wall.

'What sort of heat would be required to do this?'

McGill asked, also glancing at the riven safe door and the signs of scorching around it.

'Far beyond anything we've ever dreamed of,' Royston murmured.

'What about oxyacetylene cutters?' McGill offered. 'Or some kind of thermic lance?'

'Don't forget the time element,' the American scientist reminded him. 'Whatever happened in here did so in a matter of seconds.'

'Whoever wanted that radium was determined,' McGill commented. 'And well equipped.'

For a drawn-out moment Royston said nothing. He was staring blankly at the melted door of the safe. 'It doesn't add up,' he said, finally. 'Someone breaks in here and steals, in a matter of moments, potentially lethal radium by burning through a safe thick enough to stop a missile. And no one sees them?'

'Except the radiographer and the patient who was in here with him when this happened,' Doctor Kelly muttered.

'Claire Reece, wasn't it?' McGill asked. 'Perhaps we'll find out more when we speak to her.'

Kelly shook his head.

'I'm afraid she won't be speaking to anyone, Mr McGill,' he said.

'You mean she won't be able to tell us what happened?' McGill said.

'She'll be lucky if she can tell you her own name,' Kelly replied.

'Was she injured too?' Royston asked.

'There were relatively few physical injuries,' Kelly

told him. 'Some minor radiation burns to her hands and arms – but the psychological damage seems irreparable.'

Royston looked at McGill and then again at the devastated room. He drew his hand across the top of the leather couch and looked at the white powder that covered it. 'The same sort of residue that we found in the laboratory back at the base,' he commented.

'And in that tower out in the marshes,' McGill added. 'What could it be?'

Again Royston paused as if considering his answer before he spoke. 'The residue must be significant,' he said eventually. 'It's almost like a trail. A kind of finger - print left behind by whatever did this.' He motioned to the shattered safe, then turned and looked around again, his attention caught by a ventilator grille on the far side of the room. There was more of the white powder on the floor in front of it and some scorch marks on the grille itself. Royston knelt beside the metal and ran his finger over the mark.

There was a loud beeping sound and Kelly dug a hand into his pocket to retrieve his pager. Royston glanced at him as he read the message, his expression darkening. When he finally pushed the device back into his pocket his face was pale.

'You said that none of this made any sense,' the doctor murmured. 'Well, here's something else that doesn't. The examination performed on Claire Reece showed that there were no traces of cancer in her body. She was here undergoing radiotherapy to reduce a lump in her breast before it was removed and yet there are now no signs of that tumour. It's as if it's vanished.'

'Just like the radium,' McGill said.

'Wait,' Royston said. 'She had cancer before this happened?' he asked, waving a hand around in a gesture meant to encompass everything inside the room. 'And now she hasn't?'

'What the hell are we dealing with here?' McGill wanted to know.

Royston shook his head, then glanced down once more at the white powder covering the floor around the ventilator grille. 'Has the body of Ryan Dickinson been examined since he died?' he asked. 'Has the autopsy been done?'

'I'd have to check,' Kelly told him.

'Can you do it now?' Royston said, a note of urgency in his voice.

Kelly looked perplexed but nodded before stepping out of the room.

'What's the death of that boy got to do with what happened in here?' McGill asked.

'Maybe nothing,' Royston said vaguely. Once more he knelt beside the ventilator grille, tracing one index finger around the outline of the dark shadow on the metal there.

'Another burn?' McGill asked. 'The metal looks scorched.'

'As if a source of heat had passed through it,' Royston commented. 'And yet the grille isn't melted.' He stroked his chin thoughtfully. 'I think whatever got into this room got in through this air vent. It's the only way into this room other than by the door and yet no one saw anybody come in or out so how could that be? This vent has to be the answer.'

'But it doesn't open – it's cemented to the wall,' McGill protested. 'That's impossible. Whatever did all this damage wasn't small enough to come in through there.'

Royston was about to say something when Kelly walked back into the room, the expression on his face as grave as it had been a little earlier.

'They did the autopsy on Ryan Dickinson,' he said, quietly.

'And?' Royston asked.

'That boy had tumours in his lungs, liver, pancreas and bowel,' Kelly said. 'Large aggressive ones. And yet the autopsy revealed no sign of any cancer at all. Every tumour was gone. Every last trace of it.'

'Just like Claire Reece,' McGill murmured.

'Whoever or whatever came into this room didn't just consume the radium in the safe,' Royston said. 'I'd say it also absorbed Claire Reece's tumour and those inside Ryan Dickinson too.'

Thirty-Five

'Do you know how insane that sounds?' Kelly said. 'Something that feeds on cancer?'

'It might sound insane but is it any crazier than some-thing that moves around through ventilator grilles?' Royston countered.

McGill looked from one man to the other, unsure who his questions should be directed at.

'The same white residue found in here was found at the laboratory on the base,' Royston went on. 'Another supposedly secure location. It was found out on the marshes where Ryan Dickinson received his radiation burns and, as far as we know, his cancer too. Three places, Kelly. Whatever this is it's highly mobile.'

'Perhaps it's got a getaway driver,' McGill said.

'I'm being serious, Mac,' Royston snapped.

'I'm sure you are, Adam,' McGill replied. 'But listen to yourself. An entity that feeds on radioactive material and cancer? Christ, if it wasn't so malevolent it could be used as a cure.'

'Perhaps it can,' Royston mused.

McGill shook his head. 'Are you sure you didn't have some of that old man's illegal alcohol when you visited him out in the marshes?' he said wearily. 'Because you're talking as if you're drunk.'

'What other explanation is there?' Royston demanded.

'I'm a bureaucrat, Adam, remember?' McGill said. 'We deal in facts and figures, not speculation – and certainly not speculation as wild as this.'

'We're talking about an entity,' Kelly interjected. 'A creature.' He shook his head. 'We're talking like extras from some cheap horror movie, for God's sake.'

'No, we're talking about something that has no name,' Royston told him. 'Something we've never encountered before, something unknown. It has no name and it has no precedent. There's nothing we can compare it to. Whatever it is has never been seen before. It could be a species new to us, just like the animals on the Galapagos were when Darwin first saw them.'

'But the animals on the Galapagos didn't feed on energy and cancer and inflict radiation burns,' McGill said.

'Something that moves under doors and through ventilator grilles?' Kelly snapped. 'Something that creates cancer in its victims and then feeds on the tumours it's made? Something that uses radiation to kill but also needs it to survive?'

'That's a fairly accurate description, Kelly,' Royston told him.

'But it still doesn't explain how it got in here,' McGill said. 'As the doctor said, something small enough to get through that ventilator grille couldn't cause the damage in here. It couldn't kill a man.'

'How small is ten thousand gallons of oil?' Royston asked.

'What do you mean?' McGill wanted to know. 'I'm not with you.'

'Ten thousand gallons of oil would take up a lot of space,' Royston persisted. 'And yet it could all come through the holes in that grille, couldn't it?'

McGill looked towards the vent, his eyes fixed on the scorch marks on the metal. 'Yes, it could,' he conceded.

'So this thing, whatever the hell it is, you think it's liquid?' Kelly asked.

'I don't know what it is, Kelly,' Royston told him. 'It's like I said – we've never come across anything like this before. It has powers and abilities we can't imagine. Is it so difficult to think it might have the capability to take up any shape it needs to?'

The other two men were silent for a moment. Then Kelly spoke again. 'So where did it come from in the first place?' he asked.

'Who knows?' Royston answered. 'But it didn't appear until after that crack in the ground out on the moors opened up. My guess is it came from down there.'

'From inside the Earth?' McGill mused.

'I know it sounds ridiculous, Mac. But what other explanation do we have?' Royston said. 'That split opens up and suddenly radioactive material is being stolen or consumed. People are getting sick with radiation poisoning or they're being burned. We've got soldiers who look as if they were at ground zero when the Hiroshima bomb was dropped and all since that business out on the moors. It's a hell of a coincidence.'

'If you're right, where do you think it is now?' McGill asked.

'Somewhere out on the moors or the marshes,' Royston said. 'It's a good job that Major Cartwright didn't take my advice and station men out there.'

McGill looked sternly at the American scientist and when he spoke there was uncertainty in his tone.

'Unfortunately,' he said quietly, 'he did.'

Thirty-Six

Each of the thirty rooms inside Willen Hospice was identical. All were immaculately decorated and maintained by the ten-strong staff and each resident was allowed to add their own photographs, pictures, ornaments and paintings to the decor. The rooms were self-contained little homes for the people who were living out their lives within the confines of the building. The most important thing to those who worked in the hospice was that their residents should be comfortable and able to maintain a measure of dignity in their final days and weeks or in some cases months.

There were no set visiting hours. Relatives and friends were allowed to turn up whenever they wished and this helped to give the place a feeling of informality that was appreciated by everyone concerned, especially the residents.

Each room had a television and was relatively self-contained, even down to tea and coffee-making facilities, but there were also communal areas on the ground floor where residents could mingle. There was a large television room as well as a canteen. Many residents did not wish to be alone and the possibilty of interaction with others was thought to be as beneficial as some forms of therapy or medication. It was encouraged, but those who wanted their solitude were allowed it too.

It was important that residents should not feel that they had been placed in the institution to die. They should realise that they were being cared for by staff who specialised in catering to their specific needs and who were well able to serve them on both a physical and psychological level. Contrary to the myth associated with Willen Hospice and so many like it those inside weren't all dying of cancer. There were, of course, those stricken with that particular disease, those who had passed beyond the capabilities of an everyday hospital and who needed more constant care. But there were also those housed within Willen who were suffering from renal failure or cardiac problems and those too who were struggling with that most insidious of illnesses, Alzheimer's Disease.

All were cared for with the compassion and expertise required of such an establishment. Set as it was on the outskirts of Broughton, the hospice was within easy reach of the town centre and many of the residents were able to travel to and from there on the local buses. Those who had more trouble moving about could avail themselves of the two mini-coaches that the hospice owned. Sometimes the residents were taken further afield in these vehicles and at least twice every year, during the summer months, trips to the seaside were arranged for all the residents. It was a small gesture but it was appreciated by all.

As well as the full-time staff there were a number of

volunteers who worked at the hospice. Caring souls who helped out two or three times a week, at least three of whom had relatives resident at Willen. It gave them another opportunity to be near their loved ones while helping others at the same time.

However, it wasn't a volunteer but a regular nurse who stood at the rear of the building disposing of used dressings as the first clouds of evening began to darken the sky. She lifted the lid of the large wheeled metal bin and dumped the first of the waste materials inside, recoiling slightly from the smell that rose. She was about to deposit more waste when something on the side of the large black container caught her eye.

There was a thin layer of white powder on the side and lip of the bin.

It looked as though talcum powder had been spread there.

She saw more on the ground beneath the container. There seemed to be a trail of it leading from a drain cover nearby. The nurse dropped to her haunches and gazed at the trail more closely. It was glistening in the dull light cast by the lamp above the container.

She frowned, sure that this white residue hadn't been there two hours earlier on her previous visit to the bins.

It was particularly thick on and around the drain cover.

Puzzled, she continued to dispose of the waste, wondering whether or not she should mention her discovery to anyone inside the building. She dumped the last of the refuse and prepared to head back inside the hospice.

As she did she looked up and noticed that the trail actually led several feet up the wall of the building and then disappeared – as if whatever had left it behind had simply vanished.

Thirty-Seven

The cool breeze that had been blowing for most of the afternoon had developed into a chilly wind by the time night fell.

It whipped and whistled along the streets of Broughton but in exposed areas trees rattled and sometimes bowed, so powerful were the gusts that blew across the land.

The moor and marshland a few miles outside the town formed such an area and some of the soldiers who found themselves out there exposed to the gusting wind wandered about in an effort to restore some warmth to their bodies. Others looked for somewhere to shelter amidst the more undulating stretches of ground. How - ever, most of the terrain around the large rift in the earth that they were guarding was flat and offered precious little in the way of respite from the increasingly strong wind. A low chain fence had been temporarily erected to keep anyone away from the edge of the crevice and add emphasis to the signs stuck in the ground for two hundred yards in all directions that proclaimed KEEP AWAY.

Whether any of the locals had bothered to visit the rift none of the soldiers knew and if they were honest they didn't really care. All the men on the moor that night knew was that they wished they hadn't drawn this particular detail. Barracks seemed even more preferable when the wind blew at its strongest and several of the men feared they'd felt the first drops of rain on more than one occasion. Who the hell was going to trek out here to look at a bloody hole, anyway? That was the main consensus of opinion among the men. Others had whispered about the chain of events that had followed the initial opening of the split. The death of Don Lansing and the injuries suffered by others. Words like radio-activity, contamination and infection had been used a little too often for the liking of some of the men out on the moor that night.

One of those men was Private Andrew Morrell.

He walked back and forth close to the fence that separated the overly curious from the rim of the chasm, glancing occasionally at the rift in the ground and wondering like the others how it had appeared in the first place. He'd been a close friend of Don Lansing and the death of the man had affected him more acutely than he would have imagined. Bad enough to lose a comrade in a firefight or to a terrorist bomb, he thought, but to have him die here in the Buckinghamshire countryside killed by God alone knew what was even more intoler -able to Morrell. He prowled the perimeter of the rift now and watched it with almost accusing eyes.

'Andy.'

The sound of his name being called startled him and he turned in the direction of the shout.

'Andy.'

When the call came again, Morrell moved towards the low ridge from behind which the voice had come. He stood at the top of the incline and looked down, smiling thinly as he saw what lay beneath him.

On the opposite slope, crouching over a small Calor gas cooker was Private Nick Blake.

'Do you take that bloody thing everywhere?' Morrell asked in his strong Scots accent, pointing to the stove.

'They don't call me chef for nothing,' Blake told him. He indicated a small metal container full of bubbling brown fluid. 'Tea up.'

'Great,' Morrell answered, propping his rifle against a large rock where Blake's weapon was also resting. Then he pulled a tin cup from his pack and held it out to Blake who filled it for him.

'Just because we're stuck out here doesn't mean we can't have a cuppa, does it?' Blake smiled.

'You English and your tea.'

'One of the things that made us great,' Blake told him, taking a sip from his metal mug. 'It's just that it's whisky with you Jocks, isn't it?' He raised his mug. 'Cheers.'

Morrell nodded and lifted his own cup in salute, tapping it gently against his companion's.

'Anything happening?' Blake enquired, nodding in the direction of the slope and the rift that lay beyond it.

Morrell shook his head.

'Who the fuck is going to come out here to look at that hole in the ground?' he wanted to know. 'No one with any sense – but we have to stay out here freezing our bollocks off just in case.'

'Could be worse,' Blake commented.

'How?'

'We could be on guard duty out in fucking Helmand or somewhere like that. Dodging IEDs or some raghead with a fucking rocket launcher. At least here we're safe.'

'Tell that to Don Lansing or the guys who are in the hospital. They probably felt the same way a few days ago.' Morrell sipped his tea, gazing off across the wind-swept moor. 'What the fuck is that thing?' He hooked a thumb over his shoulder in the direction of the split.

'Don't ask me, Andy, I'm no expert. I heard some of the guys say something about an earthquake but you don't get earthquakes in this country, do you?'

'There's been talk about radiation and shit like that too. Some kind of infection or virus that might have been released when that thing opened up.'

'Maybe the scientists at the base have been fucking about with chemical weapons and one of them went wrong. I've seen reporters and TV news vans hanging about near the base – they obviously think there's some - thing going on,' Blake shrugged and sipped at his tea.

'Great,' Morrell murmured. 'Just bloody great. And we have to sit out here like fucking idiots just to make sure none of the locals decide to come and have a look around.'

'Not all the locals are that bad,' Blake told him. 'I went into town the other night on a twenty-four-hour pass and some of the local girls were pretty presentable, I must say.'

'I thought you were married?'

'I am. But just because you've bought the goods it doesn't stop you window shopping, does it?'

Both men laughed.

'What about you, Andy? Is there a Mrs Morrell?' Blake wanted to know.

'Not any more. I got divorced about a year ago.'

'Sorry. How long had you been married?'

'Six years. Five of them good.'

'My mum and dad got divorced when I was sixteen. My old man was a right cunt. Out with a different fucking woman every week, pissing all his wages up the wall. My mum was well shot of him. I always made sure I was nothing like him.' Blake looked contemplatively at his mug of tea as if searching for his next sentence on the surface of the steaming brown fluid. 'What happened with you and your missis – if you don't mind me asking?'

'It was nobody's fault, really. She just got fed up with being on her own. Me being away for so long at a stretch and she didn't want me to go to Afghanistan. She was scared I wouldn't come back. Scared I'd get hurt. Blah, blah, blah. All that kind of crap. She wanted me to leave the army and there was no way I was doing that.'

'So no one else was involved?'

'What's that supposed to mean?'

'Well, it's hard on the wives, like you say. They get lonely, don't they? Just like we do.' Blake nudged the Scot who glared back at him.

'Nobody else was involved,' Morrell told him flatly. 'What about your missis? How do you know what she's up to while you're away?'

'I don't – but I have to trust her, don't I? That's what

marriage is all about, isn't it? Trust?' Blake sipped his tea. 'I know, I read it on the back of a matchbox.'

Again the two men laughed.

'Which part of London are you from?' Morrell asked.

'Bermondsey. Down by the docks.'

'It's pretty rough there.'

'Well, Glasgow's not exactly a walk in the fucking park, is it?' Blake raised his tea in salute.

'I'm not from Glasgow, you cheeky fucker. I'm from Lanark.'

'You lot all sound the same to me.'

'Don Lansing used to say that.'

'You were pretty close, you and Don.'

The Scot nodded. 'He was a good lad. He didn't deserve what happened to him,' he said quietly.

'Radiation burns, I heard – same as the other guys who were out here that night.' Blake pointed towards the ridge and the rift beyond. 'Let's hope that whatever came out of there is gone now, eh?'

Morrell nodded, shivering as a particularly strong gust of wind blasted across the open ground.

'Oh fuck, no, look at that,' Blake exclaimed. 'It's going to piss down in a minute.'

'What makes you say that?' the Scot wanted to know.

'Because I just saw lightning.' Blake pointed up at the cloud-filled night sky again. 'There, look.'

Morrell glanced up and saw what his companion was indicating. There was a faint silver tinge to the clouds above them which seemed to be growing brighter. He squinted more intently at the glow, then rubbed his eyes.

The silver tint was still there.

'Lightning but no thunder. That's weird,' Blake muttered.

'That's not lightning,' the Scot said quietly.

Blake looked again, getting to his feet this time. 'Shit, no, you're right,' he acknowledged. He looked towards the ridge and realised that the cold white luminescence was coming from just beyond it.

'Something's glowing over there, Andy,' Blake said. 'And whatever it is it's coming from that fucking hole.'

Thirty-Eight

Blake got to his feet and picked up his rifle, moving towards the slope. Morrell did the same, moving ahead of his companion as they reached the low crest.

The crack in the ground lanced away before them, about two hundred yards from where they stood.

Both men gazed in the direction of the rift, squinting first at the hole itself and then up at the sky. The glow that had lit the night sky had faded.

'I saw something, I know I did,' Blake said, his stare fixed on the rift.

'Maybe it was an aircraft or something passing overhead,' Morrell suggested.

'So where did that glow come from? You saw it too.'

'It could have been landing lights or anti-collision lights.'

'There's no airport for miles.'

'Something from the base? A chopper?'

Blake considered the options for a moment, looking away from the rift and glancing up at the sky.

'Look,' Morrell snapped, pointing ahead.

There was a dull white glow coming from the hole. It wasn't as strong this time, as if the source of the light was deeper in the ground and barely reaching the surface but it was visible nevertheless.

Both men stood gazing towards it.

'What the fuck is that?' Blake wondered.

'We'd better check it out,' Morrell suggested.

As quickly as it had come, the glow vanished and the darkness spread across the land once again, black and unbroken.

'*You* check it out,' Blake said.

'Why not you? Are you scared?'

'Yeah – and I don't mind admitting it. Perhaps we should radio through for help.'

'And tell them what? We saw the ground glowing? They'll lock us up. They'll think we've been drinking more than tea out here.'

Blake hesitated.

Morrell looked at his companion for a moment, then nodded. 'I'll have a quick look,' he said. 'Go and make us some more tea, I reckon it's getting colder out here.'

Blake nodded and retreated back down the slope. Morrell advanced towards the flat open ground that would lead him to the rim of the split. As he moved closer he looked back and forth but could see no sign of light, however faint, coming from the rift. He walked to the edge and peered down, pulling his torch from his belt with one hand. He flicked it on and shone it into the hole. There was nothing to be seen but bare rock and the Scot switched the torch off.

A few yards ahead of him he saw light. Faint and barely visible but he saw it and he was sure it was coming from the rift in the ground, seeping out like fluid from a crack in a container. He moved on.

Back behind the ridge, Blake looked up again towards the sky.

The glow that he'd seen hadn't come from a passing plane or helicopter, he was almost sure of it. He checked the magazine of his L85A2 rifle, pulling it free of the weapon and glancing at the 7.62mm rounds inside for a moment before slamming it back into position.

He looked back in the direction of the ridge.

'Hey, Blakey.'

He heard Morrell's voice cut through the night.

'There's something here,' the Scot called. 'Come and look at this.'

Blake was already moving towards the top of the ridge again. He was halfway up when he heard the scream.

It was a sound that chilled him to the bone. A loud cry of despair and agony that rose on the wind like a banshee wail and then died just as suddenly.

With a shaking hand Blake flicked his weapon's safety catch off and ran on. 'Andy,' he bellowed. But there was nothing but silence now.

The darkness was impenetrable and he pulled his torch from his belt and flicked it on. The implement sputtered and only gave off a sickly yellow glow that barely penetrated more than a few feet ahead. He cursed under his breath when he realised the batteries were dying. Nevertheless he advanced towards the source of the cry, the hair on the back of his neck rising. The scream that Morrell had uttered had been a combination of fear and pain and the sound still seemed to reverb - erate inside Blake's head as he walked across the open ground, the barrel of his rifle pointing ahead of him.

The torch grew even dimmer and Blake shook it angrily as if that action would coax more light from it.

It didn't.

'Come on, you bastard,' he hissed, the words carried away by the powerful gust of wind that suddenly swept across the open ground.

Carried on that wind there was a strong smell that made Blake recoil. Something acrid that he thought he recognised. 'Andy,' he called again.

There was only silence.

Blake moved on, eyes alert for the slightest movement. He glanced towards the rift in the ground but there was no glow. No dull light. Nothing. Again he shook the torch and for a moment it actually seemed to burn more brightly. He aimed the beam ahead of him and it picked out something lying on the muddy ground a few yards away. Blake hurried over to it, his heart now beating harder against his ribs.

Lying on the ground at his feet was Morrell's rifle.

'Andy,' Blake murmured under his breath, dropping to his haunches to inspect the weapon.

There was a thin white powder on the stock and parts of the barrel.

It came away on his fingertips as he brushed them through the residue wondering just what the hell this stuff was.

Blake stood up, his breath rasping in his lungs now. He tried to swallow but his throat was bone dry. 'Andy,' he shouted, his stare darting around anxiously now. 'Where the fuck are you?'

The sound came from behind him. A loud crackling noise that stung his ears and echoed inside his head. He turned to find its source, his eyes widening madly as he saw what was making the noise. He took a couple of steps backwards, dropping Morrell's rifle and swinging his own up to his shoulder, his entire body shaking now. The sound became deafening and, as he staggered back, he realised what had been causing the glow he'd seen earlier. His eyes hadn't been playing tricks on him – although in those final seconds he wished they had.

Blake managed to get off two shots before it was upon him.

Thirty-Nine

Lieutenant James Bannerman watched as the Land Rover approached, bumping over the uneven ground as it drew nearer to him. As the vehicle slowed down he could pick out the faces of the passengers, one of whom he recognised immediately as his superior officer.

Major Cartwright was sitting in the front seat beside the driver who brought the car to a halt a few yards away from Bannerman.

Cartwright and the other passengers in the Land Rover scrambled out.

'Wait here,' Cartwright said to the driver and the man nodded.

Adam Royston and a smaller man whom Bannerman didn't recognize – McGill – joined the two officers.

'Where are they?' Cartwright asked immediately, his expression grave.

'We lost radio contact about an hour ago, sir,' Bannerman explained. 'Morrell and Blake had been reporting in every thirty minutes. When there was no contact I came out here myself. There's no sign of either of the men.'

'What was the last message?' Cartwright asked.

'Just the usual report that there was no activity in this area,' Bannerman replied, indicating the open wind-swept terrain around the rift. He and the other men looked towards the split in the ground. 'When they didn't answer a call I came to find them. There was no signal from their radios, you see. Nothing at all. That's why I came to have a look. I notified you as soon as I realised they weren't here.' He leaned closer to the major, his tone lower and more secretive. 'There was a lot of interference on the radio before that, sir.'

'Like the night this thing opened up?' Cartwright said.

The lieutenant nodded. 'Worse, if anything,' he conceded.

'Where could they have gone?' McGill asked, looking around.

'There was no reason for them to leave their posts,' Cartwright said, walking towards the make-shift fence that had been erected around the perimeter of the rift.

'Were they reliable men, lieutenant?' Royston asked.

'All of my men are reliable, sir,' Bannerman told him. 'They wouldn't have left their posts without permission.'

Royston nodded.

'That may be, lieutenant,' McGill said. 'But they're not here now, are they?'

Bannerman eyed the smaller man angrily for a moment, then turned towards his superior officer.

'I know these men too, Mr McGill,' Cartwright said. 'The lieutenant's right – they're good men, both of them.

If they're not here then there's a good reason why. I suggest we try and find that reason.'

Cartwright stepped over the fence and moved closer to the rim of the split. Royston waited a moment then joined him, prodding the ground close to the edge with the toe of his shoe. 'The ground seems stable enough here,' he murmured.

'Has there been any more seismic activity or radioactive presence since the hole opened?' McGill asked.

'No,' Bannerman told him. 'Men were posted here purely as a precautionary measure to prevent any civilians or media from approaching and endangering themselves.'

'It looks as if they weren't the ones in danger,' McGill murmured.

He and Bannerman joined the other two men close to the edge of the rift.

'Could I borrow that torch, lieutenant?' McGill said, indicating the item on the officer's belt.

Bannerman handed it to McGill who switched it on and swept the beam over the ground around them.

'I've already checked for footprints,' Bannerman told him. 'There are none. No one's been into this area.'

'I think someone has,' Royston said urgently, pointing. 'Look there.'

McGill aimed the beam in the direction that the American scientist had indicated but it was Cartwright who knelt to retrieve the object. He stooped close to the edge of the hole and pulled what looked like a piece of fabric from the ground there. It was a thick woollen glove with one finger missing.

'Army issue?' Royston asked.

There was something else in the earth close to the glove and Cartwright pulled that free too.

He straightened up, brushing dirt from the beret, nodding when he recognised the cap badge upon it. 'This belongs to Morrell or Blake,' he said quietly.

'Does that look familiar?' McGill said, glancing at Royston as he aimed the torch beam at the beret, the light picking out something they had both seen before.

Royston looked more intently at the item Cartwright was holding and nodded.

The headgear was covered in a thin white residue.

Forty

One of the symptoms of clinical depression is the desire to sleep an inordinate amount. The sufferer isn't necessarily tired – although the constant stress that the body and mind is subjected to can be exhausting – but the problems that are causing the depression can be temporarily left behind when the sufferer is asleep. Sleep is an escape from the woes of the conscious mind that are simply endured under normal circumstances.

Nikki Cross had come to know this fact well in the last few days.

She remembered it as she woke from a fitful slumber and glanced at the clock on the bedside table.

She'd slept for less than forty minutes, lying there in her clothes on top of the duvet. She sat up slowly, running a hand through her hair, trying to clear her head. She wished she could clear it of the worries that tormented her. As she lay propped against the head - board she allowed her hands to slide over her belly. It was inside *there*, not inside her head that her problems lay. She waited for a moment, then wondered about heading downstairs to make a cup of tea. If she stayed in the bedroom she knew she would just fall off to sleep again in time and she didn't really want to do that. She felt as if she'd spent most of the last three days sleeping.

She certainly hadn't spent much of that time talking. She hadn't gone into work during that time and she'd hardly said a dozen words to Paul even though she knew they desperately needed to discuss matters. But what, she reasoned, was the use of talking? Was it going to help her or her baby? Was a long discussion going to remove the problems she had? No, it wasn't. She was the only one who could decide the outcome of this situation and she had no wish to bring about that outcome by killing her child.

No matter what was wrong with it she couldn't bear to do that. She had a life inside her and she wasn't about to end that life prematurely. She knew of a dozen good reasons why she should and she was aware that her decision to keep the baby was in some ways a selfish one – but it was her body and her child. No one but she had the right to decide the conclusion to this scenario. No one else would have to lie on the operating table while the baby was taken from her womb. No one else but she would have to cope with the feelings of guilt and despair once the deed was done.

And what of the baby itself? Even if she managed to go full term and have it, what future was there for it? A deformed baby with a life-threatening disease would have no life at all, would it? No matter how much love it was surrounded by. Love didn't cure cancer, did it?

Nikki brought her knees up to her chin and bowed her head.

Was she to blame in some way for what had hap - pened to the child inside her? Had she done something during the short pregnancy that had caused it to be affected so badly? She hadn't smoked since finding out she was pregnant. She hadn't even touched a drop of liquor. Or was it deeper than that? she wondered. Was there something defective about her ovaries or her womb or the eggs she carried? Or was it the fault of her partner?

Nikki swung herself off the bed and padded out to the landing where she hesitated a moment before heading into the bathroom.

She looked at her reflection in the mirror there, shocked at how rough she looked. Her eyes particularly were swollen and red from so much crying and her skin was in a terrible state. There were several spots on her cheeks and chin and much of her skin was very dry too. She looked down as if anxious not to look at the young woman who stared back at her from the glass. Nikki pulled down her jeans and knickers and sat on the toilet, gazing blankly ahead.

When she'd finished, she told herself, she'd go back into the bedroom and lie down for a while. Just until she felt a little stronger. And if she fell asleep again then so what?

She heard her mobile ringing somewhere in the bedroom but she merely shook her head. It would be Paul checking on her, or her mother, or one of her friends. Let them wait.

She finished in the bathroom and padded slowly back across the landing to the bedroom where the mobile had stopped its electronic chirping by now. She glanced at it and saw familiar words on the screen:

YOU HAVE 5 MISSED MESSAGES.

Nikki didn't bother to check them – she just pushed the mobile into a drawer and lay down once again.

She was asleep in ten minutes.

Forty-One

'If there was any way I could get away I would.'

Adam Royston wedged the phone between his ear and his shoulder and continued scribbling away on the piece of paper on his desk.

'What's going on, Adam?' Sandra Morgan asked on the other end of the line. 'Or can't you tell me?'

'If I knew I'd tell you, Sandi, but to be honest I'm not even sure what the hell is going on around here.'

'Is it something to do with what happened at the hospital today?'

'The incident at the hospital, the break-in here, the deaths of Ryan Dickinson and Don Lansing and the radiation sickness suffered by those soldiers – I think they're all linked somehow. But proving it is going to be the real son of a bitch.'

He sat back at his desk, looking at the books and papers before him with something akin to desperation. The screen of his computer was also full of figures and numbers but they seemed as baffling as the rest of the information he'd accumulated in the last few hours.

'Nothing seems to add up,' Royston told Sandra wearily. 'We're dealing with something that no one has ever encountered before. There are no precedents, no examples that I can go back and check. It's like I'm starting at the beginning. I feel like a caveman seeing the sun for the first time and wondering what the hell it is.' He laughed humourlessly.

'Where did they take Claire Reece?' Sandra asked him finally.

'I don't know,' Royston confessed. 'Doctor Kelly didn't tell me. I was hoping you might be able to.'

'Sorry, Adam. Kelly wasn't too happy with me for mentioning the children. He was very clear about that after you left.'

'What exactly happened to them?'

'On each ultrasound scan there was evidence of cancer in each child, some of it so advanced . . .' Sandra allowed the sentence to trail off.

'I can understand Kelly's attitude,' Royston told her. 'He wants to protect the mothers as much as anything. I assume that in each case the babies will be aborted, right?'

'That's what the medical staff are advising. To be honest, if you'd seen those scan pictures, Adam, you'd know why. There's no way they'll survive, probably not even until the time they were due to be born.'

'Have any of the mothers undergone terminations yet?'

'Two of them.'

'When?'

'Today, as far as I know. Why?'

'What was done with the foetuses?'

'They were disposed of in the same way as usual.'

'Incinerated?'

'Adam, why are you asking about this?'

'Were the aborted foetuses incinerated, Sandi? If you know then please tell me.'

'That's standard procedure,' she informed him. 'You know that.'

'Good,' he said, flatly.

'Why, Adam? What possible interest could you have in them?'

Royston took a deep breath, not sure whether he should share some of his thoughts with her. After all, he reasoned, some of his theories were so insane he could barely countenance them himself at the moment. Why burden Sandra with his lunatic postulations? The more he told her the more she'd probably retreat from him – and he wouldn't have blamed her.

'How well did you know the women with the infected babies?' he asked finally.

'Two of them I've only known since they started coming here to the hospital but I knew Nikki Cross and one of the others by sight,' Sandra told him. 'We'd chatted in the past. Nothing too serious. Just passing-the-time-of-day stuff. Broughton is a small town, you know; there aren't many secrets here, Adam.'

'There are enough,' the American murmured.

'So what are you going to do?' she asked.

'I've set a meeting for tomorrow morning. I'm going to try and make some sense of what's been happening and hope that I don't come across as a complete lunatic.'

'If you decide to leave early you can still come and see me, you know,' she said quietly.

'I know and I appreciate that but I can't leave my

office now.' Royston glanced at his watch and saw that it was approaching midnight. 'I have to stay here until I've got something I can use, something that might help clarify this business. But I'm not too hopeful. Like I said before, it's as if I'm starting at the beginning again and no one else can help me.'

'What about Professor Elliot?' Sandra asked. 'What does he think?'

'I think he's got his own theories,' Royston sighed. 'I'm not sure he cares for mine. I can't say I blame him.'

'Call me tomorrow – let me know how your meeting goes,' she insisted.

'I will. I hope I'll have some good news for you.'

There was a moment of silence. Then Sandra spoke again. 'How dangerous is this situation, Adam?' she asked warily.

'I wish I knew,' he confessed. 'But if we don't find a solution soon it's going to get worse. Much worse.'

'Be careful,' she said.

Royston didn't answer.

Forty-Two

The bright autumn sunshine that was streaming through the windows of Adam Royston's office did little to lighten the mood of the men gathered inside.

The chilly and windy night had given way to glorious sunshine but thick banks of cloud building further away in the sky threatened to suffocate that source of warmth the longer the day went on. Now, with the clock on Royston's wall showing almost ten a.m., he sipped at his coffee, hoping that the latest caffeine boost would banish his lethargy.

He'd snatched five or six hours of fitful sleep the previous night but had woken early and found himself unable to drop off again even though it had still been dark outside. Instead, he had tossed and turned for almost thirty minutes before finally dragging himself out of bed and sitting at his kitchen table with a black coffee and some cereal. With so many ideas tumbling through his mind he'd been amazed that he'd been able to sleep at all and he was beginning to wonder how long it would be before he once more enjoyed a full and satisfying night of slumber. He hadn't slept soundly for days now. There was too much on his mind. The beginning of a headache gnawing at the base of his skull wasn't helping, either. He dug in the pocket of his jacket and fished out a bottle of aspirin. He swallowed two with some more coffee and let out a long sigh.

'You look how I feel,' McGill told him and Royston almost managed a smile.

He looked at each face before him in turn, well aware that the men who confronted him wanted something that he feared he couldn't give them, namely answers. He took another sip of his coffee and cleared his throat.

'I suggested this meeting because I think I might have an idea of what we're dealing with,' he began.

'Let's hope so,' Major Cartwright said. 'We've all been in the dark for long enough.'

Royston shrugged, catching the edge to the officer's voice and also aware that the gazes of McGill, Professor Elliot and Peter Elliot were trained on him as intently as that of the major.

'I've been as anxious to discover the truth behind these events as you, major,' Royston said, holding the officer's stare. 'It hasn't been for want of trying.'

There was an awkward silence. Royston eyed each of his audience individually before continuing.

'Perhaps one of you will have a solution,' he began. 'You may think I'm talking a lot of nonsense – maybe you reckon one of you can offer a more logical conclusion.'

'Logic hasn't really featured in much that's happened around here in the last few days,' Peter Elliot said.

'That's very true, Peter,' Royston conceded. 'But whatever's going on there has to be a way first to understand it and then to deal with it.'

'And you're going to tell us how to deal with it are you, Doctor Royston?' Cartwright asked.

'I told you, this is just a theory based on my calculations and what we've seen. I intend to present you with what I've been able to deduce and calculate.'

'So is this fact or theory, Adam?' Professor Elliot asked.

'Partly fact, mostly theory,' Royston admitted.

'I see,' the professor said, nodding. 'Carry on. We're all listening.'

'I'd like to resurrect, if I may, a thesis I did when I was a student,' the American began. 'It has to do with the cooling of the Earth's surface.' He glanced at his audience to check that he still had their attention, then went on. 'Billions of years ago the Earth was like the sun: no form, no solidity to it. It was just a blazing mass of energy. And then the Earth started cooling and as it cooled a crust was formed. The energy was still there but it was being compressed beneath this crust. As time went by the crust grew deeper and the compression became greater as its energy was being squeezed into an ever-decreasing space.'

'May I interrupt for a moment, Adam?' Professor Elliot said wearily. 'What you're telling us is something every schoolboy knows. What's it leading to?'

'I'm sorry – maybe I should skip the preliminaries,' Royston snapped.

'No, don't skip anything, Adam,' McGill interrupted. 'I was never very bright at school.'

Royston smiled at the other man gratefully, then continued.

'Well, then, in a comparatively short space of time – a matter of a couple of hundred thousand years – man has evolved,' the American stated. 'And man has evolved from nothing to become the most intelligent creature on the face of this planet.'

'That depends on your point of view,' Cartwright snorted.

Royston eyed him for a moment and raised one eyebrow. The major nodded and raised a hand as if in apology at his interjection.

'Considering the far greater span of time involved,' Royston went on, 'isn't it reasonable to assume that the forces contained in the centre of this Earth have developed an intelligence of their own?'

The other men in the room continued to look at him as he spoke.

'If we accept this,' he continued, 'then we must consider what these forces would think. Their world is being compressed out of existence. Therefore survival would be uppermost in their thoughts.'

'Wait a minute,' Professor Elliot said. 'You're asking us to accept that something is living at the centre of the Earth that is sentient and possesses the capacity to reason?'

'I'm not asking you accept anything, John,' Royston told him. 'I'm telling you what I think may be a suitable explanation for some of the events we've seen during the last few days. Just run with me on this for a little longer.'

The professor raised his hands in a supplicatory gesture.

'The goal of any species is survival,' Royston went on.

'So what's more natural in the survival of this species than that they should return to the face of the planet on which they once lived?'

For once there was no comment from the others in the room so Royston seized his chance and pressed on, warming to his subject even more.

'Now, if you check you'll find that every fifty years, by virtue of the position of the Earth within the Solar System, a greater pull is exerted on the surface of this planet. It's unnoticeable to us but two thousand miles down . . . who knows? And during the short period of time when this pull is at its most powerful you'll find there's always been a freak earth tremor or some kind of seismic shift in the Earth's crust and on each of these occasions a fissure has opened in the surface of the Earth.'

'How severe have these tremors been?' Cartwright wanted to know.

'Some of them have been catastrophic,' Royston stated. 'The eruption of Krakatoa in 1883. The San Francisco Earthquake of 1906. The eruption of Mount St Helens in 1980. The undersea quake that caused the tsunami in Thailand in 2004 and the Fukushima disaster in Japan in 2011. All these incidents have occurred as a result of the gravitational pull on the Earth being greater at some point than others—'

'They occurred because the tectonic plates beneath the surface of the Earth shifted,' Professor Elliot interrupted.

'And they shifted because of an increase of power beneath them,' Royston told him.

'An increase of power caused by this force you're talking about?' McGill asked.

'Why not?' Royston responded.

'But there wasn't a fifty-year gap between all those incidents,' the professor said. 'Your theory of a shift in the tectonic plates happening every fifty years doesn't hold water. The tsunami in Thailand and the disaster at Fukushima were only seven years apart.'

'It's not a flawless theory, John,' Royston countered. 'I never said it was – but at least consider what I'm saying.'

The professor merely shrugged as Royston continued.

'If these forces were trying to reach the surface isn't it safe to assume that they would have to break through the Earth's crust to do so? If this caused breaks in the Earth's surface as huge as those then it's easy to accept how easily it could have caused that rift we saw out on the moors. On each of the occasions I've mentioned, this force emerged looking for a way to sustain its existence, looking for nourishment. Now these forces are almost pure energy. What does energy need to sustain it? What does it live on?'

'Energy,' Peter Elliot said.

'Exactly,' Royston said. 'Energy can only be fed with more energy. In this case, radiation. A hundred and fifty years ago they emerged looking for energy, the same fifty years later and again fifty years after that and now they need that energy once more. They became unstable without it and that was when they broke free from beneath the Earth's crust to find sustenance. There was radiation in the hospital.

214

Radiation here in the laboratory. As long as this thing lives it will feed and the more it feeds the more it will grow. And if it consumes enough energy it'll become unstoppable.'

Forty-Three

'But there are much larger sources of energy than the radium stored in a small town hospital or at a military research plant,' the professor said dismissively. 'Why doesn't this creature or force or whatever it is attack a nuclear power station? Why settle for such a meagre supply of radiation when it could find something much more satisfying?'

There was a note of scorn in the professor's voice that Royston wasn't slow to detect.

'I agree,' Cartwright said. 'Why doesn't this thing go and consume somewhere like Sizewell? If it's predatory as you say it is, surely it would go after the biggest source of sustenance? Otherwise it would be like a lion passing up the chance of an antelope to get at a mouse.' The major chuckled at his own joke and glanced around at the others in the room to see if they shared his amusement.

The expressions of the other men remained impassive.

'I don't know why,' Royston said defensively. 'Just as I don't know what this thing is. I gave you a theory and that's all I can offer. I know it sounds far-fetched and ridiculous but it's all I've got. If anyone has a simpler explanation for what's going on I'd be grateful and relieved to hear it.'

'Are you trying to tell us that some kind of creature came up out of the fissure?' McGill wanted to know.

'Mac, I'm not trying to tell you anything,' Royston said. 'I'm just trying to offer a theory based on the facts that we know.'

'So what do we look for?' McGill persisted.

'I don't know,' Royston admitted.

'And what do we do if we find something?' McGill asked.

'I'm afraid I don't know that, either,' Royston confessed.

'You don't know very much at all, do you, Doctor Royston?' Cartwright cut in. 'You're supposed to be an expert in this field and yet the best you can offer us is something that sounds as if it came straight out of a 1950s horror movie.'

'There are no experts in this field, major,' Royston snapped, 'because this field didn't exist until a few days ago. What we're dealing with here is a new species, a new kind of organism that's never been seen, let alone studied.'

'How big is this thing supposed to be?' the major asked.

'It could be the size of my fist or it might be bigger than a house,' Royston said.

'Well, we can't wait around here,' McGill said. 'We've got to find this thing and destroy it.'

'How, Mac?' the American asked. 'What are you going to do? Shoot it? Burn it? Blow it up?'

'Listen to me,' Professor Elliot interrupted, irritably. 'We've just been told a story based on very little fact and a great deal of fiction. I'm surprised any of you give it credence. It's fantastic. A flight of fancy.'

'What's your theory, then, John?' Royston snapped. 'I said I'd be happy to hear what anyone else had to offer.'

'I don't have a theory,' the older man told him.

'But you're willing to shoot my ideas down without a second thought,' Royston said.

'Your ideas are wild speculation, Adam,' the professor countered. 'Unsubstantiated by facts or figures and supported only by conjecture and, it seems, a highly overactive imagination.'

'That's the way all scientific ideas begin, isn't it?' Royston told him. 'People thought Pasteur was mad for his theories, likewise Jenner and Fleming or any other scientist you want to name. They thought that at the beginning but they came to realise these men were right.'

'But the theory you're putting forward is ridiculous,' the professor insisted.

'It's all we have,' Royston reminded him. 'I'm not saying it's flawless. I'm not even saying it's correct – but a vague starting point is better than none at all, isn't it?'

'An organism that lives at the centre of the Earth and emerges periodically to feed on energy,' Cartwright added, his gaze fixed on the American. 'That's what we're facing? That's what killed my men and that little boy?'

'As far as I can work out, yes,' Royston told him. 'As far-fetched and difficult to comprehend as that is.'

'I'm amazed that this story has been accepted by the

rest of you without the slightest doubt or hesitation,' the professor said sharply. 'I said a moment ago I thought the idea was fanciful. Well, I'll go further: it's absolute rubbish. Adam, you're a scientist, you deal with facts. A man of your intelligence and capabilities has no right to talk as you have. You astound me.'

'Don't you think I'm aware of how this sounds, John?' Royston snapped. 'I didn't ask for your support or your belief – I merely put forward the only theory I could based on the facts I had before me. If you disagree with that theory, then that's your prerogative. But don't try to belittle me and if you've no alternative theory to mine then I suggest you keep your mouth shut.'

'How dare you?' the older man rasped.

'Gentlemen,' McGill said, a conciliatory tone to his voice. 'Please.'

Royston and the professor locked stares for a moment.

'So how were that boy and those soldiers burned?' Peter Elliot asked. 'How do you explain what happened at the hospital and here in Doctor Royston's laboratory?'

'We've been through that already, Peter,' the pro - fessor said dismissively. 'There must be a perfectly logical explanation for it; I suggest we allow the police to find out what it is.'

'This is beyond the scope of a local police force,' Royston insisted.

'Who do you suggest we call to solve the mystery, then, Adam?' the older man taunted. 'From what you've told us perhaps we might be better off contacting Doctor Who or Thunderbirds.'

'You pompous bastard,' Royston snapped. 'What's it going to take to make you believe that what we're up against doesn't fit into any of the neat little boxes you'd like to pop it into? How many times do I have to say it? This is a new and highly dangerous organism we're dealing with.'

'The police investigation will uncover the truth,' the professor said.

'Will it?' muttered Royston. 'I'm not so sure.'

'Well, I'm an investigator and I want to know what's behind all this,' McGill said. 'And I came here to get Doctor Royston's advice.'

Professor Elliot got to his feet. 'In that case I'll waste no more time,' he snapped, heading for the door. 'Good day, gentlemen.'

Royston merely shook his head, watching as the professor left and closed the door a little too hard behind him. 'I'm sorry if anyone else feels that way,' he commented.

'He doesn't mean to be rude,' Peter Elliot suggested almost apologetically.

'Why is he so resistant to these ideas, Peter?' Royston asked. 'You know him better than I do – he's your father.'

'He has nothing but respect for you and your work, Adam, you know that,' Peter asked. 'But he's stubborn.'

'I can see his point of view, trust me,' Royston told the younger man. 'But everything I said was intended to get to the bottom of what's going on here.'

'Supposing you're right about this thing, whatever the hell it is, feeding on energy,' Cartwright said. 'How does that tie in with those who've come into contact with it developing cancer so quickly?'

'Again, I wish I knew,' Royston said. 'All I can think is that exposure to radiation often causes cancer and this thing is innately radioactive. It feeds on radioactive material too, so anyone coming close to it would be subjected to such high doses that tumours would grow very quickly inside their bodies.'

'And it feeds on these too?' McGill said. 'On the tumours it creates?'

'Cancer cells have their own kind of energy,' Royston told him. 'They use that energy against the host body when they destroy the cells within that body.' He raised his hands. 'It's energy feeding on energy again, isn't it?'

McGill nodded thoughtfully.

'Let's try and get a look at this thing,' he said.

'The only way we can do that is by going to the fissure,' Royston told him.

'But we've been there more than once already,' McGill reminded him. 'We've seen nothing.'

'You misunderstand me, Mac,' Royston said. 'I mean this time someone has to go down into the fissure.'

'But my father and I did that when it first opened – you know that, Adam,' Peter told him.

'I know, Peter,' Royston said. 'But this time, whoever goes in has to go to the very bottom of that fissure. No matter what's down there.'

Forty-Four

The small chapel that served the religious needs of Broughton Green Military Research Facility was multi-denominational, reflecting the many and varied beliefs of the men who served there.

Predominantly Christian, though, it sported a large crucifix behind its altar, featuring a figure of Christ that was almost life-size. At its base were vases of fresh flowers and, as he sat in the front-row pew, Adam Royston could detect the pleasing scent of the blooms. It was mixed with the smell of polish from the pews themselves and the wooden lectern just in front of him. The silence inside the chapel was pleasing and it was as if the modern and brightly coloured stained-glass windows on either side of the nave acted as sound - proofing against the outside world, shutting out unwanted noises and leaving those who visited the chapel enveloped by the peace and solitude they sought in such a building.

It was here that services of remembrance and dedication were carried out when victims of the war in Afghanistan were brought back, their coffins draped in the flag of their country. They called it repatriation, Royston mused. That at least was the current euphemism. He had seen three such repatriations during his time at Broughton Green. Each time he had been touched not just by the depth of emotion and dignity shown by all involved but by the evidence of the sheer waste of life. Men had died in a needless conflict thousands of miles away and now all their families had by way of thanks were a folded flag and the empty words of politicians. Death was tragic at any time, Royston thought, but when it was so needless it was almost obscene.

'War is all hell,' he murmured to himself. He remembered those words from something he'd read once. They'd been spoken by William Tecumseh Sherman during the American Civil War. A military man himself condemning the uselessness and futility of his life's work. And now, a hundred and fifty years later, that futility was still as keenly felt. Death in battle was a calculated risk, though; sudden death away from a war zone was unexpected. And death seemed to be running free in and around this small town of Broughton, Royston thought. Death delivered by God alone knew what. By a creature or force thousands of years old? He shook his head as if struggling to accept his own hypothesis.

'I didn't expect to find you in here.'

The words echoed around the inside of the chapel and Royston turned to see Major Cartwright striding down the aisle towards him.

Royston started to get to his feet but the officer motioned for him to stay seated. Cartwright sat down next to him.

'One of my men said he saw you coming in here, I hope I'm not disturbing you,' the major said.

'Of course not,' Royston told him.

'I didn't know you were a religious man, Doctor Royston,' Cartwright said.

'I'm not.' The scientist shrugged. 'Not really.'

'It just depends on the situation, does it?'

Royston nodded and smiled.

'How about you, major? Are you a religious man?' Royston asked.

'Well, as any soldier will tell you, there are no atheists in foxholes – as the saying goes.'

'Or in Afghanistan?' Royston said.

'Quite so.' Cartwright smiled.

'My father was a priest, a preacher, a padre. Whatever you want to call it.'

'That must have made for some interesting conversations over the dinner table. You being a man of science. Was there any conflict?'

'If he disapproved of my career he never told me. He was a remarkable man.'

'Do you keep in touch?'

'He died ten years ago.'

'I'm sorry.'

'He took his own life. An overdose. Something of a contradiction for a man of God, you would think, but he'd left the church two years before.'

'Why? If you don't mind me asking.'

'Not at all. He lost his faith. My mother was killed in a car crash. She didn't die straight away – she lived for a day or two afterwards – but she was never going to survive with the injuries she'd sustained. My father prayed for her to be spared. When she wasn't I guess he just gave up on God because he felt God had given up on him.' Royston lowered his gaze. 'He never went near a church again until the day he died.'

'I'm very sorry,' Cartwright said.

Royston was looking fixedly at the cross behind the altar now.

'He said to me once that one day he looked at a crucifix and all he saw was a man dying on a cross. Nothing more.' He attempted a smile. 'I don't know if God ever forgave him but I'm damned sure my father never forgave God.'

Royston got to his feet and the major joined him.

'I apologise for the reminiscences, major. What was it you wanted?' the scientist asked.

'It's about this descent into the fissure,' the officer said as the two of them headed towards the main doors of the chapel. 'We have the men and equipment in place. We can move as soon as you're ready. The area has been prepared. I spoke to my superiors earlier. They're aware of the situation. They don't like it but they're aware of it. It's up to you now.'

The two men stepped out into the evening, struck by the chill in the air. On the horizon, the sun was sinking rapidly, staining the heavens with its blood-red colour.

'Good,' Royston said.

'There's just one thing,' Cartwright reminded him. 'We have to decide who actually goes into the fissure.'

'It should be me,' Royston said. 'I know what to look for and I'm the senior man here.'

'You can take one of my men with you, just in case.'

'In case I'm right and there *is* something down there?' Royston smiled. 'I thought you weren't going to sacrifice any more of your men, major.'

'I'm hoping not to, doctor, but you might need help.'

'If I am right about what's in that fissure, major, it might not help me if I took a whole regiment down there, let alone one man.'

Forty-Five

Night lay like a black blanket over the land and only the illumination from the dozen or so arc lights that had been set up around the rim of the fissure cut through the gloom.

In the cold white glow that they cast Adam Royston surveyed the scene before him and exhaled deeply, his breath frosting in the air.

'Are you sure you want to do this, Adam?' McGill's words cut through the cold air.

'Someone has to, Mac,' Royston told him. 'I think it should be me.'

He stood motionless for a moment, the stares of the other men fixed on him.

Behind him the fissure yawned wide and Royston couldn't resist a glance towards it. It reminded him of a mouth, open and ready to devour him. He tried to shake that particular simile from his mind and chose instead to re-examine his equipment, more anxious by the second that his descent into the crack in the ground was due to begin very shortly. Despite the chill in the air he felt hot because of the protective suit he was wearing and the weight of the equipment he was carrying. He actually felt a bead of sweat pop out on his forehead.

Fear? Go on, admit it: you're scared.

In one hand he held a Geiger counter and in the other a powerful torch. Attached to his belt there was a two-way radio, a small green light pulsing on its top. He had already checked it twice, satisfied that the frequency was clear and static-free, but now he hefted the Motorola once more and looked at Major Cartwright who was standing a few feet from him.

'It's in perfect working order,' the officer assured him.

'Humour me,' Royston said, clicking the transmit button. 'Come in, Cartwright; get me out of here as quick as you can.'

The major smiled and nodded, speaking into his own radio.

'Received and understood,' he said, still smiling. 'We'll take good care of you, Doctor Royston – won't we, sergeant?' He turned and looked at the NCO on his left. Sergeant Peter Grimsdyke nodded. He was a small man with pinched features and a nose that looked as if he'd collided at high speed with a brick wall but there was a kindness in his expression that Royston found reassuring at this particular moment in time.

'You tell us what to do and we'll do it, sir,' he told Royston who glanced at the man, then looked over towards the platform that had been lowered for him from the boom arm of the LTM 1055 mobile crane. 'We can have you out of there in seconds if that's what you want.'

Royston turned and began walking towards the platform, the other men accompanying him.

'That suit you're wearing is designed to protect you

against biohazards, corrosive material and blunt trauma impact,' Cartwright told him. 'Just be careful you don't split it on any pieces of rock.'

Royston nodded.

'Don't take any chances down there, Adam,' McGill told him.

'Trust me, Mac,' Royston said. 'Being a hero was never top of my list of priorities. I just want to get in and out as quickly as possible. But I have to see inside that thing.' He gestured towards the fissure.

'You should have let me go down, Doctor Royston,' Peter Elliot said. 'I did volunteer, you know.'

'I know and I appreciate that, Peter,' Royston told him. 'But you're father isn't my greatest fan at the moment – I don't think allowing his son into a seismic and possibly radioactive fissure housing some kind of prehistoric force would endear me to him right now, do you?'

Peter shook his head. 'I could come down with you,' he suggested. 'I've already seen the inside of the fissure once.'

'I know,' Royston conceded. 'And again, I appreciate your offer. But I'll do this myself – there's no point in possibly endangering two lives.'

Royston paused beside the platform, glancing up at the cables that supported it. He gripped one and pulled on it, the high-tensile cable feeling cold against his flesh. Then he pulled on his protective gloves and took the Geiger counter from McGill who had been holding it for him. Royston pushed the probe towards the lip of the fissure.

There was no reading from the machine. Only silence.

He could feel his heart beating a little quicker now, the blood surging in his ears as he stepped onto the platform. It shuddered a little but Royston found that he could stand upright with no problem. He glanced below him and wished he hadn't. The chasm below gaped blackly, a yawning gash in the Earth that was about to swallow him. How deep it was he could only begin to imagine.

No backing out now. Get on with it. Get down there and see.

He drew a deep breath.

'We're ready, doctor,' Sergeant Grimsdyke told him.

'If any radioactivity shows up on that Geiger counter tell us immediately and we'll get you out of there,' Cartwright said.

'Radioactivity or anything else,' Royston murmured. He turned and glanced in the direction of the crane operator who was perched high above him in the cab of the LTM 1055. The man was waiting for orders.

'All right,' Royston said. 'Let's do this.'

'Lower away,' Grimsdyke said into his own radio and there was a loud grinding noise as the cables began to extend. The platform started to descend with infinite slowness.

'I thought you said this thing was fast,' Royston said, raising his voice over the sound of the grinding.

'Faster coming up, I hope,' McGill said under his breath.

The platform bumped gently against the lip of the fissure and Royston steadied himself momentarily.

Then it began to descend more evenly. He jammed the two-way onto his belt, gripped the torch in his left hand and flicked it on, allowing the beam to play over the walls of the fissure as he was dropped lower and lower into it, his descent's speed more measured now. At his feet, the Geiger counter remained silent. Royston was relieved about that, at least. He took another deep breath, his heart rate still fast, but as he was lowered further he began to concentrate on what he saw around him. He swept the torch slowly back and forth.

'Are you OK, Adam?' The voice on the two-way belonged to Cartwright.

'If I'm not you'll be the first to know,' Royston said, his voice catching slightly.

There was a low rumbling sound as the platform moved lower and Royston could feel the vibrations running through the platform beneath his feet. He touched the cables above him and felt the vibrations there, too. Again he swept the torch beam over the walls of the fissure. Large portions were smooth, he noted. Other sections seemed to be composed of jagged rock. The smooth sections were covered with an all too familiar white residue. He reached out and ran his fingers through the powder, examining its traces on his gloves.

'The powder we saw at the hospital and the base is here,' he said into the radio. 'Lots of it.'

'Can you see anything else, Adam?' This question came from McGill.

'Not a great deal,' Royston answered. 'Not yet.'

Another bead of sweat formed on his forehead.

You're getting more scared. The deeper you go, the worse it will get.

'The temperature seems to be rising,' Royston said. 'It'll be like the goddam tropics down here soon.'

'Any sign of radioactivity?' Cartwright wanted to know.

Royston checked the Geiger counter, pushing the probe towards the white residue on the wall of the fissure. There was no reading. 'Nothing so far,' he said.

He shone the torch below him. 'There's a kind of ledge about twenty feet below me,' he said into the two-way. 'Tell them to keep lowering – I want to take a closer look.'

The torch beam flickered and Royston muttered under his breath as the bright white light suddenly faded to a sickly yellow glow. 'Son of a bitch,' he snapped, shaking the torch.

'Adam,' McGill said urgently.

The torch flickered again but then glowed with its customary brilliance.

'It's OK,' Royston assured him, relieved that the light was back to its brightest.

The platform bumped into a jutting outcrop of rock and he grunted as it swayed slightly.

'I thought that the fissure would become narrower the deeper it got but that doesn't seem to be the case,' Royston said. 'It could be even deeper than we initially thought.' He blew out his cheeks. 'And it's still getting hotter down here.' Again he shone the torch around, moving it slowly so that he could pick out every single detail of the rock around him. 'Tell them to stop lowering – I'm almost level with the ledge now.'

The platform swayed again slightly but then remained still. Royston aimed the torch at the flat outcrop of rock beside him. The white residue that covered it was thick and looked almost glutinous. He pushed one finger into it but saw that when he withdrew the digit the trace on the glove appeared quite dry.

'I think that the white powder could be some kind of excreted matter,' he said. 'Either that or this organism exudes it and uses it to move about on like a carpet to aid locomotion, the same way as a slug's slime trail helps it get around.' He swallowed hard. 'There's lots of it here.'

'Be careful,' Cartwright told him.

Royston didn't answer. His heart was thudding hard against his ribs now, his stare fixed on the residue and the ledge before him. He swept the torch beam over it again, his eyes narrowing in the gloom. He reached out once more and ran his fingers through the almost translucent white matter but this time when he inspected it on his gloves he saw something else there.

At first he thought he was mistaken but, as he looked more closely, he realised that unfortunately he wasn't.

Royston's breath caught in his throat. He brushed more of the residue away, aware now that there was something beneath it, something that his probing had uncovered.

'Jesus Christ,' he murmured.

Forty-Six

It was human flesh.

The more Royston looked at the matter sticking to the fingers of his gloves the more he was certain of it.

It was thin and membranous, some of it almost liquefied, but he was certain that what he saw before him was skin. He shuddered at the realisation. Beneath a thinner covering of the white residue he could see something else familiar. A shape that he recognised. He reached for the small object with a shaking hand, pulling it from the powder and holding it in front of the beam of the torch.

'Oh, God,' he whispered.

The ear was almost intact.

A portion of the lobe was missing but apart from that it was unmistakable.

'Adam, what is it?' McGill's voice asked.

Royston dropped the ear and reached for the two-way with his free hand, pushing it close to his mouth. 'There are body parts down here,' he said, his voice shaking. 'From the soldiers who were guarding the fissure, I think.'

'Are you sure?' Cartwright asked.

'Sure enough,' Royston told him.

Royston aimed the torch downwards, to the rocks below the ledge. There was more of the white residue down there but it was mixed with darker matter now.

'Lower me,' Royston said, once more steadying himself as the platform bumped against the wall of the fissure. He reached for the Geiger counter and held the probe close to the rock. The needles on the machine's dials didn't move.

'There's still no sign of radiation or any activity of that nature,' he said, his eyes scanning the walls of the fissure as he was lowered ever deeper. There was a crackle of static on the two-way and he looked at it warily. Again he waved the probe of the Geiger counter around but still nothing registered.

'Have you got any idea how deep you are, Adam?' McGill asked, his voice breaking up slightly.

'Seventy or eighty feet,' Royston informed him, his attention caught by something that was smeared on the wall of the fissure to his right. He moved carefully towards the mark on the rock and pointed the torch directly at it. The light reflected strongly back at him and Royston narrowed his eyes, clicking off the torch for a moment. There was a dull glow emanating from the rock now that faded slowly as he looked at it. He flicked the torch on again, then reached for the two-way.

'Some of the white powder this thing left behind has luminous qualities,' he said. 'It absorbs light for a short period of time. Stores it.'

'Any idea why?' Cartwright wanted to know.

'Absolutely none,' Royston admitted, rolling some more of the residue between his thumb and forefinger.

He shone the torch downwards as the platform continued to descend. He swallowed hard, perspiration now beginning to sheath his face and most of his body. 'The heat down here is getting more intense.'

'How deep are you now?' Cartwright asked, the words blurring behind a crackle of static.

'I must be a hundred feet down by now,' Royston told him. 'There's another ledge just below me. It looks big enough to stand on.'

'Adam, don't get off the platform,' McGill told him. 'Whatever you do stay on there – do you understand?'

'I understand,' Royston told him, his gaze fixed on the next ledge. It too was covered in the familiar white residue but there was a familiar shape lying among the powder. Even from where he was now he could see that it was an army rifle. As the platform brought him closer he caught sight of some pieces of dark material mixed in with the residue that he knew must be fragments of uniform. There was a boot too, the sole of which was burned black and most of the leather seared away.

'Keep lowering until I say,' Royston said. He recoiled violently when a loud hiss of static erupted from the radio. The sound reverberated inside the fissure, bouncing off the walls and throbbing inside his ears. 'Stop.' The platform came to a halt just below the ledge. Royston reached up and pulled a piece of cloth towards him, shining the torch at it as he held it in his hand. The material was dark with what looked like dried blood. He dropped it back onto the stone and inspected the remains of the boot too. As he was replacing it he saw something gleaming whitely in the torch beam.

It was a human skull.

There were still pieces of flesh attached but there was no way to identify who the skull had belonged to. Portions of it were scorched black and the area around the jawbone had been crushed almost to powder. There was a thin film of residue over the entire thing.

The Geiger counter began to crackle.

Royston looked down at the machine and saw that the needles were beginning to jerk into life, moving slowly at first but then faster as the crackling became louder.

'There's a reading on the Geiger counter,' he said sharply, wiping his forehead with the back of his hand. The perspiration was now running down his face, stinging his eyes when he blinked it away.

'. . . Did you . . . say . . . hearing you . . .'

The words spoken by Cartwright broke up so badly that Royston could barely make them out.

'The Geiger counter is showing activity,' he snapped, raising his voice. 'And the temperature is increasing too. I can hardly breathe.'

A low hiss came from the radio. Nothing more.

'Can you hear me?' Royston called into the mouth-piece. 'Come in, Major Cartwright. Anyone, can you hear me?'

'Adam? Adam? It's Mac,' a voice said and Royston breathed a sigh of relief at the sound. 'We thought we'd lost you for a minute. There's interference on this frequency.'

'I know,' Royston told him. 'I said that the counter was showing activity and it's increasing.'

'How deep are you now?' McGill went on.

'Well over a hundred feet,' Royston told him, glancing at the Geiger counter again. It was crackling loudly now, the sound unbroken. The needles on its readout were flashing backwards and forwards frantically. And then he heard another sound, this time from below him. It was a steady hiss that was growing louder by the second, as if some huge angry snake was loose beneath him. He leaned over and aimed the torch downwards in the direction of this new noise, trying to see what was adding to the cacophony.

'Get me out of here,' he said abruptly, his stare still fixed on what lay below him. 'Get me up. Pull me up now.' There was an urgent edge to his voice and McGill wasn't slow to catch it.

'What is it, Adam?' he said, his own voice almost drowned by a blast of static.

'Pull me up,' Royston shouted.

The platform began to rise.

'Faster,' Royston urged, still peering down towards the bottom of the fissure – and what was rising up from it.

The cables creaked as the crane jerked him upwards, lifting him higher.

'Come on, come on,' Royston shouted. 'Faster.'

He guessed he was about sixty feet from the surface now and he allowed himself a quick glance upwards to see if he could make out the glow of the arc lights that were blazing up there on the rim of the chasm.

The Geiger counter crackled madly and beneath him the hissing grew to deafening proportions.

Fifty feet to the surface.

Inside the protective suit the sweat was soaking into his clothes now as the heat within the fissure seemed to become intolerable. Royston was gasping for air and every time he inhaled he tasted something acrid on his dry tongue.

Forty feet.

He wondered if the heat would become so intense that he would merely combust. He could feel his body growing hotter and he imagined it exploding in flames. That thought filled his mind and stuck there no matter how much he tried to shift it.

Thirty feet.

'Come on,' Royston yelled madly into the radio.

The platform struck a jutting outcrop of rock and stopped dead.

It wouldn't move an inch.

Forty-Seven

The platform swayed beneath him and for one appalling second Royston thought he was going to overbalance and fall.

He sank to his knees and grabbed one side of the platform, dropping the torch which rolled away and tumbled into the depths.

Plunged into darkness, he heard the whirring of the motor above him as the crane continued to try and haul him free of the fissure. The cables groaned loudly and Royston had one fleeting thought that they were going to snap and send him plummeting downwards to certain death. If the fall didn't kill him then what was surging up the chasm after him most certainly would.

He crawled to the edge of the platform, not daring to stand up in case he toppled over, and from his prone position he looked down into the abyss.

Whatever the hell it was was still rising from deep within the fissure. Royston had no words to describe the organism that was seemingly filling the hole and rising higher by the second. It gave off a faint glow as it drew nearer to him and he couldn't stop himself shaking as he realised that he was only moments from certain death. The nature of that death was worse than anything he had ever imagined even in his wildest nightmares. He was going to die as Ryan Dickinson and the soldiers had died, burned and engulfed. Devoured by a source of power and energy so old and nameless that it was beyond his understanding and comprehension. He wiped more sweat from his eyes as if he needed to see his killer more clearly.

The cables creaked and groaned again and the whole platform lurched violently to one side, almost tipping him off.

'Adam!'

Royston heard his name shouted through the two-way and he snatched the radio from his belt. 'The platform's stuck,' he shouted back frantically.

'Is there any way you can free it?' the voice demanded. He couldn't even identify its source any more. It was just another disembodied sound in an already ear-splitting cacophony: the crackle of the radio and the Geiger counter and that infernal hiss that was growing ever louder as its source crept closer.

The platform moved again and Royston clung on to the edge for dear life as the cables creaked once more. Something from above him fell and he realised that it was a piece of rock.

'Keep raising it,' he roared desperately. 'Raise the fucking platform.'

He looked up and saw that more fragments of stone were falling. A piece the size of his fist thudded down and hit the platform inches from his head but that final impact seemed to have had the desired effect. The platform rose a foot or so, stopped once again, then began to rise as it cleared the obstruction that had been holding it back. Royston looked down again.

The glow beneath him was growing brighter and he wondered if this creature possessed enough intelligence to know that it was about to consume him. Was it aware of its prey's helplessness? Was it like a spider creeping slowly along its web towards a helpless fly? All these thoughts tumbled through Royston's mind as he held tightly to the platform, realising that it was rising once more but unsure whether it would be lifted clear of the fissure in time. He closed his eyes tightly, the combination of sounds around him now overpowering. He shouted in fear and desperation. It was an unashamed bellow of terror, torn raw and bloody from the base of his spine. He didn't want to die now, not like this, but it seemed that he was doomed. He wondered if there would be much pain before he finally died.

There was a sudden rush of cold air against his skin and Royston realised that the platform had been dragged free of the fissure.

The Geiger counter was suddenly silent. The hissing from below him receded, then disappeared, and now he heard men shouting. The voices were filled with concern and anxiety.

Royston opened his eyes. He sucked in deep lungfuls of fresh cold air, so glad to taste that now instead of the stinging acrid atmosphere that he'd inhaled deep inside the chasm. He tugged at his protective suit, anxious to feel the cool air against his burning skin too. As the platform was lowered towards the edge of the fissure he rolled off it, dropping two or three feet onto firm ground.

It was a wonderful feeling and he lay there staring at the sky for a moment as figures crowded in around him.

'Adam!' McGill called, kneeling beside him.

Peter Elliot was there too. So was Major Cartwright. Royston was grateful to see all their faces. Only moments earlier he had feared that he would never see any of them again. He was vaguely aware of the boom arm of the crane swinging above him as it lifted the platform away. Then he allowed himself to be helped into a sitting position by those clamouring around him.

'Adam,' McGill said again. 'Are you all right? What the hell was happening down there?'

Royston sat forward, rubbing both hands across his face, wiping the sweat away. He shook his head. 'Jesus Christ,' he murmured. 'I've never been so scared in my life.'

'Did you see it?' McGill persisted. 'Did you see what was down there?'

Royston nodded. 'Your men are dead, major,' he said, breathlessly, looking up at Cartwright. 'There are remains everywhere down there.' He jerked a thumb over his shoulder in the direction of the fissure, his hand shaking violently.

'What did you see down there?' the officer asked.

'I don't know what it was,' Royston admitted, his entire body still trembling. He smiled crookedly. 'It was like something from a nightmare.' He shook his head.

'Get him back to the base,' Cartwright snapped, gesturing to two soldiers who were standing nearby.

The men approached warily, one of them offering his hand to Royston to help him up.

'He's in shock,' Peter Elliot said. 'We need to get him to the hospital.'

'I'll be fine,' Royston protested, glancing over his shoulder towards the fissure.

He looked closely at the rift in the ground, his heart still hammering against his ribs so hard that he feared it would burst free. 'It's stopped,' he said, his voice little more than a whisper. 'It stayed inside the fissure.'

'And that's where it will stay now,' Cartwright snapped.

'What do you mean?' Royston wanted to know.

'My orders were to kill whatever was in there and then seal the hole,' the officer told him. 'Concrete it over.'

Royston looked at him, aghast.

'It's not your concern any more, Doctor Royston,' the major told him. 'Come on, you need to get away from here. You need to rest.' He gestured and the two soldiers approached Royston again. 'This is over now. We'll finish this thing once and for all.'

Royston opened his mouth to say something but no words would come.

McGill nodded at him, as if in agreement with Cartwright's words. 'Come along, Adam,' he said softly.

Royston looked towards the fissure once again, his head spinning. He felt weak and dizzy and he tottered uncertainly for a moment.

'Get him to back to the base,' Cartwright said more forcefully.

Peter Elliot slid a comforting arm around Royston's shoulders. 'There's nothing else you can do now, Adam,' he said quietly. 'Let's go.'

'It's over,' Cartwright said again. 'All over.'

Royston felt the blackness rushing in upon him. He passed out.

Forty-Eight

'I didn't expect to see you tonight.'

Sandra Morgan smiled down at Adam Royston and ran one hand across his bare chest as he lay in bed beside her. Royston reached up and softly stroked her red hair, playfully winding some strands around his index finger before pulling her closer and kissing her.

When they broke the kiss both were breathing more heavily and they looked at each other intently for a moment before Sandra ducked her head and kissed Royston's chest.

'Are you sure you're all right?' she asked him.

Royston nodded. 'I was thinking about what happened tonight,' he told her quietly, watching as she reached towards her bedside table to retrieve a glass of water from which she sipped. 'What I saw inside that fissure.'

'It's probably best if you don't think about it,' Sandra told him. 'All you have to think about now is that it's gone – whatever it was. Didn't you say that the army were going to seal it inside the rift?'

Royston nodded slowly.

'They know what they're doing, Adam,' Sandra

assured him. 'Stop worrying.' She nestled closer to him. 'It's all over now.'

Royston jerked his head around, his attention caught by something in his peripheral vision. He sat up, looking towards the bedroom window.

'What's wrong?' Sandra asked, seeing the concern on his face.

'Look,' he said, pointing.

She followed his pointing finger but saw nothing.

'The street lights have gone out,' Royston said. 'They were on a minute ago but now they've gone out.'

Then the lamp on the bedside table flickered once and went out.

'It must be some kind of power cut,' Sandra suggested, watching as Royston hauled himself out of bed and crossed to the window, peering out into what was now total blackness.

'There are no lights on in any of the houses, either,' he murmured, glancing up and down the street.

'I'm not surprised,' Sandra told him. 'It's late.'

Royston crossed to the light switch beside the bedroom door and flicked it a couple of times, his eyes on the shaded bulb that hung from the centre of the ceiling. It remained unlit.

'Power cut,' he muttered sceptically.

'What else could it be, Adam?'

He didn't answer. He was still standing beside the bedroom door, his gaze now fixed on the slight gap at the bottom of the doorway. There was a very faint glow showing there. Just a strip of barely visible luminescence that was obviously coming from some source of light on the stairs and landing. Royston put his hand on the door handle and prepared to turn it.

'Adam, what are you doing?' Sandra called.

Royston didn't answer her. He noticed that the strip of light was getting brighter.

He also noticed that the handle of the door was warm. The metal felt as if something hot had been pressed against it and held there. Royston glanced back towards the bed where Sandra was now sitting upright, watching him.

'Adam,' she said again.

Royston eased the door open and looked out onto the landing.

As he did he heard the fizzing, crackling noise he had come to know only too well. The stairwell was filled with a dull glow and as he stepped out onto the landing he saw why.

The hallway and most of the stairwell was covered in a seething mass of what looked like undulating, bubbling mud. The entire bulk gave off a lurid glow as it moved higher up the stairs, the crackling sound it emitted now growing louder by the second.

Royston ducked back inside the bedroom and slammed the door behind him, standing with his back to it, aware that the heat was becoming more intense now.

'We've got to get out of here,' he barked. 'It's here. It's inside the house. What I saw inside the fissure is here.'

Sandra seemed paralysed by his words and remained motionless on the edge of the bed, her only movement being to point at the bedroom window. Royston glanced in that direction and saw that the dull glow was now visible there too.

'It's everywhere,' he shouted. 'Come on.'

Sandra screamed and pointed at the gap beneath the bedroom door.

Some of the glowing ooze was beginning to seep beneath the door into the room itself.

Royston leaped away, desperate to avoid the touch of the reeking matter which spilled across the bedroom floor with startling speed. Smoke was rising from the floor as it incinerated whatever it touched. The bedroom door itself was now smoking, the wood actually bowing inwards and Royston could only imagine how much of the organism was building up beyond it. He knew that the barrier wouldn't hold much longer.

'We'll have to get out the window,' he snapped, dragging Sandra with him and sliding the sash open. As he stuck his head out he saw that the street outside was also filled with the same thick ooze. The hissing sound it gave off was now almost deafening.

The bedroom door exploded inwards, pieces of splintered and charred wood spraying across the room as what looked like tons of the sludge slopped inside like a river of black and rancid liquid excrement.

More and more of it spread across the bedroom floor, some engulfing the bed itself, igniting the sheets there. Flames had begun to dance wildly and the heat inside the room was growing more intense with each passing second.

'We've got to get out,' Royston shouted.

Sandra merely stood there looking blankly at him, her eyes bulging wide in horror.

'Come on,' he roared, desperately trying to galvanise her into action.

Most of the bedroom was ablaze now, flames leaping madly and adding their own roar to the ever-growing sound that the sludge was emitting as it filled the room, turning everything it touched to ash with terrifying speed. Royston hauled himself out onto the window ledge and glanced up towards the guttering. If he could just get a grip on it then he could haul himself upwards and onto the roof, he thought. He had to try. There was nothing else to do. The bedroom was an inferno now. They had to get out or they would either be burned alive where they stood or engulfed by the organism that was still spilling through the shattered bedroom door.

'Come on,' Royston screamed at Sandra who wasn't moving.

He could see the ooze sliding across the floor towards her bare feet.

Royston grabbed her hand and tugged her towards him.

Her arm came away at the shoulder.

Royston held the disembodied limb in his hands for what seemed like an eternity, glancing at the stump. There was no blood, only thick black matter that oozed out and dripped into the sludge that was creeping up Sandra's legs, searing the flesh there. She looked at him and opened her mouth to scream but inside that yawning cavity he saw only a swollen, bulbous red growth. There was another on her forehead now, two more on her breasts and belly. They rose like huge blisters but then remained on the skin, throbbing and pulsing obscenely like animated tumours.

Royston dropped the arm and clambered further out onto the window ledge, reaching up to grab the guttering, using it to pull himself up and away from the horrendous scene inside the bedroom.

Below him, the glowing sludge was beginning to rise higher.

Royston could feel the heat on the soles of his feet. The obscene hissing filled his ears as he struggled vainly to pull himself up to the roof.

The guttering cracked under his weight and began to give way.

'No,' he screamed.

He shot out a hand and tried to claw at the roof. Anything to stop himself falling. But it was useless.

He plummeted towards the waiting mass.

Forty-Nine

Royston sat bolt upright, the nightmare still fresh in his mind.

He was gasping loudly as he sat there, propped against the metal frame of the bed, his back soaked with sweat.

'Adam.'

He heard the voice but at first he didn't recognise it.

He reached out both hands and touched his face, half expecting the flesh there to be burned and charred. He looked at his upturned palms, relieved when he saw no damage.

'Adam,' the voice said again.

This time he turned his head in the direction of the sound and saw Peter Elliot standing there. The younger man smiled reassuringly at him and Royston nodded as if to acknowledge Peter's presence.

'Are you feeling better?' Peter asked.

'I had a nightmare,' Royston told him.

'We gathered that.'

The second voice belonged to Professor Elliot and Royston saw that the older man was standing near the door of the hospital room.

'You were a little confused when you were brought in,'

the professor went on. 'Raving about something you'd seen in the fissure. Something that tried to kill you.'

Royston nodded and reached for the jug of water on his bedside table. Peter filled the plastic beaker there and handed it to him. Royston drank deeply, then let out a long sigh.

'I don't know how to describe it,' he said finally. 'It seems to have organic life, whatever it is.'

'How can you be sure of that, Adam?' the professor asked.

'Because it came after me,' Royston told him. 'It killed those soldiers. I saw remains down there, John. It killed them and it tried to kill me.'

'That still doesn't make it organic,' the professor said on.

'It was moving,' Royston reminded him. 'It had a purpose.'

'Molten lava moves but it's nothing more than melted rock,' the professor told him. 'It has no intelligence. No instincts. No purpose, as you put it.'

'I know what I saw,' Royston told him defensively.

'But unfortunately none of the rest of us do,' the older man said.

Royston regarded the professor silently for a moment, then took a deep breath. 'That was what killed the Dickinson boy,' he said. 'And the soldiers. I'd bet my life on it.'

'They suffered radiation burns,' the professor reminded him. 'Why didn't you? You say you were in close contact with it. If this thing is so deadly why aren't you burned too?'

'It didn't touch me,' Royston reminded the older man. 'There has to be direct physical contact between this thing and its victims to cause radiation burns as severe as those that killed that boy and those soldiers.'

'But the men who suffered radiation poisoning – as distinct from burns – weren't in direct contact with it,' said the professor. 'Why aren't *you* suffering from radiation poisoning?'

'Are you saying I imagined what I saw inside that fissure?' Royston snapped.

'I'm not saying anything, Adam,' the professor countered. 'But you've been through a stressful situation and perhaps your imagination is a little over-active. I don't doubt you saw something but you know what the human mind is like, what tricks it can play. It was dark inside the fissure wasn't it? It's a wonder you didn't see little green men down there.'

Royston glared at the older man.

'What did it look like?' Peter Elliot asked.

'Mud,' Royston said flatly. 'Thick slime, sludge. Call it what you like. It had no discernible form but it has more substance than just liquid.' He swung himself out of bed, swaying a little when he stood up.

'The doctor said you should spend the night here, Adam,' Peter Elliot told him. 'Just until they're sure you're OK.'

'I'm fine,' Royston told him. 'Just a little shaky.' He drank some more water. 'I always react that way to near-death experiences.' He rubbed a hand across his face. 'How long was I out?'

'Not long,' Peter said. 'A helicopter brought you

straight back here from the fissure. The doctor said it would be better for you to just rest. You've been sleeping for the last hour or so.'

'Until I had that nightmare,' Royston added, managing a thin smile. 'Where's Mac?'

'He stayed with Major Cartwright at the fissure,' Peter said. 'They're going to seal it tonight.'

Royston shook his head. 'They're wasting their time,' he snapped.

'They're going to destroy whatever's down there, Adam,' the professor informed him.

'They're using explosives,' Peter added.

'And once they've done that they'll seal the rift with concrete,' said the professor.

'It won't work,' Royston insisted. 'Whatever that thing is it's too powerful to be destroyed by explosives. Besides, if they don't set them deep enough it won't even be touched.' He looked at the professor. 'You know how deep that fissure could be.'

'The army know what they're doing, Adam,' the older man stated.

'I'm not sure any of us know what we're doing where this organism is concerned,' Royston protested.

'They'll deal with it,' the professor assured him.

Royston didn't answer.

'Well, we'd better leave you alone,' the professor said. 'Let you get some of that rest you so badly need.'

'I'll go back to my quarters,' Royston said. 'Spend the night there.'

'I'll go and inform the doctor, then,' the professor told him.

'You might be better off here, Adam,' Peter said. 'Just so they can keep an eye on you.'

Royston shook his head. 'I'd rather be in my own quarters,' he said. 'Besides, there's something I've got to do.'

Fifty

The explosion woke him up.

At first the old man who had been sleeping so soundly inside Fisher's Folly thought that he had been dreaming, that the blast he'd heard had been part of some bizarre nightmare. But as he swung himself upright on his rickety wooden bed he realised that the noise was real and not part of his imagination.He sat there for a moment, pulling the blankets he slept in more tightly around him. It was cold. The wind was whipping around the folly and across the marshes tonight, wailing mournfully in the trees that grew so thickly around the great stone monument. The old man shivered and got to his feet, crossing the room in the darkness to retrieve one of the many jars of clear liquid that were arranged on the shelves opposite where he slept. He took one down and unscrewed the top, sniffing the liquor inside as a wine connoisseur would test the bouquet of a fine claret. Then he took a large swallow of the home-made alcohol.

It burned its way down his throat to his stomach and he let out a deep sigh of appreciation. He felt a warm sensation deep within his belly that he hoped would spread throughout his entire body. The temperature inside the tower was dropping and had been for most of the night. He'd ventured into Broughton earlier that evening in an effort to sell some of his brew but he'd only managed to get rid of two jars. Perhaps the next evening he'd try and sell some in Monkston. It was further away and he didn't enjoy such a long trek but if he could sell half a dozen of the jars then the trip would be worth it. He sipped more of the alcohol and walked across to the doorway that led out onto the stone steps.

As he reached the steps he heard another loud blast and as he stood there he could tell that the sound came from somewhere away to the eastern side of the folly, away from the marshes and on the moor itself. The sound echoed through the chilly night air like a muffled thunderclap and, still carrying his jar of liquor, the old man began to climb the stone steps towards the top of the tower.

Two more blasts sounded and he paused for a moment, wondering just what the hell could be making the noises. He had seen army trucks heading across the moor as he'd made his way back from Broughton. Were the soldiers from the base responsible? He smiled suddenly as he thought of the base. Surely someone there would be interested in his home-made brew? Perhaps, he told himself, he'd take a trip to the research facility one of these days. He was still considering that possibility when he reached the door that led to the very top of the folly. He pushed it, shoving his shoulder against it when it wouldn't open immediately and the added impact caused it to swing open, the hinges squealing in protest. The old man stepped out onto the roof of the folly. The wind was blowing so hard that it almost lifted him off his feet.

He waited until the savage gust died down. Then he wandered across to the battlements and peered through the darkness in the direction of the blasts.

Fisher's Folly was tall enough for him to be able to see easily over the tops of the trees in the marshes and, if he'd had a pair of binoculars or something like that, he would have been able to see as far as the moor. It was a remarkably clear night, the moon having emerged from behind what tiny wisps of cloud smeared the heavens. The entire area round about was bathed in cold white light and the old man looked down like a king surveying his empire. He took another slug of liquor and held onto the stone embrasures as the wind once again swept across the land with incredible ferocity.

As it died down again he heard movements in the trees and on the overgrown ground around the Folly. Predators were out hunting. A fox was slinking through the trees and bushes in search of prey and the hooting of an owl could be heard every now and then. But it was that far-off sound of explosions that concerned the old man and he jerked his head around in the direction of another one that came moments later.

Along with the noise this time he also saw a vivid orange and yellow flash from the same direction. It was followed seconds later by another.

What the hell were they doing over there, he wondered? He stood for a few minutes longer, supping his alcohol and trying to figure out what was causing the blasts. Was it some sort of exercise? He shivered as the cold wind seemed to penetrate to his very bones. Who cared what was happening? Why should he stand here in the cold when he could be wrapped up in his blankets sleeping? He drained what was left in his container and dropped the empty receptacle over the side of the folly, smiling when he heard it strike the ground a second or two later. He took one last look towards the source of the blasts, his ears now assaulted by a new sound.

It was the unmistakable noise of helicopter rotor blades and he ducked involuntarily as the Lynx swept through the air high above him, heading in the direction of the explosions he'd heard.

He watched as the chopper disappeared into the night, the lights on its skids and tail winking at him as he watched.

As the sound of the rotors receded too the old man turned and prepared to head back down the steps.

He paused for a moment, his attention caught by something much closer to Fisher's Folly itself. Some - thing at ground level. About three hundred yards away he saw what appeared to be a dull glow between some gnarled and decaying trees. He narrowed his eyes, trying to make out what was causing the strange light, but before he could focus properly it faded again and only the darkness of shadows and the rays of the moon stained the terrain.

The old man paused and, sure enough, the glow appeared again. Closer to the tower this time. It seemed to be pulsing slightly, almost like some kind of illuminated heartbeat.

He shook his head, wondering if he'd perhaps downed a little too much of his home-made liquor. Perhaps this batch had been stronger than usual, he thought. It must be the rays of the moon causing the strange light, he told himself. What else could it be?

When he reached the room where he slept he peered through one of the embrasures in the wall and squinted in the direction of the glow he'd seen.

There was nothing there. No peculiar dull luminescence to be seen now.

He shook his head dismissively and turned towards the containers of liquor on the shelves. Just a few more sips, he told himself, smiling. It would help him get back to sleep.

The terrain around Fisher's Folly was silent. The darkness was total once more. Nothing moved except the surface of one of the pools of rancid water. It was bubbling gently as if warmed from beneath by an incredibly powerful source of heat.

Fifty-One

Adam Royston was sitting at his desk when he heard the knock on his office door.

He glanced from the computer screen before him to the pile of papers stacked in such a haphazard fashion on his desk and sighed wearily. He'd been in his office since early that morning, refreshed by a good night's sleep – albeit one assisted by a couple of sleeping pills given to him by one of the doctors at the base hospital. But the pills had kept his nightmares at bay and for that alone Royston was thankful. Now he looked in the direction of the door as a second knock sounded.

'Come in,' he called, smiling when he saw the rotund figure of Leo McGill enter the room.

'Morning, Adam,' McGill said.

'Morning, Mac – I was expecting you earlier.'

'I've been at the fissure.'

'Have they finished down there now?'

'They've done as much as they can do, I'd say.'

'Really? Like what?'

'About fifty pounds of high explosive and a neat little concrete tombstone.' McGill smiled.

'Rest in peace, huh?' Royston said.

McGill studied his expression for a moment, then sat

down in the chair opposite. 'You don't think it's done any good, do you?' he asked.

Royston shrugged. 'I'd like to believe it has, Mac,' he began. 'But let's look at the facts here shall we? This thing – this X, this unknown quantity – has forced itself through miles and miles of solid rock. How are a couple of feet of concrete supposed to stop it?'

'But the explosive would have had some effect on it, surely.'

'How can we know that, Mac? This thing is unlike anything we've ever encountered before. It isn't a living organism as we know it.'

'But it *is* alive?'

'It moves, it needs to feed, it has a rudimentary instinct for survival so that would seem to suggest it possesses some kind of life – or life as we would define it when displayed by any other organism. But beyond that we're still in the dark. We don't understand it and as long as it remains beyond our comprehension we can't hope to stop it. Until we know its life source we can't hope to end its life.'

'Thanks for cheering me up,' McGill said, and shrugged.

'You see my point?'

'Unfortunately I do.'

'We know as much about this thing as we do about this.' Royston reached down and pulled a small fragment of dark material from his shoe. 'Mud.' He held it up between his thumb and index finger. 'What I saw in that fissure last night looked like this. It looked like mud. How the hell do you kill mud?'

McGill smiled in spite of himself. 'I see what you're driving at, Adam, but I have to believe this thing is dead,' he stated.

'Why, Mac? Because the thought of it still being around is too terrible?'

McGill nodded almost imperceptibly.

'What the army did might have been enough to destroy this thing,' Royston said. 'Covering the fissure with concrete may well be sufficient to prevent any more activity.' He spread his hands in a 'Who knows?' gesture.

'But you're not convinced?'

Royston raised his eyebrows. 'Have you informed anyone in London about this?' he asked.

'No more than half a dozen times,' McGill told him wearily. 'At first they were interested although that interest seemed to be confined to keeping the story away from the media.'

'And now?'

'As far as they're concerned my job here is done. I had a phone call this morning telling me to return to London.'

'When?'

'Tonight. They want a full report on what happened here.'

'And what are you going to tell them?'

'I haven't a clue, Adam. I don't even understand what I've seen here myself.'

'Join the club, Mac.'

'If I go back and tell them that a force from the centre of the Earth that is at least hundreds of thousands of years old has been slithering around the countryside feeding on radiation they'll lock me up. And, to tell you the truth, I wouldn't blame them.'

'When you put it like that . . .' Royston shrugged. 'So what *are* you going to tell them, Mac?'

'Whatever I have to in order to keep my job, Adam.'

Royston nodded, then got to his feet and extended his right hand, which McGill shook warmly.

'I'm going to miss you, Mac,' Royston said. 'It's been good having you around. You've been one of my staunchest allies – or, at least, one of the few people around here who doesn't seem to think I'm crazy.'

The two men regarded each other evenly for a moment. Then McGill spoke again. 'This thing's going to break out again, isn't it?'

'In my opinion, yes.'

'And there's nothing we can do to stop it?'

'It isn't your problem any more, Mac. Or it won't be when you're back in London.'

'As long as it's here it's a problem, Adam. As long as it's alive it's a threat.'

Royston nodded. 'There is something I've been work - ing on for a long time now,' he began. 'It's a method of disintegrating atomic structure while obviating the resultant explosion.'

McGill shook his head and circled one hand over it to indicate his incomprehension.

'Sorry.' Royston smiled. 'Do you know how an atomic bomb works, Mac?'

'It's something to do with fusion or fission. Breaking up or joining atomic particles to create energy.'

'That's close enough.'

'I told you before I wasn't the brightest kid in my chemistry class.'

'I've been working on something that breaks up these atomic particles but without causing an explosion.' He motioned McGill towards the computer, then hit a number of keys. 'I can show you the data here.' A diagram appeared on the screen, a mass of multi-coloured images that might as well have been a foreign language to anyone not familiar with what they were seeing.

McGill sighed. 'You're going to have to keep this simple, Adam,' he said almost apologetically.

Royston smiled and he moved the computer mouse so that the pointer on the screen was aimed at a gleaming cylinder.

'Now just suppose that lead container there is full of radioactive material,' he began.

McGill nodded.

Royston tapped the mouse and the diagram enlarged to reveal the inside of the structure on the screen.

'The matter inside is an atomically unstable com- pound,' he went on. 'Two things can happen to it. Either it can continue to give off radiation for the next two hundred years or it can be subjected to an outside force which will disintegrate it in a fraction of a second.' He looked at McGill. 'With me so far?'

'A bomb, in fact?' the other man said.

Royston nodded. 'If you like, yes,' he added. 'But that's what I'm trying to prevent.' He touched the mouse again and another page of data appeared.

'It's a pity Oppenheimer didn't have one of these,'

McGill chuckled, glancing at the new images before him.

'If he had he'd probably have been able to end the war four years before he did.'

'Typical American – trying to credit one of your own with single-handedly ending the war.'

'You know as well as I do, Mac, that the Japanese would have fought to the death without the kind of power that the atomic bomb made available against them to the Allies. Hundreds of thousands of lives – military and civilian – would have been lost storming Japan itself. Oppenheimer saved more lives than he destroyed with his work.'

'You would say that – you're a scientist too.'

Royston nodded and indicated the next diagram. 'If an unstable compound is drawn between the scanners pictured here and those scanners are adjusted to a certain pitch then it should be possible to neutralise any compound within their range,' he explained.

'Is this equipment viable?'

'I've used prototypes on a very small scale. In fact, there's one in my laboratory now.'

'You mean to say this apparatus would neutralise an atomic bomb?'

'In theory. I can't stress that strongly enough, Mac. Most of this work is theoretical but the one I've used should certainly be powerful enough to neutralise or destroy certain types of energy.'

'That's incredible.'

'It's a step in the right direction if nothing else. They always used to say that the greatest deterrent to the use of nuclear weapons was nuclear weapons themselves.'

'You mean that no one could win a nuclear war?'

'Mutually Assured Destruction,' Royston confirmed, nodding. 'If this equipment worked on a large scale then nuclear weapons would become obsolete purely and simply because they wouldn't work. They couldn't be a threat because there would be a way of disarming them, rendering them useless.'

'Who else knows about this?'

'Most of the American government. They weren't as supportive as your lot. Much of America's economy is built on the manufacture and sale of arms. An invention that would wreck that economy was never going to be popular. Why do you think I came here instead of continuing my work in the States?'

'Why weren't they interested?'

'They said that nuclear power isn't the threat it was twenty years ago. They couldn't support a project like mine because it was too expensive. But it has practical uses for peacetime too. Something like this would have helped neutralise the Fukushima power plant that was on the point of blowing up after the tsunami in Japan in 2011. It could be used in so many ways.'

'Could it be used against that thing out there?'

Royston didn't speak at first; his gaze was still fixed on the computer screen.

'Adam, did you hear what I said?' McGill persisted. 'Could this apparatus be used against that organism? Could it be used to destroy it?'

Royston drew in a deep breath, then let it out slowly.

'I think so,' he said finally. 'It would be a gamble but if I'm right it might be the only chance we have.'

Fifty-Two

Nikki Cross folded more clothes and pushed them into the suitcase.

Paul Coleman stood beside the bed, watching her.

'Nikki, for Christ's sake,' he said despairingly. 'You can't go through with this.'

At first she ignored him, seemingly more intent on what she was pushing into her already overstuffed suitcase. But finally she let out a deep sigh and turned to look in Coleman's direction.

'And what am I supposed to do, Paul?' she asked wearily.

'Let's talk about this,' he implored.

'We've already talked and where's it got us? You know how I feel. I'm not going to have an abortion.'

'I understand the way you feel but—'

'You don't understand.' She cut across him. 'And I don't think you really care, either. If you did you'd support me in this decision.'

'That's not fair.'

'Fair? Since when has any of this been fair, Paul? I'm carrying a child that's deformed and that may well die before it even has the chance to be born. But it's still my child.'

'It's *our* child.'

'Then why do you want it killed?'

'Come on, Nikki, be logical about this.'

'You mean sit down and calmly draw up the pros and cons for having or not having my baby and then do what you want me to do – which is get rid of it?'

'You haven't thought this through. We haven't talked about it.'

'What's the point, Paul?' Nikki snapped, slamming the suitcase shut. 'We could talk all day, every day and you'd still say the same thing. You don't want me to have the baby.'

'We're not talking about a normal baby,' he reminded her.

'We're talking about *our* baby,' she shouted.

Coleman let out a deep sigh and took a step towards her. 'The baby is ill, very ill,' he began. 'Like you said, you don't even know if it's going to survive until it's born and then, if it does survive, it's going to be deformed. What kind of life is that going to be for you or for the baby?'

'Or for you?' Nikki said harshly. 'We couldn't have a kid that was anything less than perfect, could we, Paul? It would be embarrassing, wouldn't it?'

'Oh for Christ's sake, be sensible – it's got nothing to do with that. I care about your health and what this might do to you.'

'And have you thought about what having the abortion might do to me?'

'The baby's ill, it might die. It's not as if we can't have another one, is it?'

'So scrap this one? Throw it away as if it was some kind of broken radio and just get another one – is that it?'

Coleman glared exasperatedly at her.

'I can't stay here, Paul,' she told him.

'And where are you going?' he asked.

'I'll go and stay with my mum for a few days – talk to her, think things through,' she told him.

'Why can't you stay here and talk to me?' he snapped.

Nikki closed the locks on the suitcase and dragged it upright. 'I'll ring you when I get there to let you know I made it safely,' she told him without looking at him.

'Nikki, please . . .' he began, his tone gentler now.

She merely shook her head, still not meeting his gaze. 'I just want to go,' she told him quietly. 'Don't make this any harder than it already is, Paul.'

He swallowed hard, turned and headed towards the stairs. She heard his footfalls on the steps as he descended.

Fifty-Three

The Westland Lynx AH7 banked sharply to the left as
it swept over the moorland and marshes.

'Take her around once more, will you?'

Lieutenant Bannerman glanced down towards the
ground as he spoke, pushing the helmet-mounted
microphone closer to his mouth with one hand.

The pilot nodded, tapping his headphones.

'I said—' Bannerman began but the pilot raised his
hand and smiled.

'I heard you, sir,' he told the officer. 'It's just that I'm
getting some interference through these cans.' Again he
tapped the headphones. 'It's been like it for the last
twenty minutes or so.'

Bannerman nodded. 'One more circuit should do it,'
he said, the crackle of static momentarily filling his own
headphones.

'What exactly are we looking for, sir?' the pilot asked
as they descended smoothly, the Lynx cutting effort -
lessly through the air above the marshes.

'The same thing we were looking for half an hour ago
when we first started circling this bloody area,'
Bannerman reminded him.

'And what was that?'

'My orders were to ensure that the area was stable and that there was no activity so that's what we're going to do.'

'If you don't mind me asking, sir, what kind of activity were they expecting us to find?'

Bannerman smiled thinly and indicated for the pilot to take the chopper lower. 'To be honest, I couldn't tell you,' he admitted, forced to raise his voice over the loud thrashing of the overhead rotor blades and the roar of the twin Rolls-Royce Gem turboshaft engines.

As the Lynx descended Bannerman manoeuvred the spotlights of the helicopter himself, ensuring that the beams were trained on the reason for their little excursion. He nodded to himself when he saw the thick grey concrete that had been used to cover the fissure.

'I can land if you want me to, sir,' the pilot offered.

'No, just circle again,' Bannerman told him. 'If there was any damage we'd be able to see it from here.' He hissed under his breath as a particularly powerful surge of interference tore through the headphones, causing his ears to ring momentarily.

'Any idea what's causing that?' the officer asked.

The pilot could only shake his head. 'Some of the instruments have been playing up, too,' he added. 'Some of the lights on the dash have been flickering on and off. It's like we're flying through an electrical storm but it should clear soon. It's nothing to worry about.'

'I'll take your word for that,' Bannerman said, his stare still fixed on the huge plug of concrete below them. The fissure had been filled with the fast-drying com - pound. How many tons it had taken to seal the rift in the ground he had no idea but he told himself that it must have been a huge amount, considering the depth of the chasm.

The pilot took the Lynx a little lower, then allowed it to hover as Bannerman played the powerful lights all over the concrete below. Satisfied with what he saw, he made an upward movement with his index finger. 'Let's get out of here,' he added. 'I've seen enough.'

The pilot nodded and the Lynx began to rise once more, climbing higher and higher into the darkening sky away from the fissure, the moor and the marshland around it. As the helicopter rose several of the internal lights in the cabin dimmed and both men winced as more powerful static hissed through their headphones. The pilot tapped his, relieved when the sound abated somewhat. Bannerman pulled his off for a moment, his gaze still fixed on the sealed fissure below, but as the chopper swung away he replaced the headphones and contented himself with gazing out at the evening sky.

If the downdraught caused by the Lynx's rotors hadn't been so strong then perhaps Bannerman would have noticed the wisps of smoke rising from the edges of the concrete sealing the rift. If the helicopter had landed then perhaps he would have felt the vibrations in the earth around the hole. The sounds that accompanied these vibrations came from deep underground and had been growing steadily louder for the last hour or so. But, as it was, the lieutenant saw and heard nothing.

If he'd been there thirty minutes later he would have seen the concrete begin to crack.

Fifty-Four

Adam Royston gazed at the display screen of his mobile phone and shook his head irritably.

MESSAGE FAILED

He hit the RETRY option and waited but still the text wouldn't send. He hit the CONTACTS key and found Sandra Morgan's number. There was nothing but a forlorn beeping sound from the phone, followed by a dismal crackle of static. Royston regarded the phone with something approaching disdain, his attention diverted momentarily by the arrival of Peter Elliot who had emerged from his office further down the corridor.

'Adam,' the younger man called.

'Sorry, Peter, I was just trying to send a message. But my phone either can't get a signal or just won't do what I want it to do,' Royston said.

'Neither will mine,' Peter said. 'It's been like it for the last hour or so. Could it be something to do with the work that's going on in the laboratory?'

'No, I wouldn't think so. Cleaning cobalt rods isn't going to cause problems with mobile phones.'

'But radioactivity *can* interfere with radio waves, can't it?'

'True,' Royston acknowledged. 'But as you say, it's only been a problem for the past hour and the men are sealed inside the laboratory with the cobalt rods. That shouldn't have an effect on apparatus outside.'

'What do you want to do with the rods once they're ready? There's a truck standing by outside.'

'Take a quick reading and then we'll load them,' Royston told him. 'By the way, Peter, where's your father? I wanted to speak to him about a couple of things.'

'He was expecting a call from the Atomic Energy Commission earlier this afternoon but I haven't seen him since.'

'What about?'

'What's been going on here, I would imagine.'

'But McGill is going to give them a full report when he gets back to London.'

'I suppose they wanted another perspective – and my father is in charge here isn't he?'

'Thanks for reminding me,' Royston said, smiling grimly.

'I know he's been a little edgy lately, Adam, but you have to see his point of view. He sees what goes on here as his responsibility and any problems are ultimately laid at his door.'

'I understand that, Peter. I just don't understand his hostility sometimes.'

'It's just his way.'

The two men continued up the corridor, their

footsteps echoing on the brightly polished floor inside the walkway.

'I'm going to miss Mac now he's gone,' Royston said as they walked. 'He was a good guy.'

'He seemed it. What do you think he'll tell the AEC?'

'I really don't know, Peter. How the hell would anyone explain the things we've seen and experienced during the last few days?'

'How would *you* explain it?'

'I couldn't,' Royston said. 'I wish I could. There's probably a PhD waiting for anyone who could explain what the hell was down in that fissure. What it was, where it came from and what it wanted here.'

'Thank God the army dealt with it.'

Royston didn't answer. He reached for his mobile again and tried once more to send a message. Again he had no luck. This time there wasn't so much as a light on the display panel. It was as if the phone had been drained of power.

'I would say use mine,' Peter Elliot told him. 'But look.' He held up his own mobile and Royston saw that the display screen on that phone too was lifeless.

'I'll use a landline,' Royston said.

'Good luck,' Peter said. 'The landlines aren't much better. For the last hour all over the base we've barely been able to make or receive calls.'

Fifty-Five

'Turn it off.'

Constable Edward Chapman winced as a particularly loud burst of static erupted from the police radio and seemed to fill the patrol car.

'Bloody typical,' Chapman went on. 'They finally give us a new car and the radio's up the shoot.'

'It's only been like it for the last hour or so,' Constable William Lucas reminded him, leaning forward to twist the dials on the radio in the hope that the interference would stop.

'Well, it's no good to us like that, is it?' Chapman insisted.

'We can't switch it off, Ed – how will they get in touch with us?'

'They can't get in touch with us *now*. We can't hear a bloody thing.'

Chapman guided the car along the road, his gaze ever watchful. They passed a small garage where he could see a man filling his car at one of the two pumps on the forecourt. 'Wasn't that the place that was robbed last month?' he murmured. 'Or was it the one out on the road into Monkston?'

'They were both done in the space of three days,

weren't they?' Lucas reminded him, still fiddling with the controls of the radio. 'A couple of kids no more than fourteen. They only got about fifty quid from each place.'

'Little bastards,' grunted Chapman. 'What the fuck is wrong with kids these days?'

'They're not all bad, Ed. Just *most* of them.'

Both men laughed.

'There's a lad of about sixteen lives next door to my mum and dad,' Chapman went on. 'He's a good kid. He lives with his parents. He goes round to my mum and dad once a week and cuts their grass for them. My mum gives him a fiver and he's happy enough. It's a pity there's not more like him.'

'How's your dad?' Lucas enquired.

'No better,' Chapman sighed. 'But then again, he's not going to be, is he? Fucking Alzheimer's doesn't improve once you've got it. He's just going to get worse.'

'Is it definitely that?'

'Early-stage Alzheimer's, the doctor said. There's nothing they can do for him – or nothing they can be bothered to do for him. I reckon the National Health just gives up on people once they get past a certain age and my dad's nearly eighty now. They couldn't give a fuck.'

'How's your mum coping with it?'

'She'd be able to cope better if she could get a decent night's sleep. But my old man gets out of fucking bed four or five times a night to go for a piss but then he can't remember where the toilet is so he goes and asks my mum and she has to show him. She looked so tired last time I saw her. It really gets to me, Bill. I just wish there was something I could do to help. I feel so bloody useless.'

'Will you have to put him somewhere?'

'In the end we won't have any choice, I suppose. The thing is he's fine most of the time but then he just sits there and it's like he drifts away into his own little world.' Chapman shook his head. 'He keeps asking when he can go home and my mum keeps telling him he is home and then two minutes later he's asking again.'

'I'm sorry, Ed,' Lucas said quietly.

'So am I, mate. So am I.'

There was a particularly loud blast of static from the radio and Lucas reached for the handset, shaking it irritably as if that simple action would alleviate the problem.

'Are the two-ways the same?' Chapman enquired, watching as his companion pulled the Motorola from his belt and clicked it on. A similarly harsh burst of static came from that, too.

'What the fuck is going on here?' Chapman grunted. He was about to speak again when the headlights of the car illuminated something in the road ahead. He stepped hard on the brakes and the police car came to an abrupt halt.

'You could have warned me, Ed,' Lucas snapped.

'Look,' Chapman said, pointing ahead.

Lucas squinted through the windscreen, following his companion's pointing finger.

He pushed open the passenger-side door, pulled a torch from the glove compartment and swung himself out of the vehicle. Chapman left the engine running and did the same, joining Lucas. Both of them were transfixed by what lay only yards ahead of them now.

There was a crack across the road about two feet deep that cut through the tarmac from one kerb to the other. The drain cover on one side of the road had been torn from its housing and the tarmac all around the crack was practically liquid – as if it had been subjected to an incredible amount of heat. Even the tyres of a car that was parked nearby had melted, the rubber having pooled like thick black blood around the rims.

'Gas explosion?' Chapman wondered, looking at the damage.

'There's no debris,' Lucas said. 'If there'd been an explosion there'd be bits of concrete all over the place.'

'But what else could have created this much heat?' Chapman muttered. 'And what the hell is this stuff?' He drew the toe of one boot through the white powder that covered much of the road and the parked car.

'I don't know.'

'I'll call it in,' Chapman said, turning back towards the waiting police car. As he did so, the headlights on the vehicle first dimmed and then went out completely. The engine died seconds later.

'What the fuck is happening here?' Chapman wanted to know.

Lucas had no answer. He was still staring at the melted and gouged road before him.

Fifty-Six

The drive from her home in Broughton to her parents' house in Monkston would normally have taken Nikki Cross less than thirty minutes. As she guided the Renault onto the main road that joined the two neighbouring towns she turned on the radio in the forlorn hope that music might distract her from the other thoughts tumbling through her mind. The reception was bad on the first station so she switched to another but the crackling that interrupted the broadcast every few seconds was no better on that one. Four times she pressed the button to find new wavebands but the result was the same. Always that incessant hiss and crackle from the radio and Nikki tired of it quickly. She switched the radio off and pushed a CD into the player instead. Music began to fill the car but she still couldn't seem to banish the thoughts from her mind. Thoughts about her baby and about her future. In the end she switched off the CD as well and drove in silence, con - centrating on the darkened road, wondering why the sodium glare of street lights wasn't relieving the gloom.

The lights on both sides of the road were off.

At first it didn't strike her as too strange. The local council was always trying to save money somehow and choosing not to light certain parts of the town and its approaches was something that they had tried before. However, this particular stretch of road that was flanked on both sides by fields was particularly gloomy. Not aided by the fact that hedges protecting the fields rose as high as five or six feet on both sides of the tarmac. Nikki slowed down, aware that animals were prone to dart across the road out here in the more countrified surroundings. Apart from the distant farm houses that lay hundreds of yards off across the fields no one lived out here. It was pitch black without any roadside lighting. She switched her headlights to full beam.

What she saw bathed in their cold white glare almost caused her to swerve.

She stepped hard on their brake, clutching the steering wheel more tightly.

Whatever was lying in the road was much larger than the usual casualties such as hedgehogs, birds or rabbits. Nikki narrowed her eyes to see what the poor unfortu-nate creature was but then realised that there were two of them. The carcasses of both were lying almost nose to tail on the road, making it impossible for her to drive on without hitting one or both of them. She exhaled hard, realising that one of the dead animals was a badger and the other was either a large fox or a dog. Had one of the dogs from the farm chased the other creature onto the road where they'd both been struck by a passing vehicle?

As she sat behind the steering wheel trying to make sense of the little tableau she realised that her path was blocked. She could either drive over one or both of the dead animals or she could move one enough to allow her clear passage. The prospect of shifting roadkill didn't exactly appeal to her but neither did the idea of crushing dead animals beneath the tyres of her car. She told herself that she could always hook one of the unfortunate creatures clear of the road with the umbrella she had in the boot – she didn't have to touch it.

Nikki switched off the engine, then got out of the car and moved around to the rear of the vehicle, shivering as a particularly powerful blast of chilly wind swept across the open countryside. She opened the boot and took out the umbrella, inspecting the handle and judging that it would be strong enough to hook the smaller of the two carcasses clear of the road. With that done she could continue on her way and, unsavoury as it might be, the task should be completed quickly enough. She swallowed hard, hoping that there wasn't too much blood. Moving the dead animal was going to be harrowing enough but if it had been pulverised by whatever had hit and killed it then it would be worse if there were entrails all over the road. Gripping the umbrella tightly she turned and advanced up the road towards the two dead creatures.

If Paul had been with her he would have moved them both.

Well, he's not with you, is he? You're on your own.

Nikki swallowed hard, buffeted again by the wind that blew ferociously in this exposed area of countryside. There was a gate to her left that led into one of the fields and the wooden structure was creaking on its rusty hinges, making a low squeaking noise that became more noticeable as she drew closer to it. As Nikki glanced that way she also saw that there was a dull glow coming from the field. A barely visible pulsing display of sickly light that faded as she glanced towards it.

She moved on towards the animal carcasses and saw that they were indeed a badger and a dog.

However, neither seemed to have been hit by a car or lorry as she'd thought at first. There was no blood around the animals as was usually the case after such a collision, just a light dusting of white powder that seemed to cover most of the road. Looking down at the unfortunate creatures Nikki recoiled slightly at the smell rising from their bodies. It was a strong odour of burning and, as she looked more closely, she could see that the fur on both animals was scorched off in several places to reveal seared red flesh beneath.

Both of them looked as if they'd been pushed into a furnace, then dragged out again and laid across the road like some kind of charred barrier. There was even smoke rising from the bodies in thin wisps. Nikki put her hand to her nose, trying to blot out the foul stench and wondering what could have caused this kind of damage.

She was still wondering when she heard a low hissing sound off to her left.

It grew louder and now she was aware once again of the dull glow she had seen previously.

The hissing became a louder crackling sound and Nikki felt her heart thudding harder against her ribs.

Suddenly the idea of driving over the dead animals didn't seem so bad. She wanted to be in her car and away from this place. Away from whatever was making that scary sound and whatever was giving off that dull sickly glow. She turned and hurried back towards her car, sliding behind the steering wheel.

She turned the key in the ignition and pressed down hard on the accelerator.

The engine sputtered once, then died. As it did, the headlights went out, plunging the entire area into blackness once more.

At least, it would have been blackness but for the glow that was coming from the field to her left.

Nikki twisted the key again but still nothing happened. She grabbed for her mobile and hit Paul's number. He would come and get her. He would help her. She didn't want to be out here alone any more. She just wanted him to help her.

There was no signal on the phone. In fact, the display screen was unlit. Dead. She hurled the mobile down in terrified frustration and turned to her left as she heard a series of loud snapping sounds and realised that the high hedge there was being broken down by whatever was approaching from the other side.

Whatever it was it must be giving off an incredible amount of heat, Nikki thought, because the air in and around the car suddenly seemed to be unbearably hot. It was like sitting inside an oven.

She wondered what could be causing this terrifying change in the air temperature.

When she saw what it was she screamed.

Fifty-Seven

'**B**loody thing,' Leo McGill hissed irritably, glaring at his mobile phone.

He pressed it to his ear again and shouted into the mouthpiece. 'I'm due to catch a train at just after eleven tomorrow,' he bellowed. 'I should be back in London around one.'

There was no answer from the other end, only the steady hiss and crackle of static that he'd come to expect and which had been plaguing him for the last hour or more.

'Hello,' he shouted. 'Hello, can you hear me? I'm going to try again from a landline, see if that's any clearer.'

There was no answer, just that infernal static.

'To hell with it,' McGill snapped and shoved the phone into the pocket of his jacket.

He guided the rental car down the road past some houses and a well-lit pub and saw Broughton's main police station to his right a hundred yards or so further on. The train station was a short walk beyond, across a concrete bridge. He swung the vehicle into the car park in front of the police station and hauled himself out, heading for the main door. He pressed the buzzer there and the door opened to allow him access to a small reception area. There was a raised counter protected by plexiglas and behind it stood a tall, sallow-faced man in a sergeant's uniform. He looked McGill up and down and nodded officiously.

'Good evening,' McGill said. 'I was wondering if I could borrow your phone.'

'There's a phone box just down the street,' the sergeant told him.

McGill fished his ID from his jacket and pressed it to the plexiglas. 'It is official business,' he said.

The sergeant glanced at the ID. Then he nodded and pressed a buzzer below the counter. The door to McGill's right opened a fraction.

'Come round,' the sergeant instructed and McGill did so. There was a phone on the wall and another on the desk close to the uniformed man who pointed to the device on the wall.

McGill smiled gratefully and took the receiver down, wedged it between his ear and his shoulder and began dialling.

'Have you been having trouble with your phones?' he asked while he waited for the call to be answered. 'I've been trying to call London but I can't get through because of all the interference.'

'It's been like it all night,' the sergeant told him. 'Even our patrol cars are having trouble keeping in contact because their radios have been affected.'

'What do you think it is? An electrical storm?'

The sergeant could only shrug.

At the other end of the line McGill heard a voice he

recognised despite the ever-present hiss and crackle of static. 'Sorry about that,' he said. 'It's me again. I had to call it a day with the mobile, no signal. Now, as I was saying, I need one more night here if that's possible.'

The person at the other end said something.

'Why do I have to speak to him? Can't you authorise it?' McGill protested.

The voice apparently couldn't.

'All right, you'd better put me through, then,' McGill said, watching as the desk sergeant answered a call of his own.

'Duty sergeant speaking,' the uniformed man said.

On the other end of his own line, McGill heard another voice he recognised and he stiffened at the sound. 'Yes, sir,' he said. 'Just one more night. If nothing happens I'll catch the first train back to London in the morning.'

'Yes,' the duty sergeant said, continuing with his own conversation. 'You're going to have to speak up. The line's terrible – it has been all night.'

McGill saw the expression on the man's face darken.

'What about the occupants of the car?' the sergeant asked, scribbling something down on a piece of paper.

'Yes, sir,' McGill went on, intrigued now by the other call he could hear in the background. 'First thing tomorrow morning. Thank you, sir.' He hung up, replacing the receiver slowly, his attention now caught by the duty sergeant's words.

'That's impossible,' the uniformed man said. 'Where are you calling from? And where's the car?'

McGill hesitated a moment longer.

'Melted?' the desk sergeant snapped. 'How could the body be melted?'

McGill shot the man a perplexed glance.

'There's a patrol car in that area,' the desk sergeant went on. 'They can be there in five minutes. You stay there until they arrive.' He hung up.

'What did you say?' McGill asked.

'There's been an accident,' the desk sergeant went on. 'A burned-out car has been found about five miles from here on the road between Broughton and Monkston.'

'You said something about the occupant being melted. What did you mean?'

'The caller said the inside of the car looked as if somebody had turned a flame-thrower on it and that the driver must have been melted.'

'Where is this? Where did it happen?'

'I can't tell you that.'

'It's official,' McGill insisted, flipping his ID wallet open again. 'Give me that address.'

Fifty-Eight

He could smell the stench of burned flesh as soon as he climbed out of the car.

Leo McGill closed the door and glanced down the road towards the burned-out hulk of the Renault. There was smoke still rising mournfully from it and, even from a hundred or so yards away, he could see that most of the paint had been burned from the chassis, exposing bare metal beneath. The windscreen and rear window were gone, as was the roof of the vehicle, missing as if they'd simply been vaporised. The hedge to the right- and left-hand side of the country road was also scorched in several places. In others it had been flattened.

There was a single police car parked near the remains of the Renault and, as he moved closer, McGill could see that there was a man seated inside the emergency vehicle who was busy on the radio and seemed not to have seen him. McGill approached the Renault and peered more closely at the wreck. He recoiled from the acrid stench of charred human flesh and he could see fragments of white matter stuck to the driver's seat and also to the dashboard. He realised with revulsion that it was bone. Pieces of seared flesh were also in evidence inside the car and the lumps of yellowish material that he could see he surmised were pieces of human fat. Whoever had been inside the car had been subjected to a source of heat so ferocious that it had literally melted them as easily as a candle melts before a flame.

McGill dropped to his haunches and ran his finger through the white residue that covered the tarmac around the car and also the chassis itself. It looked uncomfortably familiar to him and he let out an almost painful breath as he straightened up.

'Hey, you.'

The shout came from behind him, from one of the large open fields that stretched away into the darkness on either side of the road.

McGill turned to see another uniformed policeman advancing towards him from the field.

'What the hell are you doing?' Constable Chapman wanted to know, running an appraising gaze over McGill. 'You're not supposed to be here.'

McGill fumbled for his ID and showed it to Chapman who glanced at it and nodded.

'When did this happen?' McGill asked, nodding towards the smouldering wreckage of the Renault. 'How long ago?'

'We got here about ten minutes ago,' Chapman told him. 'It was like that when we arrived.'

'No sign of the driver?'

'No. I knew her, too.'

'You knew her?'

'We checked who the vehicle was registered to. Nikki Cross. Lovely girl. She came from Broughton. Christ knows where she is now.'

'From what I can see in that wreck I wouldn't hold out much hope of seeing her again,' McGill said flatly. He fumbled in his pocket for his mobile and jabbed some buttons. But the display screen merely glowed weakly for a moment, then faded completely. 'Not again,' he hissed irritably.

'Are you having trouble getting a signal?' Chapman asked.

'I'm having trouble getting anything at all. Even on landlines there's appalling interference.'

'I know, we've been getting it on our radios all night. There's a call box just down the road – you might have more luck there.'

'Thanks,' McGill said, turning to look at the flattened and charred hedges on either side of the road. 'Any idea what could have done that?' he murmured, gesturing towards the destruction.

Chapman merely shook his head.

McGill had his own theories about what had bulldozed its way through the hedges and enveloped the car but he thought it best to keep them to himself at present. Trying to convince a policeman that some kind of primordial force was crawling across the countryside, consuming objects in its path, might not be appreciated at the moment, he reasoned.

'We've seen other stuff burned up like that tonight,' Chapman said.

'Like what?' McGill demanded, the hairs on the back of his neck rising.

'Other cars and sections of road,' Chapman informed him.

'Where?'

'In other parts of Broughton.'

'When did you see these?'

'Earlier tonight. The damage looked very similar.'

The knot of muscles at the side of McGill's jaw pulsed nervously. 'You said there was a public call box near here,' he reminded the policeman. 'I have to use a phone now.'

'It's down the road about a mile. You can't miss it,' Chapman told him.

McGill was already heading for his car. As he reached it he turned and looked back at the watching policeman. 'Seal this area off,' he called. 'And if there are any houses in the vicinity tell the occupants to stay inside. In fact, get a message to the other men on your force and get them to spread the word around Broughton. Tell everyone to get inside and stay there.'

Chapman was about to ask why but McGill slammed his door and started the engine. He swung the car around and sped off into the night.

Fifty-Nine

'**D**octor Royston.'

The American scientist heard his name echo across the laboratory and he turned slowly towards the owner of the voice that had called it, aware that there was an edge to the tone. He knew without even looking that the voice belonged to Professor John Elliot and he also suspected that Elliot's mood wasn't of the best. Something else he'd come to expect during the last few days.

'What have I done this time?' he murmured under his breath.

As the professor descended the stairs from the upper level of the laboratory his footsteps echoed through the large room.

'Adam,' the older man said as he moved closer to Royston. 'What's been going on in here?'

'We've just taken the cobalt out of the pile, John—' Royston began.

'I'm fully aware of that,' the professor snapped. 'On whose authority?'

'I tried to find you but you were otherwise engaged,' Royston said.

'Work of that kind is not supposed to be undertaken

without my express permission,' the professor reminded him.

'As I said,' Royston went on, attempting to keep his tone even, 'I would have waited until you gave your permission but you were busy.'

'Yes, I was busy speaking to the head of the Atomic Energy Commission in London, attempting yet again to explain what's been happening here.'

'You were lucky you could speak to anyone, considering the state of the phones,' Royston reminded him.

'That's as maybe,' the professor replied irritably. 'The fact is that you still undertook work that was unauthorised. Do you know how long it takes to get that pile started again?' He looked at his son reproachfully. 'And you stood by and let this happen, Peter?'

'Peter assisted me in removing the cobalt from the rods,' Royston announced.

'Well, he shouldn't have,' the older man said. 'He shouldn't even have been in here in the first place.'

'I was trying to help,' Peter said.

'Your job at this base is administration,' the older man snapped.

'There wasn't time to wait until you signed the appro - priate forms or gave your permission,' Royston insisted. 'I acted on my own initiative. No harm has been done.'

'That isn't the point,' the professor said. 'There are routines and protocols that should be followed on a base like this and when materials such as this are concerned.'

'Everything was conducted with the utmost regard for safety,' Royston went on.

'You put the cobalt bombardment weeks behind schedule.'

Royston nodded, tiring of this tirade.

'What's done is done, John,' he said wearily. 'Next time I'll make sure I get an order in triplicate signed by you before I do anything – is that OK?'

'Entirely on your own initiative you break in on an official experiment,' the professor continued. 'You deactivate the pile without consulting me. This isn't your workshop, this is a government establishment.'

'I'm well aware of that,' Royston told him. 'You're constantly making me aware of that fact, John. But a fact that *you* seem to forget is that you have no seniority over me.'

'I run this establishment,' the professor snapped.

'You supervise an establishment that is run by the army,' Royston reminded him. 'There's a difference. I take my orders from people like Major Cartwright because he's the one with the real authority around here.'

'That may be – but there's always the question of ethical behaviour,' said the professor.

'For Christ's sake,' Royston sighed dismissively. 'If you want a written apology I'll have it on your desk in the morning. I promise never to act without the full permission of the director again. How's that? Humble enough for you?'

The two men glared at each other for a moment longer. Then Royston turned his head when he heard the phone in one corner of the laboratory ringing.

'I'll get it,' Peter Elliot announced, heading across to

the phone and lifting the receiver. He recoiled as a savage blast of static filled his ear. 'Hello. Hello. You'll have to speak louder – it's a terrible line.'

At the other end of the line the voice barely penetrated the haze of static but it cut through enough for the caller to identify himself.

'Oh, hello, Mr McGill,' Peter answered. 'I thought you'd gone back to London. No, Doctor Royston is busy at the moment. This is Peter Elliot.'

McGill tried to explain what he'd seen on the outskirts of Broughton.

Peter gripped the receiver more tightly, his expression darkening. 'I see,' he murmured. 'Wait a minute, I'll get him.' He allowed the phone to dangle by its cord and hurried over to where Royston and Peter's father were still facing each other. 'Doctor Royston,' he cut in. 'It's Mr McGill on the phone. It appears that what you were afraid of has happened. That thing from the fissure has just killed someone in a car. The line's terrible but I'm sure he said they'd been killed in the same way as the soldiers whose remains you found inside the fissure. He said they'd been melted.'

Royston shot an angry glance at the professor, then hurried to the phone. 'Mac, can you hear me?' he said, cursing the interference on the line. 'It's Adam. What the hell is going on out there?'

McGill told him as best he could.

'And where have these incidents happened?' Royston asked.

Through a haze of static again, McGill told him.

Royston pulled a pen and a piece of paper from his

jacket and scribbled details down as the other man relayed the information.

'OK, I've got that,' he said finally. 'Where are you now, Mac?'

McGill told him.

'All right, listen to me: make your way back here to the base as soon as you can,' Royston instructed. 'Got that?'

There was a fearfully loud explosion of static on the line.

'Get back here now, Mac,' Royston repeated.

Now there was only static. The line was dead. He replaced the receiver and turned to the professor who had ambled over towards him.

'John, do you have a local survey map in your office?' Royston enquired.

'Yes,' the professor told him.

'We need to take a look at it now.'

'What's going on?' the older man asked.

'Show me that map and I'll try to explain,' Royston said, already heading for the door.

Sixty

'This point right here is the fissure.'

Royston pressed the point of the pencil into the map that was spread out on Professor John Elliot's desk. As the professor and Peter watched he drew the pencil along the edge of the ruler he'd also laid on the map. He pressed the point in again.

'Here is the hospital,' he said. Then he did the same again at another point on the map directly in line with the first two locations he'd indicated. 'According to what Mac told me on the phone this is where the burned-out car was found.' He shifted the ruler, sliding it across the map and drawing another line against its straight edge. 'Over here is the base and, if we follow the line, right here is the old tower where the Dickinson boy was burned.'

'Do you think this thing from the fissure is following some kind of pattern?' Peter Elliot asked.

Royston shrugged.

'Whatever it's doing it can obviously sense radio - activity and once it does nothing can stop it,' he said. 'It makes straight for it and then returns to the fissure. And from these lines it's pretty clear that it returns by the same route.'

'Don't most predators hunt in the same areas every time?' Peter Elliot offered.

'That's right,' Royston confirmed. 'And this thing is no different.'

'Don't you think we're attributing qualities to it that it might not actually possess?' the professor interjected. 'It's an amorphous mass of matter. Calling it a predator hardly seems appropriate.'

'It feeds and it hunts what it feeds on, John,' Royston told him. 'It has a food source that it has to consume and it does just that. In my book that makes it predatory.' He looked down at the map again. 'Mac said that the burned out-car was here.' He pressed the pencil into the map again. 'Now, if we extend the line to the fissure through this point then somewhere along this extended line is where it's headed.' He jabbed the point of the pencil into the map, indicating an area they all saw only too clearly: Broughton Green Military Research Facility.

'It's coming here,' Peter Elliot said quietly.

'That's right,' Royston exclaimed. 'It's on its way to the biggest meal of its life.'

'You can't know that for sure,' the professor said.

'It's a logical assumption, John,' Royston exclaimed. 'The amount of energy here that it could consume makes this base the next logical target.'

'If that's true then Major Cartwright should be informed,' the professor stated.

'I agree,' Royston said, nodding. 'He might have some ideas about how to stop this thing.'

'According to you that's impossible,' John Elliot said.

'Let's get Cartwright in here, see what he thinks,'

Royston suggested, watching as Peter reached for the internal phone on the professor's desk. He hit the required button and waited.

McGill was sure that there were more soldiers than usual in evidence as he pulled the car up to the main gate of Broughton Green Military Research Facility.

There were four men in the concrete building that stood close to the main entrance, all of whom looked at him questioningly as he sat outside the large wire-mesh gate with his car's engine idling. At first none of them moved towards him so he hit the horn a couple of times. 'Come on,' he shouted.

One of them finally headed out of the gatehouse towards him.

'Open the gate,' McGill called.

'I need to see your pass, sir,' the private said.

'Oh come on, you know me. Open up,' McGill replied.

'Sorry, sir, I have to see your pass first,' the private insisted.

Muttering under his breath, McGill dug inside his jacket and pulled out his ID.

'Sorry, Mr McGill,' the private told him. 'But there are procedures I have to follow.'

'I know that,' McGill said, handing him the ID. 'What's with all the extra men?'

The private glanced perfunctorily at the ID, nodded, then handed it back.

'It's like it all over the base,' he said. 'Orders from Major Cartwright.'

'It looks like he's getting ready to fight off an invasion.'

The private nodded and waved towards the gatehouse. There was a loud whirring sound and the gate opened, swinging back on its hinges. McGill guided the car through, pausing momentarily when he was level with the private.

'Can anyone tell me what's going on?' he asked.

'We know as much as you do, sir,' the private told him. 'We're on alert, that's it. No one said why. I was hoping *you* might be able to tell *me*.'

McGill raised an eyebrow quizzically, then drove on. Behind him the gates swung shut once again.

Sixty-One

Major Edward Cartwright ran a hand through his hair and looked squarely at Adam Royston. 'So what you're telling me is that if this thing decides to attack the base then my men won't be able to stop it anyway?' the officer said quietly.

'I don't see how they can with just conventional weapons,' Royston conceded.

'So what the hell are we supposed to do?' McGill asked. 'Just sit here and wait for this thing to arrive?'

'How can you be sure that it is heading for the base?' Cartwright enquired.

'Because of the cobalt here,' Peter Elliot interjected.

'If Doctor Royston is right and it feeds on that kind of energy,' Professor Elliot added. 'That's what's drawing it here.'

'What if the cobalt was removed from the base?' McGill asked. 'Taken away?'

'There must be a limit to how far away this thing can sense or detect radiation,' the professor suggested. 'If we could get the cobalt beyond that range then we might have a chance of stopping it.'

'Unless you're right about how it's evolved, Doctor

Royston,' Cartwright added. 'Perhaps the cobalt isn't its only target.'

'Listen, most of the theories concerning this creature are pure speculation,' Royston admitted. 'My theory about it evolving is, too. At least, I hope it is.'

'But you said that all predators adapt according to their prey,' McGill said. 'Surely that's the case where this thing is concerned. If it can't feed on radiation or radioactive material then it will find something else to sustain it.'

'And that something else could be human beings, yes,' Royston said. 'Not only does this base have a supply of radioactive material for that thing to feed on, it also has a large number of people which it could decide to consume. It killed the driver of that car, didn't it, Mac? It didn't attack because of any radiation coming from the vehicle; it attacked because it wanted what was inside. Namely the driver.'

'If that's true then no one is safe,' Cartwright stated. 'Not the personnel here on the base and not the residents of Broughton or Monkston or any of the other centres of population near here.'

'If something large enough to consume the population of a small town is roaming the countryside then why haven't we heard reports of sightings?' the professor asked. 'How could something that huge keep out of sight for so long?'

'It might alter its form and become almost invisible, isn't that a possibility?' Royston suggested. 'It came from beneath the ground and it might even have gone below again to move around. Perhaps that's why no one's seen it.'

'Like a shark under the water?' McGill asked.

'Why not?' Royston said.

'So you're telling me we might not even see this thing until it attacks?' Cartwright said.

'I don't know that for sure, major,' Royston told him. 'It's just a—'

'Theory, I know,' the officer cut in. He got to his feet and wandered over to the window in Royston's office, gazing out into the night. 'I'm going to order some reconnaissance,' he announced. 'If we've got helicopters in the air then at least we might get a glimpse of this thing before it actually gets here. If any of the choppers see it they might even be able to destroy it.'

'How?' Royston asked.

'Each of the Lynx helicopters we use is equipped with eight anti-tank missiles. If they hit it with those then it should at least slow it down,' Cartwright told him.

'No,' Royston said. 'If this thing absorbs energy, feeds on it, then missiles won't kill it or damage it. They might even make it stronger. If it absorbs the energy from the helicopters' missiles it could grow stronger. Tell your men not to fire at it, major; just track its movements if they see it.'

'We can't contact the helicopters,' the professor reminded him. 'That interference we've been getting has made communication virtually impossible.'

Royston gave a frustrated groan.

'What about the security around the base?' McGill

asked. 'I saw extra men when I arrived.'

'The whole base is on alert,' Cartwright told him.

'Then all we can do is wait,' Peter Elliot said.

McGill reached for the phone on Royston's desk and jabbed one of the buttons.

'What are you doing?' Royston asked.

'Ringing the gatehouses around the base,' McGill told him.

Cartwright nodded and all eyes turned towards McGill as he began to dial.

At the other end of the line a phone began to ring.

And continued to ring.

Sixty-Two

'I'm going to take a walk around the perimeter.'
The first of the soldiers in the gatehouse got to his feet and swung his rifle up onto his shoulder.

'What for?' the second man asked.

'Because it's better than sitting in here doing fuck all,' the first man said. 'I might even see something.'

'Like what?' the second man said.

'I don't know – whatever they've put us on alert for.'

'If there was anything happening we'd see it on these,' the other soldier assured him, pointing towards the bank of closed-circuit TV screens on one side of the room, each one supplied with a picture by a surveillance camera that overlooked the approaches to the main gate.

'I'm going to have a walkabout, anyway,' the first man repeated.

'So where are you going?'

'I'm just going to wander a hundred yards or so in each direction, just to get the old blood pumping.' He smiled and tapped his legs.

Outside he heard the roar of rotor blades as another helicopter passed overhead.

'How many's that in the last fifteen minutes?' the first

private muttered, glancing out of the window of the gatehouse towards the dark sky. 'Three?'

'Do you reckon this is anything to do with what happened to Don Lansing and those other guys out on the moor?' the second soldier asked.

'Nobody ever seemed to know what happened to them for sure. At least no one said anything. Some of them are still in hospital, aren't they?'

The second man nodded. 'I heard they were still in a pretty bad way,' he said.

The first private raised his eyebrows and sighed deeply. 'I won't be long,' he said wearily, pulling open the gatehouse door. He stepped out into the night, his breath clouding in the air. He peered out into the gloom beyond the high wire fence that surrounded the base but saw nothing. He had no idea exactly what he was expecting to see but there was no movement of any kind beyond the perimeter fence and the night seemed still, despite the comings and goings of the helicopters, which seemed to be taking off every couple of minutes. He set off away from the gatehouse, his steps slow and measured as he continued to scan the terrain beyond the fence.

Thirty or forty yards away he thought he saw some - thing. Just the faintest glimmer of light in the periphery of his vision. A dull glow as if from a distant candle.

He tried to focus on the light but as he gazed more intently into the darkness he could see no sign of it again and he wondered if one of the spotlights mounted on the high perimeter fence was causing some kind of visual disturbance. He walked on, further from the gatehouse, never straying more than ten yards from the perimeter fence, his eyes always alert for any signs of movement.

Behind him, the private inside the gatehouse glanced from one of the CCTV screens to the other. There were four surveillance cameras mounted on the main gate, all equipped with infrared and all trained on the approaches to the perimeter fence or the land close by. The images on each screen weren't as clear as normal and the private wondered if the same interference that had been disrupting radio and telephone communications that night was somehow responsible for the break-up of the pictures that was happening sporadically. Even as he watched the first screen began to flash, the images on it fading and then glowing almost unnaturally brightly.

He muttered something under his breath and watched as the picture on the second screen began to distort too.

'You're having a laugh,' he grunted to himself, glancing irritably at the monitors. When the third and fourth screens began to show broad bands of inter - ference he shook his head in disbelief.

The first screen was now completely blank and he wondered whether it was the monitors or the cameras themselves that were at fault.

The third screen went blank.

The private could hear a low crackling sound and he turned up the volume on the two remaining monitors, trying to identify the source of this latest disturbance.

He decided that the sound didn't seem to be coming from the monitors. It was coming from outside the gatehouse.

Taking one last look at the bank of screens he turned and headed for the gatehouse door, pushing it open.

Sure enough, the sound was louder now.

At first he thought it was coming from beyond the perimeter fence but as it grew louder and more insistent he realised it was closer than that.

The ground beneath him shuddered and he let out a gasp, shocked and suddenly frightened by the tremor. He dragged his rifle from his shoulder and swung the weapon up to the ready position, his eyes now fixed on the ground beneath him. Tiny wisps of smoke were rising from several small cracks that had criss-crossed the dark ground.

The crackling sound he had heard initially was still growing in intensity and so too was the sudden warmth that had enveloped him as he stood gazing down transfixed at the ground beneath his feet. There was more movement from below and this time the soldier struggled to remain upright. He shook himself from his paralysed state and bolted for the gatehouse.

As he reached the door the ground erupted behind him. Lumps of earth and rock flew skywards and he saw something thick and glutinous flowing from the resulting holes, something that slithered across the ground after him. More and more of the noxious matter flowed upwards through the riven earth like blood from a fresh wound and now the soldier felt searing heat on his back.

His uniform was smoking, the material incinerated

by the incredible temperature that was enveloping him, while lower down the thick ooze that had come pumping up from beneath the ground now covered his boots and shins as it sought to consume him. He felt excruciating pain where it touched him, the skin peeling away as easily as if it had been subjected to the blast of a blowtorch. Flesh on his hands and the back of his neck blistered and as he stumbled across the threshold of the gatehouse he felt his head spinning. He knew he was blacking out but the pain kept him conscious for a precious few seconds.

He shot out a scorched hand and using all his remaining strength he managed to hit the red button on the wall near the door. The strident wailing of the alarm klaxon began to fill the air.

Sixty-Three

All eyes turned in the direction of the alarm when the sound tore through the night.

Royston shot McGill a worried glance, then turned to Peter Elliot.

'That's coming from the main gate,' he said, his face drained of colour.

'I'll check if I can see anything,' Peter told him, sprinting off.

The men had emerged from the relative warmth of Royston's office and were crossing the wide-open area in front of the laboratory complex. The main gate lay more than two hundred yards away and other buildings on the base now blocked their line of sight.

'It must be the creature,' McGill said. 'It must be here.'

'Adam, what about the cobalt?' Professor Elliot asked, concern etched across his features.

'There's nothing we can do about that now,' Royston told him.

'But if that thing gets to it, it might explode,' McGill protested.

'I'm ordering my helicopters to fire on it if they get a clear shot, Royston,' Cartwright said as he dashed off in another direction.

This time Royston didn't argue. His gaze was now fixed on Peter Elliot who was scrambling up a metal ladder attached to the side of a building close by. Royston watched as the younger man clawed his way up the iron rungs until he was almost at the top. When Peter reached the flat roof of the building he steadied himself and looked down at the men below him.

'Can you see it?' Royston shouted up at him.

Peter took a few steps across the flat roof and looked towards the main gate. 'Oh my God,' he murmured under his breath.

He guessed that the mass of glowing pulsating matter that was slithering across the compound from the main gate was easily fifty yards across and it seemed to be expanding by the second, oozing in all directions in a bid to consume whatever it touched. He could see what remained of the gatehouse which had been reduced to smoking rubble by the creature. Much of the metal fence nearby had also been melted by the passage of the entity. Now the heaving sludge moved ever nearer, always accompanied by the hellish glow and loud crackling sound that it gave off.

'It's coming this way,' Peter shouted to the men on the ground. 'It's about a hundred yards away now.' He began clambering down the ladder.

He leaped down the last few feet, slipped as he landed but kept his balance. He sprinted back towards Royston and the others who were already turning and heading away.

'Get everyone out of the laboratory complex,' Royston shouted.

'Most got out when the alarm went off,' McGill assured him.

'Was all the cobalt loaded into that truck when the rods were cleaned?' Royston asked, pointing at the Scania lorry that was parked outside the complex behind them.

'Yes,' the professor told him. 'But what does that matter now there's no way we can stop it?'

'Because that's what this thing has come to feed on,' Royston reminded him. 'The cobalt is unstable.'

'If that thing consumes it won't that make it unstable too?' McGill said.

'Yes, it will,' Royston told him.

'Look,' Peter Elliot shouted, gesturing wildly behind the men.

They turned to look towards what he was pointing at and froze as they saw it.

The creature was now on the roof of one of the buildings, sliding and oozing over it like water over a dam before heading down towards the ground and the waiting lorry.

Royston watched it with horrified fascination as it swelled and throbbed, its mass glowing with that sickly dull light as it slid effortlessly over anything it touched, incinerating it. Windows in the building shattered and the whole structure looked as if it might collapse under the weight of the sludge. Royston could only begin to guess at how much the thing weighed and he shook his head in bewilderment as it slithered closer and closer to the lorry carrying the cobalt. The noise it gave off filled the night and threatened to shatter the eardrums of all those within range of it. Simultaneously repulsed and fascinated by what he saw, Royston watched as the creature oozed around the truck and then seemed to engulf it like a fist closing around a grasped object.

Smoke and flame erupted from the lorry as the fuel tank was ruptured, the belch of flame quickly engulfed by the creature as it flooded over the remains of the obliterated truck. Even from where they stood the men could feel the heat given off by the heaving mass.

'It's getting bigger,' McGill gasped, transfixed like Royston by the sight before him.

'It's expanding to accommodate the energy it's ingesting,' Royston told him, his stare fixed on the monstrous shape as it continued to swell and seethe over the truck and its contents. 'The mass has to increase to cope with the extra radiation.'

Tendrils of the sludge moved in different directions as if seeking more sustenance but when they found none they withdrew once more to be reabsorbed into the original mass.

'This is unbelievable,' the professor gasped. 'How did we ever think we could stop *that*?'

Royston shot out a hand to steady the older man who was swaying uncertainly on his feet as he watched the creature envelop what was left of the truck and its load. The glow it gave off seemed to intensify and the watching men squinted as the luminescence increased for long seconds before finally dimming again.

'If it expands when it feeds how big will it get?' McGill asked.

'The important thing is how unstable will it get,' Royston said.

'What difference will that make?' McGill responded, his stare still fixed on the seething mass that was now sending out thick streams from the main body of matter as if it was feeling its way across the open compound. Those probing tentacles that touched nothing were again swiftly withdrawn.

'If it becomes unstable it becomes vulnerable,' Royston stated.

'Is there anything we can do?' the professor asked.

'Not here,' Royston told him. 'The only thing we can do is to let it go back to the fissure.'

'How can you be sure it will do that?' John Elliot demanded.

'Because it has done so every other time after it's fed,' Royston reminded him. 'There's no reason to think it will alter its habits now. We know the exact route it takes: that route has to be cleared, people evacuated from their homes if necessary.'

'I'll inform the police,' McGill said. 'If I can contact them through this bloody static.'

'People have *got* to be cleared from its path, Mac,' Royston insisted. 'Otherwise there could be hundreds of casualties.'

Two Lynx helicopters swooped over the compound, their spotlights trained on the heaving mass below.

'I just hope Cartwright managed to contact the pilots of those choppers,' Royston said, peering upwards into the night sky. 'If they open up on it here then God alone knows what might happen.'

Peter Elliot grabbed Royston's arm.

'Look,' he said excitedly. 'I think it's going. It's leaving.'

Royston nodded as he saw the creature slither back up the side of the building it had first appeared on. The entire oozing mass slid back over blackened bricks and shattered window frames until it was once again on the roof of the structure in front of them. One of the helicopters dived low over the entity, veering away sharply when it got too close.

'It must be heading back to the fissure, just like you said,' the professor exclaimed.

Royston nodded.

'Those helicopters can track it,' McGill added. 'If it changes direction they can tell us.'

'If they can maintain contact,' Royston murmured, watching as the last seething vestiges of the thing disappeared from sight. Only the dull glow coming from behind one of the other buildings and the low crackle that the entity gave off signalled its presence.

'I'm going to call the police,' McGill said, hurrying off towards the building behind them.

'Let's hope they can clear the people from that thing's path quickly enough,' Royston murmured.

'The areas where it's heading are mainly on the outskirts of Broughton,' the professor said. 'Not so densely populated.'

'What if they can't get them out in time?' Peter Elliot asked.

'Then a lot of people are going to die tonight, Peter,' Royston said flatly.

Sixty-Four

Saint Catherine's church was a magnificent building on the outskirts of Broughton.

Visible for miles around, it stood on a low hill that overlooked most of the town. A monument to the skill and craft of the men who had built it and died centuries ago, the church was something of an anomaly among the modern houses over which it towered. For many years it had been the centre of life in the area when Broughton had been first a settlement and then a small village but that importance to the community had been lost with the passage of time. The church wasn't the centre of Broughton's existence any more and congre - gations had diminished gradually. But now, on this particular night, the church was in demand again and people were flocking to it – but for reasons very different from those for which they would normally have attended its hallowed confines.

A steady stream of people had been making their way towards the building for the last thirty minutes now. Having left their homes in the shallow valley below, they came carrying overnight bags and small suitcases. Some drove their cars as close to the building as they could and left them on the gravelled area before the great steel-braced main door. There were policemen outside the church and soldiers too but none were able or willing to provide the reluctant visitors with any information about why they had been forced to leave their homes and come here. Many had suspected that something had gone wrong out at the military research facility. There had been whispers of nerve-gas clouds that had escaped. Of some kind of viral infection that had been manufactured at the base. But none of Broughton's residents knew the truth at present and their questions were met either by silence or shaken heads from the police and troops who swarmed around the building ushering civilians inside. There was a subdued air about the people who gathered inside the church. They wanted to know why they had been forced to come to this place but they feared what the answer might be.

The church was approachable only by two narrow roads that wound through the houses below and then terminated inside the graveyard of the church itself. It was along one of these thoroughfares that Constable William Lucas now guided the patrol car while his companion struggled with the radio in an attempt to minimise the savage interference that was distorting every message sent or received.

'It's no good,' Constable Edward Chapman snapped. 'I can hardly hear anything on this bloody thing.' He glared accusingly at the radio.

'Didn't the last message say that the interference was caused by that thing?' Lucas enquired.

'It gets worse the closer that thing is,' Chapman told him.

'What the fuck is it, anyway?'

'No one knows. Or if they do they're not saying.'

'Something from the military base?'

'Could be. Didn't one of the messages say that there'd been an attack there tonight?'

Lucas exhaled deeply and brought the car to a halt outside the church.

'Why evacuate people here?' Chapman murmured, looking up at the church towering above them.

'It's high up, isn't it?' Lucas said.

'Does that thing have trouble climbing hills, then?' Chapman said sarcastically.

'Perhaps they think God might protect them,' Lucas suggested, raising his eyebrows.

'Good luck,' Chapman said, seeing the local priest and two soldiers approaching the car.

'How close is it going to come to here?' the priest asked anxiously.

'Within a hundred yards,' Chapman told him.

'Is everyone out of their houses?' the first soldier asked.

'As far as we can tell,' Chapman said. 'How long have you got to keep them here?'

'Until someone tells us different,' the soldier told him.

Above them, one of the helicopters swept over, the roar of its rotors making both men look up.

'Why don't they just kill it?' Chapman hissed as the Lynx disappeared into the night.

The soldier didn't answer.

*

'What the hell is it, lieutenant?'

In the cockpit of the Lynx all that Lieutenant James Bannerman could do by way of an answer was to shake his head. His own attention, like that of the pilot, was trained on the slowly moving mass of matter about a hundred feet below them. Bannerman watched as the sludge passed either straight over or straight through everything it came into contact with. Stone walls, hedges, cars, trees and other objects were simply obliterated by the steadily moving entity.

'No one seems to know,' the officer murmured, his gaze still fixed on the creature which was now approaching an open field.

It crashed through the wall surrounding the field and slithered on across it.

The pilot took the Lynx a little higher, conscious of the electrical pylons that were ahead of them.

The creature seemed untroubled by them and ploughed into the first one, buckling and melting the steel at the base. The entire structure wobbled then fell, crashing to earth as the cables snapped and whiplashed through the night air. They fell onto the mass and were consumed immediately, plumes of smoke rising from the entity as it enveloped them.

Another of the pylons was flattened too, the twisted metal falling to the ground where it lay for a moment before the creature slithered over it.

'We could try having a go with the missiles, lieutenant,' the pilot suggested. 'They did say that we could try if we could get a clear shot. There's nothing around for miles.'

Bannerman hesitated, then shook his head.

'We don't know what will happen if we hit it,' he said. 'If it fragments it could spread even quicker.'

'Then what do we do?'

'We follow orders and track it,' Bannerman reminded him. 'Major Cartwright says it's heading back to the fissure where it first appeared. They're going to deal with it then.' The lieutenant glanced down at the map spread out on his lap, tracing the red line that had been drawn on it with one index finger. He frowned.

Below them, the creature crashed into a barn and brought the wooden structure down easily. More smoke billowed skyward as the planks were incinerated and consumed.

'Do you think it can see?' the pilot asked.

Bannerman shook his head vaguely. 'I really don't know,' he said. 'I know as much about that thing as you do.'

Again he checked the map before him. 'It's changing direction,' he said, a note of alarm in his voice. 'It's not following the course they said it would.'

The pilot glanced worriedly at him, then looked down again at the mass of sludge that was now about to crash through a high fence.

'If it continues on the course it's on now it'll be heading straight for the centre of Broughton,' Bannerman announced.

'Can't you tell them?' the pilot asked.

'Through this static?' Bannerman said. 'I can hardly hear you, let alone anyone else.' He looked down again at the map, then tapped it with his finger, holding the map up so that the pilot could see. 'Take us to checkpoint three.'

'But I thought we were supposed to follow this thing?' the pilot protested.

'Just get us to checkpoint three as quick as you can,' Bannerman insisted.

There was a sudden loud bang from below and both men looked down to see smoke rising from the seething mass. Seconds later something large hurtled past the Lynx, missing it by a matter of feet. It left a burning trail across the sky and Bannerman realised that a lump of hot rock had been launched into the air. Another followed, then another. It was as if an artillery barrage had suddenly opened up on them as debris continued to spew skyward from the river of sludge beneath. Portions of the flow seemed to rise upwards like tentacles towards the helicopter and Bannerman realised with horror that the thing was trying to reach them.

'Get us up,' the lieutenant shouted, jabbing a finger skyward.

The pilot needed no second invitation and sent the Lynx into a climb.

The mass below them was glowing more brightly now as it poured down a narrow country track, channelled by the high grassy banks on either side. It smashed effortlessly through a wooden gate, tearing away much of the wall to which the gate was attached in the process. Smoke rose into the air and so too did small clouds of ash.

The Lynx suddenly dipped violently and Bannerman

was almost thrown from his seat. He shot an enquiring glance at the pilot who was struggling with the controls.

'We're losing power,' the pilot gasped, dragging hard on the throttle.

Bannerman looked at the dashboard of the chopper and saw that the lights there were dimming.

The Lynx lurched and dropped like a stone for twenty feet before the pilot managed to drag it upwards again.

'Get us away from here,' Bannerman shouted.

Again the Lynx dropped and both men held on fearfully.

'It's draining our power,' Bannerman shouted.

'I know,' the pilot yelled back, wrenching the cyclic so hard that he almost tore it from its housing.

The lights on the instrument panel dimmed again but then flared more brightly and as they did the helicopter began to rise. The pilot worked the control pedals and the Lynx gained more elevation.

'Go on,' Bannerman roared, seeing that they were rising higher.

The sound of the rotors merged with the ever-present crackle of static and the whine of the engines and the lieutenant swallowed hard as he saw that they were pulling clear. The pilot banked the helicopter sharply to one side and it swung away from the mass beneath it.

'Jesus Christ,' the pilot gasped. 'I thought it was going to pull us down.'

Bannerman nodded.

'Now get us to checkpoint three,' he said.

'Lieutenant, look,' the pilot interjected, pointing at the ground. 'It's changing direction again.'

Bannerman peered through the gloom towards the flowing mass beneath them. He saw that it had smashed its way through two parked cars that had been left on the roadside and was now flowing quickly towards the heavily wooded ground that masked the approaches to the moor.

'It is heading back to the fissure,' the lieutenant murmured. 'Just like they said it would. Stay with it – but keep us high.'

The pilot nodded.

Below them, the creature continued its rampage across the countryside.

Sixty-Five

L eo McGill took a sip of coffee, wincing when he realised that it was cold. He paced slowly back and forth in front of the large oak desk in the room, glancing occasionally at the rows of books that filled the shelves on three of the walls. So much knowledge contained within those volumes, McGill thought, and yet nothing in any of them was of any use in the situation in which they now found themselves.

He exhaled wearily, accepting that no one had the knowledge necessary to help them. Who *would* have answers to the types of problems they found themselves confronted with? There was no manual for coping with this type of emergency, no contingency plans for handling the kind of circumstances that had occurred in and around the base and the countryside that surrounded it. Even as he considered the gravity of the situation he knew that the absurdity of it was also a factor.

A force, a creature or whatever they chose to call it, hundreds of thousands of years old, had emerged from the depths of the Earth to feed on energy. Once satiated, it had returned to those same depths but only until its hunger was aroused again. It seemed unstoppable and it was certainly not just going to disappear of its own volition. None of them knew if it possessed even the most rudimentary intelligence – in fact, none of them knew if it was even technically an organic entity. There were so many questions and yet there were still so few answers.

McGill had considered the possibility that this thing might even be indestructible. If it wasn't technically alive then how could it be killed? he asked himself. Was it some kind of primordial nemesis not just for the men on the base and the people who lived nearby but for the whole of the human race? Thoughts like these tumbled through his mind now as he continued to pace back and forth inside the office, occasionally stopping to peer out of the window not even sure what he was looking for when he did.

He glanced at his watch and saw that it was approaching 3:11 a.m. McGill sighed and rubbed his eyes. 'How long have we been waiting?' he asked, quietly.

'Two hours now,' Professor John Elliot reminded him.

'How much longer?' McGill asked, looking again at his watch as if that simple act was somehow going to speed up time.

'This equipment that Royston has in his laboratory is only a prototype, anyway,' the professor reminded McGill. 'There's no guarantee at all that it will work.'

'It's a slim hope but it's the only hope we have at the moment,' McGill said. 'No one else has suggested a way of destroying this creature so we have to rely on Adam at the moment.'

'But if we could contact the ministry then surely they'd be able to help us,' the professor offered.

'They don't know all the facts.'

'We could at least try.'

'Every line out of this place is useless and the radios are even worse. We haven't a chance of getting through to London now and even if we could what would they do? We've got to handle this ourselves.'

'It's heading back to the fissure. We know that. As soon as it gets there we should leave it alone.'

'And hope it stays there?' McGill shook his head. 'We tried that before if you remember rightly. The army filled the fissure with concrete and the thing still got out. It can't just be ignored, professor.'

'The energy it consumed at the base may well have been enough for it.'

'*This* time. What about next time?'

The professor didn't answer.

'Adam said that the larger this thing grows the more its range will increase. No one knows how much bigger it's got since it last fed. If it keeps increasing in size it could destroy the base, Broughton and all the towns within a twenty-mile radius and after that it'll need more sustenance. It'll head for larger towns, for other targets.'

The professor nodded slowly.

'I did some calculations of my own,' he said. 'And they don't make for very good reading, I'm afraid.'

McGill turned and looked fixedly at the professor.

'If this thing is increasing in size at the rate which Royston suggested then it could consume an area the size of Buckinghamshire within less than a day,' the older man proclaimed. 'If it continues to grow it will spread across the entire country. That could happen in a little under a week.'

McGill ran a hand through his hair and reached for one of the high-backed chairs in front of the desk. 'Why didn't you say something earlier, professor?' he asked.

'To what purpose? If I'm right we're all living on borrowed time.'

'What do you mean?'

'Unchecked and with access to the nourishment it craves, this thing would be able to destroy the entire world population just over 93,000 hours from first contact,' the professor said, his voice catching. 'This creature is the manifestation of every ancient prophecy we've ever heard. The harbinger of doom.' He smiled bitterly. 'The bringer of destruction to all mankind. This could be the end, Mr McGill. The end of everything we've ever known and created as a species.'

McGill swallowed hard, the professor's words filling his head.

'And there is something else to consider,' the older man went on. 'What if it isn't alone?'

'What do you mean?'

'Royston postulated that this thing emerged from below the Earth's crust at various times, that it followed some kind of cycle when it came to the surface looking for energy to sustain it, didn't he?'

'He thought every fifty or a hundred years.'

'Didn't he mention the volcanic eruptions at Krakatoa and Mount St Helens? The earthquakes in San

Francisco, the tsunamis in Thailand and Japan? What if those weren't caused by this same entity? What if there are others? That isn't so hard to accept, is it?'

McGill shook his head.

'It would seem that the earth is being reclaimed, Mr McGill,' the professor told him, his eyes shining with tears. 'By something that evolved before man himself – and the next stage of that evolution doesn't involve the human race. Mankind may very well be obsolete nine months from now.'

Sixty-Six

'I can't do it.'

Adam Royston shook his head and leaned dejectedly against the worktop in the laboratory, his face pale. 'With the equipment I have here I can't destroy that thing,' he went on. 'It was only ever a prototype that might work in theory, not in practice.'

'So what do we do?' Peter Elliot wanted to know.

Royston shook his head, a look of defeat on his face. 'I was a fool to think it would ever work,' he admitted.

'You can't give up, Adam, not now.'

'I'm not giving up, Peter, I'm just saying that the method I thought would work against this creature is unsatisfactory. We could try but if we fail . . .' He allowed the sentence to trail off.

'But what choice do we have? If we can't use your equipment against it then what do we do? Surely a slim hope is better than no hope at all.'

'There might be another way,' Royston told him.

'What is it?'

'It's a last resort.'

'Just tell me what it is, Adam.'

'If I'm wrong I daren't even think of the consequences.'

'Will you just tell me?'

The laboratory door opened and both men looked around to see the three figures who had entered. Led by McGill the trio headed towards Royston and Peter.

'What's the news, Adam?' McGill asked.

'Not good,' Royston told him. 'The equipment I thought might be able to draw the radiation from that thing isn't powerful enough. It might destabilise it but it wouldn't destroy it.'

'So what now?' Major Cartwright asked. 'We were pinning our hopes on your theories, Doctor Royston, and now you claim there's no way they'll work.'

'My ideas were only ever theoretical – I've just explained that to Peter,' Royston said defensively.

'Professor Elliot was explaining his own theories to me,' McGill said. 'About this thing growing as it consumes more energy. It could destroy everything.'

Royston nodded.

'The helicopters tracked it back to the fissure,' Cartwright reported. 'I've got a hundred men positioned around the area. It's in there now and it's not moving. Not for the time being, anyway.'

'Not until it's hungry again,' McGill said.

'It won't stay in the fissure indefinitely, we know that,' Royston said. 'And we can't effectively destroy it while it's in there.'

'According to you we can't destroy it anyway,' Cartwright reminded the American.

'Not with the method I originally suggested,' Royston responded. 'But there could be another way.'

All eyes turned towards him.

'First we have to get it out of the fissure,' Royston began. 'We can't wait for it to move of its own volition. We have to get it out of there now.'

'And how do you propose to do that?' Cartwright asked.

'We load up a truck with radioactive material,' said Royston. 'We give it a reason to come out.'

'Bait,' McGill murmured.

'Exactly,' Royston went on. 'We draw it out of the fissure and when it's out in the open we destroy it.'

'So you say, doctor – but how?' Cartwright snapped.

'When it feeds it becomes unstable,' Royston told the watching men. 'When it's unstable it's vulnerable. In an unstable state I think it may well succumb to conventional weapons such as the rockets from the helicopters. But to make sure I think we need to add an extra payload to those missiles.'

'Like what?' Cartwright enquired.

'Cobalt,' Royston declared. 'We attach a small amount of cobalt to each of the missiles.'

'That's insane,' Professor Elliot declared. 'You'd wipe out half of the country. You might as well drop a nuclear warhead onto this thing.'

'No,' Royston said, smiling. 'This thing ingests energy, it consumes it. The cobalt on the missiles would be fired into it and it would absorb that material. The cobalt would explode inside it, making it unstable, and while it was in that state the energy from the rocket explosions would destroy it. It would be like causing it to overdose on energy. We need to force it to ingest a massive amount of energy in a very short time. That would destabilise it. The missiles will provide that speed and power.'

'How sure are you that this will work?' Cartwright wanted to know.

'I'm not sure of anything any more, major,' Royston admitted. 'But it's the best chance we have in the time we have left. That thing isn't going to stay in the fissure for ever.'

'How much cobalt would have to be attached to the missiles?' the professor asked.

'A minuscule amount,' Royston said.

'But wouldn't it be like detonating a cobalt bomb?' the older man protested. 'The results would be disastrous.'

'No, they wouldn't, John,' Royston said, shaking his head. 'This thing ingests the energy it feeds on so the result would be an implosion of cobalt inside it. The radioactivity contained in the cobalt itself would be consumed by the creature. The explosions caused by the missiles will be what destroy it. Any debris would be non-radioactive.'

'You're sure of this?' Cartwright demanded.

'As sure as I can be,' Royston admitted.

'We'd need clearance,' Cartwright said.

'From who?' Royston snapped.

'The MOD, the prime minister, the defence secretary and probably half of NATO for all I know,' the major rasped. 'I can't authorise this, Royston. It's beyond my authority.'

'We haven't got a choice,' Royston told him. 'There's no way of contacting London or anyone outside the base. This has to be done now. If this thing isn't stopped it will destroy everything it touches, you know that. Cartwright, it has to be stopped – and stopped for good.'

'I understand that. But the risks are unimaginable,' Cartwright protested.

'So are the consequences if that thing gets loose again,' said Royston flatly. 'Now: what are you going to do?'

'I'm not taking responsibility for this,' the officer insisted.

'No one's asking you to,' Royston told him. 'I'll drive the truck as close to the fissure as I can but once that thing comes out it's down to your helicopters.'

'How many missiles would it take?' McGill enquired.

'And how many does each helicopter carry?' Royston asked.

'Eight,' Cartwright told him.

'That should be enough,' Royston said.

'But it only has the capability to fire two at a time,' the officer went on. 'If you're talking about tipping these missiles with radioactive material then my men can't be handling them when they reload even if they are wearing protective clothing.'

'Two should be enough – there'd be no need for them to reload,' McGill said. 'Or we could just equip more than one of the helicopters with the right type of missile.'

'Two should be sufficient,' Cartwright told him. 'The payload is a high-explosive copper-lined charge. It's powerful enough to burn through the strongest tank armour in existence so it should be able to penetrate this thing.'

'But aren't the missiles laser-guided?' the professor asked. 'If this creature is disrupting the transmission of radio and telephone signals then it might be able to do the same with lasers and so render the missiles useless.'

'Then the helicopters will have to fire them without laser guidance,' Royston said. 'If they get close enough they won't need a guidance system.'

The major shook his head but said nothing.

'What's your answer going to be, major?' Royston persisted.

'If this goes wrong,' Cartwright said, glaring at him, 'I'll personally blow your brains out.'

'You won't have to,' Royston told him. 'If this goes wrong we'll all be dead anyway.'

Sixty-Seven

It had taken the small convoy of vehicles that set out from Broughton Green Military Research Facility less than thirty minutes to reach the area around the fissure. Now, as the leading ones pulled up on the windswept open ground, Adam Royston looked around in the gloom and saw dozens of soldiers positioned on the higher ground that sloped up around the fissure itself.

There were more men in small groups near the rift but none strayed closer than fifty feet from it and they were constantly turning towards it on the alert for the slightest sight or sound of movement. In the sky above helicopters circled constantly, the drone of their rotors mingling with the rumble of engines below.

Ahead of the lorry he was seated in, Royston could see a Land Rover that he knew contained Major Cartwright and Professor John Elliot. Behind him was another similar vehicle carrying McGill and Peter Elliot. Royston himself had spent most of the journey watching the movements of the lorry driver, talking to the man about how the vehicle handled. He was sure that he would be more than capable of driving the Scania when the time came. There was a thick lead shield between the cab of the lorry and the cargo it held and Royston periodically leaned back and tapped it almost unconsciously. Behind that shield lay the small container of cobalt that had been loaded back at the base.

'You'll be fine driving this, sir,' the driver said. Royston looked at him, his train of thought interrupted.

However, for that he'd been grateful. From the time they'd left the base he'd pictured himself behind the wheel of the lorry, being consumed by the creature as it flowed out of the fissure. He'd even imagined himself burning alive as the thing enveloped the truck. They were thoughts he didn't care to entertain but no matter how hard he tried he couldn't seem to drive them from his mind. Now the words spoken by the driver forced him back to the immediacy of his surroundings.

'She sometimes sticks a bit in second,' the driver went on. 'But otherwise it's a piece of piss, pardon my French.' He smiled good-naturedly.

Royston nodded.

'You don't have to do this, you know, sir,' the driver said. 'You don't have to drive it.'

'I know,' Royston told him. 'But I wouldn't ask anyone else to do it.'

'You're a brave man.'

'Brave or stupid? I'm not sure which.'

The driver brought the lorry to a halt and switched the engine off. Up ahead the Land Rover had also stopped and Royston saw Cartwright and Professor Elliot heading towards him.

'Out you get,' Cartwright said to the driver who nodded and swung himself out of the cab.

Royston slid across behind the steering wheel and clamped both hands on it. From behind him he heard movement on the running board.

'Peter's uncovering the cobalt,' Professor Elliot told him.

Royston nodded. 'Are the helicopters ready?' he asked.

'Lieutenant Bannerman has orders to wait until the thing is completely clear of the fissure before firing on it,' Cartwright told him.

Royston gunned the engine, the sound reverberating through the stillness of the night. As it died down again he smiled thinly at the other men. 'Just checking,' he said.

'You don't have to do this, Adam,' the professor told him.

'Yes, I do, John,' Royston said.

'Back it up to within fifteen feet of the fissure,' Cartwright said. 'No closer.'

McGill and Peter Elliot appeared at the side of the lorry.

'Everything's ready,' McGill said.

'What if there isn't enough cobalt to tempt that thing out of the fissure?' Peter asked.

'There will be,' Royston assured him. 'Just make sure your men don't open fire until that thing is completely clear of the rift, major. If any part of it is still inside when the missiles hit, then—'

'I know,' the officer said, interrupting him. 'They know what they've got to do. You just concentrate on your part.'

'Good luck, Adam,' McGill said.

'I think I might need it.' Royston smiled but there was no warmth in the expression. 'You get away. Get clear.' He jammed the lorry into first gear.

'If you have any problems just get out,' McGill told him. 'Abandon the lorry and save yourself.'

Royston nodded.

Above him the Lynx carrying the missiles swept over, flashing its spotlights as it passed.

'That's the signal,' Cartwright told him.

Royston nodded and the lorry moved off slowly across the open ground towards the fissure.

Sixty-Eight

Royston drove slowly, his eyes scanning the fissure as he drew closer to it.

In the darkness it looked like a scar across the landscape but it appeared quiet. Deceptively so, he mused as he brought the lorry to a halt and shifted carefully into reverse. He checked the wing mirrors, then guided the vehicle backwards towards the gaping rift.

Come on, you bastard. Come out in the open.

He could feel his heart thudding hard against his ribs. It seemed to eclipse even the low drone of the helicopter's engine and the whirring of its rotor blades as it passed back and forth overhead.

Royston checked the wing mirrors again to see if there was anything visible.

Still nothing.

How long am I going to have to wait?

He turned and peered out of the window of the lorry, scanning the fissure for any sign of movement, his ears alert for any sound. Royston turned off the vehicle's engine and sat there, trying to control his breathing. His mouth was dry and he was having trouble swallowing.

Scared, aren't you?

He caught a glimpse of his reflection in the rear-view mirror and even in the darkness inside the cab he could see how pale his skin looked. He gripped the steering wheel and looked again into the wing mirrors.

The fissure was still silent.

He drew a deep breath and started the engine once more. As he did he eased the truck into reverse and allowed it to creep backwards a few more feet. Not closer than fifteen feet, Cartwright had told him, and Royston could see the sense in that. No one knew exactly how fast this thing could move if it wanted to and he didn't want to be caught out by its speed when it emerged from the rift. If it ever did. He backed up a little more, watching his own progress in the mirrors, judging the distance to the lip of the rift. When he was ten feet away he hit the brake gently, leaving the engine idling this time.

The helicopter swept over again and Royston looked up at it, then across to the higher ground where most of the troops were sheltering. He knew that McGill, the professor and Peter Elliot were also there, watching him intently. Waiting and wondering.

But down here you're on your own, aren't you?

He pressed his foot down on the accelerator slightly and the engine revved, exhaust fumes rising into the cold air.

Come on. Come on.

For a moment he feared that the amount of cobalt in the back of the lorry wasn't going to be sufficient to coax the creature from the fissure.

So what are you going to do?

Royston jammed the lorry into reverse once again and allowed it to roll backwards another couple of feet, his stare fixed on the wing mirror closest to him.

'Come on, you bastard,' he murmured under his breath, repeating his earlier unspoken order to the entity.

As the Lynx roared over the open ground below for yet another sweep Lieutenant Bannerman saw that the truck driven by Royston was getting closer to the fissure.

'What the hell is he doing?' the lieutenant rasped.

The pilot heard him say something but seemed more concerned with keeping the helicopter on its course.

'Don't get so close,' Bannerman hissed again as Royston backed nearer and nearer to the gaping rift.

The Lynx banked and swung back over the fissure once more.

'Take us down,' Bannerman snapped, grabbing the arm of the pilot who looked at him aghast. 'No, not all the way. Just hover over the lorry. He shouldn't be that near.'

The pilot did as he was instructed, the chopper dropping smoothly until it was about fifty feet from the ground.

Bannerman manipulated one of the spotlights and aimed it at the cab of the Scania, allowing the piercing beam of white light to play across the vehicle.

He could see Royston inside it and the American scientist even raised a hand in acknowledgement. Bannerman made several gestures with his own hands designed to indicate that the lorry should be moved away from the fissure. But if Royston understood the rudimentary semaphore he chose to ignore it because the lorry continued to move backwards at a snail's pace until it was less than five feet from the lip of the rift. There it stopped.

Bannerman shook his head but when Royston raised one thumb and held it in the air the lieutenant could only give in.

'Take us back up,' he told the pilot.

The Lynx began to rise once more.

Sixty-Nine

Royston watched as the helicopter gained more height. Then he settled into gazing fixedly at the lorry's wing mirrors once again.

There was still no movement from the fissure.

Did the creature know it was being lured into a trap? Was that why it was staying deep inside the Earth?

Don't be ridiculous. How could it know? It can't reason and plan.

Royston let out a weary breath. There was still so much they didn't know about the entity and the extent of its intelligence was one of the many unknown factors. Was it driven purely by instinct or was there some kind of primordial conscious purpose that governed its movements? He shook his head, knowing that these unanswered questions might well remain that way. All that mattered now was destroying this thing and the only way that was going to happen was if it ever emerged from its lair.

He tapped agitatedly on the steering wheel, then reached forward and switched off the engine. The near-silence that descended was unnerving. The helicopter was continuing to circle but it had risen so high into the skies that even the roar of its twin Rolls-Royce engines was little more than a distant drone. Royston could hear the sound of his own blood rushing in his ears as he sat there, his mouth dry.

A thought struck him suddenly and it made him reach for the ignition key.

What if the creature is aware of what's happening and it's luring you closer? You're not tempting it out – it's coaxing you in. Close enough so that when it chooses to strike you won't be able to get away.

The idea went against every shred of logic in Royston's mind but nevertheless he could not shift it.

He turned the ignition key to start the engine, wanting now to be further away from the fissure. Should the creature appear then he needed a good start on it and that entailed being further than five feet away once the chase began. As he twisted the key he looked again at the wing mirror and he was sure that he saw a faint glow rising from the rift where there had been just impenetrable blackness before. Or were his eyes now playing tricks on him?

The engine sputtered, then died. Royston frowned, turning the key harder now.

This time there was a low roar and the engine burst into life. He exhaled gratefully and jammed the Scania into first, moving forward slightly.

In the wing mirror he saw that the glow was getting brighter, a faint luminescence that rose from the fissure like dying headlights. Royston wound down the lorry's window and heard a sound he recognised only too well. A loud crackling that grew more intense by the second.

He stepped on the accelerator, certain now that the creature was rising from the fissure.

As he glanced back he saw that the glow was much brighter now. How far it had to go before it reached the lip of the fissure he had no idea but there was no doubt that the thing was dragging itself upwards towards the surface and towards him. Royston pressed harder on the accelerator and the truck rolled forward faster.

He kept his foot on the clutch, not wanting to speed away too quickly in case the creature retreated back down into the depths. It had to be drawn all the way from the cover of the rift before it could be destroyed and he knew that the only way to do that was by using the cobalt he had in the back of the lorry.

'Come on, come on,' Royston murmured to himself, chancing one quick look skyward to where the helicopter was swinging around to allow itself a clear run at the entity as it emerged.

The first seething, glutinous traces of the creature slithered over the lip of the fissure.

Royston guided the lorry further away, knowing that the bait had worked and wanting now to be as far from the thing as possible. He saw more of it come spilling into view, pulsing and undulating as it struggled to heave all of its mass free of the hole.

The crackling noise was deafening now and the glow was growing more intense with every passing second.

Royston jammed the lorry into second gear and stepped hard on the accelerator as the creature continued to rise from the fissure in waves that slid and flowed into each other as they expanded inexorably.

Royston was sure that the thing had somehow increased in size like some vast amoebic entity whose cells were constantly dividing and expanding. It looked like a wall of rancid glowing mud as it slithered across the ground towards the lorry, sometimes rising a few feet into the air as if reaching out towards the source of food it craved.

He was still thinking that when his foot slipped off the clutch.

The lorry's engine stalled and the vehicle stopped dead.

Seventy

For long moments Royston felt fear more strongly than he'd ever experienced it in his life before.

It struck him almost like a physical blow, wrenching the breath from him and causing him to let out several deep gasps.

He shot a hand forward and twisted the ignition key once again, looking with terror towards the wing mirror nearest him to check on the progress of the creature as it continued to haul its seething bulk out of the fissure. Most of it was flowing towards the stricken lorry.

Had Royston been able to see the rear of the vehicle he would have noticed that the rubber on the two back tyres was beginning to smoulder. Paint was starting to peel away from the chassis of the Scania as the heat generated by the mass grew more intense. The plastic covering of one rear headlight had already melted and the other was in the process of dissolving too. Steam was rising from the tarpaulin that covered the frame of the lorry and the soggy ground between the vehicle and the heaving form of the creature was drying out as the temperature rose.

Royston turned the key again and stepped on the accelerator, feeling relieved – to put it mildly – when the engine fired. He pressed harder on the gas pedal and the lorry lurched forward, skidding slightly on the muddy ground. But he gripped the steering wheel more tightly and guided the Scania across the terrain, trying to ensure that he didn't get too far ahead of the undulating mass behind him even though his only desire was to be as far away from this monstrosity as possible.

He again checked the wing mirror and saw that the thing was pursuing him but whether or not all of it was clear of the fissure he couldn't tell. Only those in the helicopter above would know that and only they would be able to judge the correct moment to strike. All Royston could do was ensure that the creature didn't catch up with the lorry. He felt the heat inside the cab increasing, felt sweat pop onto his forehead and cheeks, and he glanced at the dashboard to see that the engine temperature had risen alarmingly. The needle was almost nudging the red portion on the dial. Royston pressed his foot more firmly on the accelerator.

The truck continued forward and he guessed that he must be a good thirty or forty feet from the fissure by now. Surely the creature was clear of its subterranean home by now. Unless it had increased in size so dramatically that it was still oozing out of the rift in the Earth. Royston tried to force that particular thought from his mind, concentrating on keeping the thing behind him.

He smelled burning and to his horror he realised that flames were actually rising from the tarpaulin that covered the back part of the lorry.

He managed to coax more speed from the engine, aware now that he was closer to the ridge ahead than he was to the fissure behind him.

Surely the creature was clear and out in the open. It had to be.

Where the hell was the helicopter? Why didn't it attack?

He heard two loud bangs as the rear tyres on the lorry burst, transformed into smouldering rings of rubber by the nightmarish heat coming from the pursuing mass. The lorry stopped dead again but this time, with no traction from its back end there was no chance of it moving.

Royston knew he had no choice. He looked into the wing mirror then flung open the driver's-side door and leaped from the stranded vehicle.

As he hit the ground he felt the heat from the creature but he didn't dare look behind him to see how close it was. He gritted his teeth and ran for his life, legs pumping madly, the breath searing in his lungs as he raced on.

Behind him the undulating mass enveloped the lorry.

Flames rose briefly into the air and thick plumes of smoke began to billow upwards. But they were smothered immediately by the creature as it consumed the lorry and its contents.

Only now did Royston chance a look back and he saw the mass glowing more brightly, its entire glutinous form pulsing obscenely as if lit from within.

Suddenly, above him, he heard a roar and he ducked his head involuntarily.

From the darkness of the night sky, the helicopter

hurtled into view like some savage avenging angel and Royston hurled himself to the ground as it fired both its missiles in rapid succession. He turned his head in time to see them both strike the mass.

There were two small explosions as the missiles hit, tearing through the heaving entity which closed around them, the blasts muffled by its pulsing form.

Royston scrambled to his feet again and ran on, glancing back to see that the creature was glowing even more brightly now. Not just its centre but the entire mass was giving off a blinding white light that made Royston shield his eyes.

The crackling noise was deafening now and the entity's whole bulk seemed to be rising and folding in upon itself again and again as it flowed over and around the remains of the lorry.

Interminable seconds passed as the creature writhed and shuddered, its form filling the night with an ever more intense luminosity.

Then the blast came.

A shrieking plume of fire fully fifty feet high shot into the air. Orange and white flame roared upwards and a huge mushroom cloud of black and grey smoke seemed to fill the very heavens themselves. Lumps of debris spiralled skyward, then seemed to evaporate due to the sheer power of the blast.

The explosion was so massive that it blew Royston off his feet, lifting him into the air as if he'd been grabbed by an invisible hand then hurling him several yards. He slammed into the ground once more and rolled over as the concussion blast swept over him, almost tearing the breath from his lungs. He kept his head down, his fists clenched as a curtain of heat rolled over the terrain. The last vestiges of the blast shook him as he tried to straighten up.

When he sucked in a breath at last the air he inhaled was hot. Royston got slowly to his feet and looked back towards the fissure. Wreaths of smoke had formed around it and for fifty feet in all directions.

There was no sign of the creature.

He moved slowly down the slope, his stare now fixed on the rift and the open ground around it.

'Adam.'

Royston heard his name but didn't turn in the direction of the shout.

McGill caught up with him seconds later and grabbed his arm triumphantly. 'Adam, it's gone,' he said, beaming.

Royston merely nodded, watching as four soldiers sprinted down the slope towards the fissure, each of them holding a Geiger counter, the probes aimed at the ground ahead of them.

'It looks like you were right, Doctor Royston,' Major Cartwright said, appearing at his side. 'The missiles worked. The sudden introduction of so much energy was too much for that thing.'

Royston swayed uncertainly on his feet for a moment but then felt McGill's hands supporting him.

They moved further down the slope together.

'There's no reading, sir,' the first of the soldiers called, glancing at Cartwright.

'No sign of radiation,' another echoed.

'We'll have to check the fissure itself,' Royston said, his gaze still fixed on the yawning chasm in the ground ahead of them.

'But it's gone, Adam,' McGill insisted. 'Your idea worked – you should be proud.'

'I'll celebrate when I know every last trace of that thing is gone,' Royston muttered, walking towards the fissure. There was smoke and vapour rising from it that gradually dispersed as a cool breeze swept across the open ground.

The helicopter roared past overhead and Royston glanced up to see that the spotlights on the Lynx were flashing intermittently as if in celebration. The pilot swung the chopper back around and those on the ground could see that it was slowly descending on the far side of the rift. He saw Lieutenant Bannerman raise one thumb in a gesture of victory.

Royston at last managed a thin smile.

'We'll seal the fissure again,' Major Cartwright stated. 'Concrete it over.'

Royston nodded, reaching the edge of the hole where he paused and looked down into the blackness below.

'It really is gone,' McGill said quietly.

'Let's hope to God it is,' Royston replied.

'But there'd be traces of radioactivity if it was still around,' Cartwright said. 'We got it, Royston. It's gone and it won't come back again.'

Royston nodded slowly, still staring at the chasm. He dropped to his haunches and drew his fingers through the white residue that coated the rock around the fissure's lip. It was all that remained of the entity.

"I will show you fear in a handful of dust'," he said, quietly.

'What was that, Adam?' McGill enquired.

'It's a quote,' Royston told him. 'From *The Wasteland* by T. S. Eliot.'

'Very philosophical,' McGill said, and grinned. 'I'm just glad that thing is gone.' He looked at Royston. 'It is, isn't it? I mean, gone for good?'

Royston nodded slowly. 'I hope to God it is,' he murmured.

McGill glanced at him again.

'I said there'd be a PhD waiting for anyone who could work out what the hell had happened here,' Royston said. 'Maybe it's time to start work on my second doctorate.' He laughed quietly. 'We need to understand.'

'It's over, that's all that matters,' Cartwright said.

'Until we figure out what happened fully it's not over, major,' Royston replied. 'This thing has to be investigated and we have to understand it.'

'Good luck with that,' Cartwright said, smiling.

'Thanks. I think I'm going to need it,' Royston confessed, brushing the white dust from his hands.

He watched as it disappeared into the night, carried away on the breeze like a bad memory.

'The oldest and strongest emotion of mankind is fear and the oldest and strongest kind of fear is fear of the unknown'

H.P. Lovecraft.

THE POWER OF READING

Visit the Random House website and get connected with information on all our books and authors

EXTRACTS from our recently published books and selected backlist titles

COMPETITIONS AND PRIZE DRAWS Win signed books, audiobooks and more

AUTHOR EVENTS Find out which of our authors are on tour and where you can meet them

LATEST NEWS on bestsellers, awards and new publications

MINISITES with exclusive special features dedicated to our authors and their titles

READING GROUPS Reading guides, special features and all the information you need for your reading group

LISTEN to extracts from the latest audiobook publications

WATCH video clips of interviews and readings with our authors

RANDOM HOUSE INFORMATION including advice for writers, job vacancies and all your general queries answered

Come home to Random House

www.randomhouse.co.uk